A
MOST
PERILOUS
JOURNEY

A MOST PERILOUS JOURNEY

A Hanneke Bauer Mystery

Kathleen Ernst

First published by Level Best Books/Historia 2024

This novel is entirely a work of fiction. The names, characters and incidents portrayed in it are the work of the author's imagination. Any resemblance to actual persons, living or dead, events or localities is entirely coincidental.

Kathleen Ernst asserts the moral right to be identified as the author of this work.

Author Photo Credit: Scott Meeker

First edition

ISBN: 978-1-68512-692-6

Cover art by Level Best Designs

This book was professionally typeset on Reedsy.
Find out more at reedsy.com

For Laurie Rosengren Haselden

Praise for A Most Perilous Journey

"*A Most Perilous Journey* by Kathleen Ernst is more than a story; it's a compassionate lesson in history."—Nancy Cole Silverman, author, The Kat Lawson Mysteries

Characters

- Hanneke Bauer—Pomeranian immigrant living near Watertown, WI
- John Barlow—deputy sheriff
- Hiram Aubuchon—bounty hunter
- Levi Cox—bounty hunter, employed by Aubuchon
- Jacobine Ketzler—Hanneke's dear friend
- Karoline Ketzler—Jacobine's mother
- William Bluewing—Ho-Chunk scholar, farmhand, and Jacobine's fiancé
- Annie Bluewing—William's mother
- Claudette Bluewing—William's young sister
- Charlotte Stofeldt—German immigrant, abolitionist
- Beatta and Henni—Charlotte's children
- Berta, Erna, and Felix Pohl—siblings who live near the Stofeldts
- Asa Hawkins—wealthy Yankee businessman, nativist, conductor on the Underground Railroad
- Dr. Rausch—physician
- König family—German immigrants helped by Hanneke
- Angela Zeidler—proprietor, Red Cockerel Tavern
- Liesel—Angela's baby daughter
- Adolf—worker, Red Cockerel Tavern
- Celia—a legally enslaved woman traveling to find freedom
- *Nancy and Joseph Goodrich—operators of the Milton House Inn
- Gideon Sparrow—conductor on the Underground Railroad
- Daniel—a legally enslaved boy traveling to find freedom
- Clara and Charles Steckelberg—neighbors
- Gerda and Oscar Muelhauser—neighbors

*real people

Chapter One

Hanneke Bauer jerked upright in bed when a fist pounded against the back door. The night was black as pitch. Sleet rattled angrily against the windowpanes.

A neighbor must need help, she thought. Word of her interest in healing had spread through her rural community, and it wasn't uncommon for one of her fellow Pomeranian immigrants to ask for assistance when confronted with a family illness or an impending delivery.

She lit the lantern kept by her bedside for such moments, and stamped into her shoes. Her bedroom was on the house's ground floor, mere steps from the back door. She threw on her cloak before grasping the latch, eager to hasten her guest out of the foul weather. "Who's there?"

No one responded.

Wariness replaced Hanneke's instinctive concern. Something wasn't right. She lived alone on an isolated farm. Most people frantic enough to trek to her place on such a night would be yelling her name and identifying themselves.

She grabbed a heavy rolling pin and set it within reach. Only then did she crack open the door.

Although February had just given way to March, winter still gripped southern Wisconsin. A cold wind slapped her cheeks as she peered outside. No one stood on her porch. No lantern flickered in the yard.

Raising her own light, Hanneke made out a figure silhouetted against the snow remaining beyond the steps. "Who's there?" she demanded sharply.

"Please! You got to help him." It was a female voice, low but urgent.

Hanneke's jaw dropped. *Mein Gott.* She was almost certain that her desperate visitor was a Negro. She'd spoken in English, but the dialect was far from what Hanneke heard when conducting business with Yankees. The words sounded thick and were accompanied by a slight whistling sound. Hanneke needed a moment to decipher the request. "Who—" she began, then stopped. The woman had already melted into the icy night.

Freezing rain pelted Hanneke's cheeks as she cautiously stepped onto the porch. Her fingers tightly clenched the lantern's handle. She didn't see whomever the woman had referred to. She took two slow steps forward, and—*there.* A man had collapsed, or perhaps been dropped, in the slushy snow beside the porch. His clothing was dark, but beneath a wool cap, his cheek was pale.

Mindful not to slip, Hanneke hurried down the steps and crouched beside him. He was breathing, but insensible. "Sir?" she tried. "Sir!" He made no move or sound.

Hanneke sank back on her heels, blowing on her fingers, shivering. This simply would not do. She wished the man's companion had lingered long enough to help get him up the two porch steps. In this weather, there was no time to run to the closest farm for help.

Well, she thought briskly, I'll have to manage.

It was not easy. Torn between the need to get the man warm and her fear of causing more harm, Hanneke labored slowly. She was panting by the time she'd managed to drag the man into the kitchen. The parlor, which held the home's only woodstove, seemed an ocean away. For now, she thought, this is the best I can do.

Darting into the bedroom, she grabbed warm blankets and a pillow, and soon had the man settled onto a pallet on the floor. He looked to be perhaps thirty or thirty-five years of age, a few years older than her own twenty-nine. Removing his hat revealed a thatch of hair the color of ripe wheat above high cheekbones and a sharp nose.

She knelt and touched a finger to the man's eyelid. No twitch or flutter. Then she picked up one of his arms, held it low over his face, and dropped it. It landed square, and provoked no additional response. Very well, then. He wasn't faking his stupor in some bizarre attempt to gain access to a young widow's home. A hasty check for weapons revealed only an empty knife sheath.

Satisfied that she wasn't in imminent danger, Hanneke quickly kindled a fire in the cooking niche and lit all three tapers in the tin sconce on the wall. With better illumination, she saw what she had missed before—bloodstains and a small hole in his lower right trouser leg. No, two holes.

Her mouth tightened. This man had not fallen, or suffered a farm accident. He'd been shot through the fleshy part of his calf—and she was fairly sure that she knew why.

The implications prickled a warning against her skin, but she straightened her shoulders. Speculation was a waste of time. She needed to focus on what needed doing. Hanneke had no formal medical training, but she'd been watching and learning from skilled healers since childhood. Without a family of her own to care for, tending to others in need helped stave off despondency.

Now, she quickly gathered a basin of warm water, clean rags, absorbent cloth, and strips of linen. Easing up the man's trouser leg, she found a tight, makeshift bandage fashioned from a heavy cotton kerchief. She slipped a heavy towel beneath his calf so she could clean and dress the wounds.

When she'd done what she could for the gunshot wounds, she turned to the question of the man's insensibility. There was no sign of blood matting his hair, but her gentle fingertips soon discovered a lump on the back of his head. Since the skin had not broken, there was nothing more she could do about that.

His skin felt cold to the touch, and she indulged in a quick, silent fume that her home contained no true hearth or modern cookstove. The small *fachwerk* structure had been constructed in the Old World style, with a mixture of clay and straw filling in a framework of posts and beams. The nogging clenched the wet cold.

Hanneke wrestled the man from his wet coat. His arms and shoulders were well-muscled, and it took some effort, but he didn't stir. One coat pocket was filled with hard slices of twice-baked bread. The other was empty, and the pockets of his trousers as well. His shirt and vest were dry, so she simply folded another blanket over him. New socks as well, she decided, for blood had soaked into his boot. She knit professionally, and had plenty of thick, warm socks on hand. She grabbed a pair from her market basket, tugged off his well-worn boots, and made the exchange.

Then she filled the teapot, placed it on the iron stand in the cooking niche, and built up the fire. There. The man's most immediate needs had been seen to.

Instead of taking a deep breath, though, Hanneke felt a rising sense of agitation. Fanning her fingers toward the flames, she contemplated the stranger lying on her floor. *Lieber Gott*, what was she going to do with him?

There were no easy answers, for she felt certain that the African woman who'd begged for help was a runaway slave. If the man lying on her floor had been trying to help her, he may have been shot by a slave catcher from the South. Or, Hanneke reflected grimly, whoever took aim might have been a local resident who hoped to capture the fugitive woman and claim a reward.

The thought was revolting. It was frightening as well. Hanneke began to pace. If the shooter was able to trace the pair here, she and the unconscious man were *both* in danger.

Her understanding of the Fugitive Slave Act of 1850, a law passed six years earlier, only added to her growing unease. That law required that anyone aware of a runaway must help the kidnappers and lawmen bound to return that person to their owners—even if the fugitive had reached a free state such as Wisconsin.

Hanneke had never actually seen a Negro on her property before. However, after her husband's death, she'd discovered that he had been an abolitionist. Fridolin had established a secret hiding spot in the grain barn, and when Hanneke figured out what he'd been doing, she had vowed to continue his work. In the ten months since she'd immigrated to Wisconsin, she had on a few occasions found evidence that some desperate soul had found shelter among the carefully stacked wheat sheaves. Had this injured man been guiding the Negro woman toward that sanctuary when he was shot?

A cardinal's song came through the back window. With a start, Hanneke realized that dawn was yawning over the horizon. Her closest neighbors and friends were always up before the sun and—since Hanneke owned no mount or vehicle—often stopped by to offer a ride to town or help with a heavy chore. She could not risk having somebody visit and spot an unconscious stranger on her kitchen floor.

She pressed her thumbs to her temples. She must keep this man safe, but that responsibility would be a great deal easier to manage if she had any inkling of how the Underground Railroad actually operated.

Was there someone she might approach for help? Her neighbor John Barlow was steady in a crisis, but he was also a deputy county sheriff. Although a few vocal abolitionists had established an anti-slavery society in the area, they appeared to be most interested in changing laws, not breaking them. Hanneke didn't think they were the people to turn to.

An unexpected incident last spring had brought her in brief contact with three Watertown businesspeople who helped fugitives travel north. She'd had the most contact with a white Yankee man named Asa Hawkins, but going to him was out of the question. Despite the risks he took to help freedom-seekers, he was a dreadful human being with strong anti-immigrant sentiments. She felt more comfortable asking for help from one of the others, a colored laundress and a barber. She didn't know how to find the laundress, but she'd visited the barber before.

Very well, Hanneke decided. If a better solution hadn't presented itself by the time she'd finished stable chores, she'd drag the injured man into her *schwartze Küche*—a walk-in chimney—where he couldn't be seen from any window. Then she'd make her way to Watertown.

Before venturing out, Hanneke changed into a deep blue wool work dress and tied a scarf over her hair. She checked on her patient. He was still insensible.

She tried not to hurry as she crossed the farmyard, but she couldn't help wondering if someone was watching from the dense forest surrounding her cleared acres. Once inside the stable, she tended her sheep with her usual care. Then she tossed some dried corn through the door to lure her chickens and geese outside. Geese were as vigilant as watchdogs.

Normally, she checked the grain barn at this early hour, prepared to replenish the supplies she'd stashed there, but today, she hesitated. It might be best to leave it alone in case someone was watching. She worried, though, about the tin box holding crackers, warm socks, and mittens that she'd secreted there. She'd be hard-pressed to explain those items if a slave catcher or lawman found her stash. I will retrieve the box, she decided, but I will go in the front door, as if simply needing to fetch something.

She made a conscious effort to hide her jitters as she walked to the barn and slipped through the tool room door. Then she walked down the central threshing floor to the rear. The storage bay on her left was empty. The bay to her right was piled with the bundled wheat that hid the secret trapdoor in the back corner, which provided runaways access.

"I'm only here to help," she softly called in English, but there was no sign of a visitor. Well, that was not surprising. Something bad had happened near her farm. The woman who'd pounded on her door had taken a huge risk by helping the injured white man as best she could, instead of simply running. No doubt she was miles away by now.

Hanneke collected her box and tucked it beneath her cloak. Her hidey-hole was no more than a gap between the bundles in the far corner, and she took care that she didn't leave a trail as she retraced her steps.

Then she hurried back to the house. "Don't be alarmed," she called as she opened the back door, in case the man had roused in her absence.

Then Hanneke froze, half inside and half out. The pallet was empty. The coat she'd hung on a chair to dry near the cooking niche was gone. She stared at the blankets on her floor until a sharp gust of wind at her neck roused her from incredulity, and she slammed the door behind her.

He couldn't have gone far, she told herself. She circled through the kitchen area, the workroom, the parlor, and her bedroom, all the while opening cupboards and checking beneath furniture. No luck. The loft was also empty.

She whirled and raced back outside. His tracks in the snow were not discernible among the others crisscrossing the yard. Save for her fowl, the farmyard was empty. She walked around the house, scanning the horizon, checking up and down the road. No one was in sight.

Back in the kitchen, she leaned against the wall by the fire and tried to imagine a plausible scenario. The front door was still latched from within, so the man must have slipped out through the back while she was in the stable tending her sheep, before she let the geese out.

Timing, however, was only part of the puzzle. How had the man managed the physical activity? He surely had a pounding headache. The leg wound would have been painful. Even if those things hadn't stopped him, the man had been out cold when she left the house.

…Hadn't he?

Hanneke fretted her lower lip between her teeth. Reaction to head wounds was difficult to predict, but she *had* wondered about the duration of his stupor. She was quite sure he'd been unconscious when she brought him inside. Could he have come to his reason without giving any sign? The thought that he might have been awake while she dressed his wound and changed his socks was disconcerting.

All told, recent events suggested that the man had been shot while doing desperate work. His ability to conceal his returning wits, and steal away in such circumstances, confirmed that he was in danger.

Hanneke's breath had grown shallow. She needed to rid her home of any evidence of her nocturnal visitor.

Fortunately, the blankets had not been stained with blood. She folded them with trembling hands and thrust them back inside her storage trunk. The handful of bloodstained cloths and towels needed to be destroyed. Hanneke considered several options before nodding. Today would be a *very* good day to bake bread. After snatching up the telltale linens, she hurried into the *schwartze Küche*.

Hanneke generally did everything possible to avoid working in the black kitchen. The small chamber stank of smoke. The chimney bricks were black with soot. The floor was stained with juices that had dripped from the hams and the occasional deer haunch hung on poles overhead to smoke.

Her solitary culinary needs could usually be accommodated in the cooking niche in the next room. Big baking jobs, however, could only be handled in the brick bake oven, which was large enough to hold a dozen loaves.

The oven's access door gaped in the wall over the cooking pit. Hanneke began by placing logs into the oven. The bricks needed to be heated evenly, and despite her sense of urgency, she wasn't going to waste good firewood.

When the fuel was in place, Hanneke nestled the bloodied linens as far into the oven as she could reach and constructed a tower of tinder and kindling around them. She lit the tinder and blew gently toward the first sparks until the fire was burning well. Then she secured the heavy oaken oven door in place and closed up the *schwartze Küche* to keep smoke from filling the whole house.

After a deep inhale, Hanneke lifted her chin. There. She'd done what needed doing.

Soon, she'd assembled what she needed to make a dozen loaves of bread: a bit of the starter she kept alive in a crock, warm water, molasses, and caraway seeds. Leaving that mixture to become livelier, she began scooping rye flour into her dough trough. The familiar routine was reassuring.

Then she heard three firm knocks on the front door. Hanneke stiffened, for this was a rarity. Any of her friends would have come to the back.

The thought of slipping upstairs and pretending that she wasn't home flashed through her mind, but she impatiently flinched that idea away. Hiding would be ridiculous. Her chimney was smoking, and if the unexpected visitor was inquisitive enough to walk around the house, one glance through the kitchen window would reveal a busy day of baking well underway.

Her caller knocked again.

Don't dither, Hanneke admonished herself, and pushed back her shoulders. There was nothing to do but answer the door.

Chapter Two

Hanneke cracked open the door and saw a black-haired man waiting on her front porch. The stranger removed his hat and smiled pleasantly. *"Guten Tag. Sprichst du Englisch?"* When she nodded, he switched to his own native tongue. "My name is Hiram Aubuchon." His accent was unfamiliar.

She studied him with narrowed eyes. She judged him to be no more than forty, maybe less. His appearance was respectable. A carefully shaped mustache flared above his mouth, and his side whiskers reached to his jaw in a fashion Hanneke had seen on businessmen in town. The unbuttoned dark brown frock coat he wore was well-tailored, as were his white shirt, black cravat, and a pretty waistcoat made from tan and mauve brocade. His hands were empty, although Hanneke didn't miss the slight bulge of a holstered pistol under his coat. He'd tied his saddle horse to her front garden fence, and she also took note of the rifle secured behind the saddle.

She didn't like the look of him. "May I help you?" she asked without enthusiasm.

"Possibly so. May I come inside for a chat?"

"Indeed not!" His hubris left her incredulous. "I'm very busy this morning."

He nodded, as if very well-versed in a German farm wife's travails. "Of course, of course. I'm terribly sorry to trouble you. I am a policeman."

I doubt that very much, Hanneke thought. "May I see your badge?"

"I'm a private policeman," he clarified. "We don't carry badges. What's important is that I have reason to believe that a fugitive slave woman is traveling through this area."

Hanneke gripped the inside door latch so hard a pain shot through her hand. She had surmised as much, but hearing the confirmation jarred her. Had he singled her out? How much did he suspect?

She stared at him coolly. "Is that so?"

"It is indeed. Simply put, her owners want her back." Mr. Aubuchon smiled pleasantly again, as if discussing nothing more dramatic than the weather. "Have you seen any colored women passing by?"

Holding his gaze, Hanneke willed herself to remain composed. "I have not." It wasn't even a lie. In the darkness, she'd seen nothing.

"This one's about twenty years of age, black colored, with several broken teeth."

Hanneke puckered her brow in what she hoped was convincing fashion. "Should I be alarmed?"

"You should be concerned." Aubuchon stroked his side whiskers. "And watchful. The woman is dangerous. She possesses a violent temperament."

"I shall keep my doors locked." Hanneke took a step backwards, indicating the conversation's end.

Instead of retreating, Aubuchon took a step forward. It was a small step. His expression remained affable. Still, Hanneke sensed an unspoken threat.

"These runaways are devious," Aubuchon continued, as if confiding a secret to a trusted companion. His false veneer of camaraderie and polish made Hanneke feel queasy. "I've known them to ghost inside some upright citizen's home, steal food or valuables, and disappear again without a trace."

"I've lost nothing."

"Well," he said, drawing out the word, "there are signs that only an experienced man such as myself would notice. I trust you won't mind if I come in and take a look around."

Hanneke's pulse quickened. "That would be *most* inappropriate."

Aubuchon propped the toe of one gleaming boot onto the threshold. "I must advise you, ma'am, that it would be even more inappropriate for me to conclude that you might be breaking federal law by aiding and abetting a fugitive."

For the first time, Hanneke glimpsed a flicker of malevolence in his eyes.

Her heart began banging against her ribs like a mallet. Her first instinct was to slam the door in his face. Her hand trembled with the desire to do just that.

But…was that what he wanted? Did he want to claim that she wasn't providing him assistance as required by law? Would allowing him to conduct his odious search be the most expedient way to be rid of him?

She didn't know. That in itself was alarming. There's nothing for him to find, Hanneke reminded herself. The reassurance didn't make her feel any better. Seconds were ticking by, though. She had to say something.

"Very well." Her words fell like ice chips, for even false courtesy was out of her reach by now. Stepping back, she allowed Hiram Aubuchon to access her home.

Searching the small and sparsely furnished house didn't take long. Hanneke balled her fists as the slave tracker looked under her bed and inside the tall freestanding *shrank* that took the place of a clothes closet. He opened the trunk where she'd re-packed the spare blankets.

She followed Aubuchon up to the loft. He checked this space with equal care, bumping his head against strings of dried apples hanging from the rafters, squinting at shadowed corners. He paused at the window where Fridolin's precious telescope stood just as he'd left it, and leaned over as if to use it.

"Do *not* touch that," she snapped, goaded beyond endurance. "Mr. Aubuchon, as I told you, I am extremely busy this morning. It's time for you to go back downstairs."

He raised one sardonic eyebrow but turned to the stairs. Back on the lower level, he stopped at the chimney door. "What's in there?"

"A black kitchen."

Clearly none the wiser, he opened the door and walked inside. "Good God!" he exclaimed, studying the chimney walls with momentary shock. Then he noticed the dome-shaped door over the firepit. "Where does that go?"

Hanneke forced herself to unclench her teeth. "To my bake oven."

"Open it."

"I will not!"

He shot her a speculative sideways glance. "Then I will." He grasped the handle, pulled off the door—and was instantly engulfed in the wave of smoke that billowed from the oven. He stumbled backwards and dropped the oven door to the brick floor.

Hanneke took great satisfaction in his violent coughing fit. "Take care!" she barked. "That door might have cracked. Besides, you're letting the heat escape." She tossed in a few more logs before securing the wooden door back in place.

She'd hoped Aubuchon would be on his way, but once he'd composed himself, he announced his intention to check her outbuildings. "You will go nowhere near my animals without my supervision," Hanneke informed him. She strode after him to the stable.

From there, they visited the huge grain barn. Aubuchon insisted on opening the big breezeway doors. For a moment, Hanneke feared he'd go out the back and spot the small star Fridolin had carved low on the building's northwest corner as a signal of safety to runaways. Apparently, however, the slave catcher only wanted more light.

Grabbing a pitchfork, he shoved his way through the storage bays, poking at the bundled grain. Hanneke bit her tongue to keep from shrieking. *Gott sei dank* the fugitive woman had been wise enough to keep running after leaving her wounded companion. Had Aubuchon done the shooting? The thought brought a new curl of nausea. He didn't look like he'd been running through the woods all night, but there had been plenty of time for him to return to his lodgings and tidy up before heading back this way.

After taking his time, Aubuchon finally put the fork aside. Hanneke gestured him to the door and followed him out. Even the weak sunshine felt good on her face. "Very well," she snapped. "You have intruded on my time and my property for long enough. I expect you to leave at once."

He had the audacity to tip his shiny hat before walking calmly across the yard and down the drive to his waiting horse. Hanneke stood by the garden fence, watching until he'd mounted and disappeared from sight around a wooded bend in the road.

Bile abruptly rose in her throat. She forced it down before making her shaky way back inside and latching the door behind her. In the kitchen, she added more fuel to the small fire in the cooking niche. Then she sank into a chair, folded her arms on the table, and buried her face.

Hanneke had named her property Safe Haven Farm in an unspoken pledge to any desperate soul trying to reach Canada. In time, she'd come to embrace this house—wretched black kitchen and all—as her own haven as well. Now, an actual *slaver* had intruded upon the sanctity of her home.

I certainly knew something like this might happen one day, Hanneke thought. The prospect of being arrested for breaking the law had always been unsettling. She had also pushed the thought to the back of her mind. She hadn't imagined a slave catcher appearing at her door, or known how personally violated she would feel, or—

She jerked erect at the sound of booted feet climbing her back steps. Someone knocked firmly on the door. "Frau Bauer?" a man called.

Hanneke pressed one palm against her chest before belatedly recognizing the voice of John Barlow, who owned a farm just northwest of her own. She made an effort to collect herself before going to the door and ushering him inside.

"*Guten Morgen,*" he began, but a frown quickly puckered his brow. "Are you all right?"

Nein, she wanted to say. She hadn't had time to collect her own thoughts, much less decide what to share with Deputy Barlow. "Let me get a pot of coffee started," she equivocated.

He leaned against the dry sink. "You're obviously distraught."

The observation was true, but annoying nonetheless. "I'm mostly furious," she tried.

His mouth twisted with impatience. "For the love of God—"

"I just had a visit from a slave catcher."

John's face tightened as anger flared in his eyes. He was a lean man of only middling height, but Hanneke had watched him break up tavern brawls, arrest violent drunkards, and even face down an angry street mob. It was a relief to have him here...and it made her wary.

"What was the man's name?"

"Hiram Aubuchon."

They'd been speaking in the Pomeranian dialect, but the deputy muttered an English curse. "I've met him."

She blinked. "You have? Where?"

"Aubuchon came up from Missouri, and introduced himself to local lawmen when he arrived in Watertown. Said he was tracking a woman and gave us a description of her. He brought two men with him to help." John's voice was tight with distaste.

"I would have guessed that such a man would cling to secrecy."

Barlow pulled off his hat and raked a hand through his dark hair. "I suspect his primary goal in speaking to us was intimidation. He felt compelled to remind us that the government protects his work."

Hanneke glared at the floor. The situation was intolerable.

"I think we should sit down," the deputy suggested, "so you can tell me what happened."

She realized with chagrin that she'd been shockingly discourteous. The two of them usually sat in the kitchen with refreshments when they needed to converse. Now the huge dough trough claimed the table, and the yeast she'd set to quicken had foamed up in its bowl and dribbled over the sides. "Let's go into the other room," she said, and led the way.

The parlor was freezing, but Hanneke quickly lit the prepared fire in the small woodstove. They pulled chairs close. Omitting mention of her nighttime visitors, she recounted her experience with Hiram Aubuchon. "Someone vile enough to drag a human being back to a life of horrors poked through my house," she summarized. She heard the bitterness in her tone but couldn't help it.

John leaned back in his chair so he could warm his worn boots by the stove. "I must say, I'm surprised that you didn't slam the door in Aubuchon's face."

"I *wanted* to." Hanneke reached into her knitting basket and pulled out a half-finished sock. "I've always imagined slave catchers as rough men in shabby clothes following baying hounds through the woods. His dress and manner disconcerted me."

"I've no doubt that was the man's exact intention." The lawman's voice was grim.

"He told me that he was a private policeman."

"Aubuchon is a soulless bounty hunter."

She focused on the sock for a few seconds, grateful for the repetitive stitches, the familiar feel of soft yarn, and smooth wooden needles in her hands. "He threatened me as well. He said that refusing him entry would cause him to conclude that I was aiding and abetting a fugitive."

John grimaced.

"The truth is…." Feeling the rare sting of tears, Hanneke paused, furiously blinking them away. "I made a terrible mistake."

The admission prompted John's eyes to flare with something that she didn't recognize. "Do not blame yourself. Men like that are well practiced in whatever manipulations are needed to get their way." He looked away, brooding for a long moment. "Aubuchon must have reason to believe that the missing woman might be passing through this general area. He's probably going door to door, hoping someone will help him."

"I've never heard of a slave catcher in the county before."

"Bounty hunters operate more commonly in eastern states," John agreed. "But as I understand it, people fleeing from places like Arkansas and Missouri often travel up the Mississippi River. Then, they pick up the Rock River and continue their journey through Central Illinois. Once in Wisconsin, they somehow make their way to one of the Lake Michigan ports."

The Rock River looped right through Watertown. I'll never look at the waterway again, Hanneke thought, without wondering how recently someone seeking freedom had paddled through town under cover of darkness. "Will you be called upon to help Aubuchon?" The thought was repugnant.

"Federal marshals are responsible for finding runaway slaves. However, county lawmen must provide aid if asked, and would get involved if there's any kind of ruckus." He lifted his palms in a weary gesture. "Some people in these parts would be eager to help return a slave, especially if they'd receive a reward. Others would be just as eager to hinder a kidnapper. Sentiments run high. There have been incidents in other Wisconsin towns where things got ugly."

That, Hanneke mused, I do not doubt. "Take care," she murmured, and he nodded.

Hanneke's relationship with John Barlow had not always been companionable. He was stubborn and often irritable. The day last May when she'd arrived in nearby Watertown, he'd ordered her to leave. Subsequent interactions had been confrontational. Even now, they often argued.

She had, however, come to understand that the deputy was a good man at heart. He was already struggling to manage his small farm, excel in his law enforcement work, and care for his beloved but frail wife. As a Yankee who'd married a Pomeranian woman, he straddled two sometimes contentious worlds. Hanneke felt sorry for John, and angry that the government had placed him in such a wretched position.

"Well," John said, "I must soon be on my way, Frau Bauer." They'd agreed to converse on a first-name basis, but old habits died hard. "I'll stop at home and tell Ulricke not to open the door to any stranger today. I also need to talk with a woman who believes that someone stole her best-laying *Ostfriesische Möwe*. The bird produced over two hundred eggs last year."

"Gracious." Egg money was often the backbone of a farm woman's economy. No wonder the owner wanted the chicken returned.

"And," John continued, "I haven't even told you why I'm here."

"Oh!" Hanneke felt chagrined anew. Honestly, she thought. This was most disconcerting. She took pride in presenting herself as a capable and hospitable woman. "How may I help you?"

"You can assist me with a case."

"Of course." She was relieved to change topics and pleased by the request. After she'd helped solve two horrid murder cases, the deputy had resigned himself to the fact that her unique perspective and efforts had value. Now, in cases affecting women or families, he sometimes asked for her assistance. She didn't get paid for her services, of course, but her involvement was satisfying, nonetheless.

"I've received notice that a Pomeranian servant named Charlotte, who broke her bond and left the Old Country without permission, has taken up residence in the county. Out near Clyman's Corners, if you happen to know it. I need to discover the truth of that charge, but when I visited her, she was less than helpful." His mouth twisted to one side with annoyance. "To say the least."

And how brusquely did you speak with this Charlotte? Hanneke wanted to ask but refrained. Sometimes, John Barlow got in his own way. She tipped her head, considering. "What will happen to the woman if she admits to the charge?"

"Her employer wants her returned. He said he'd also be willing to accept financial compensation, but I doubt she can pay. Pomeranian officials won't come and retrieve her, and it's difficult to believe that her former employer would invest any more time and resources on the matter. He probably wants to get some revenge by giving her a fright. Nonetheless, I have an obligation to learn what I can, and write back to the man. I'm hoping that she'll be more willing to confide in you."

"Where does the woman live?"

"Charlotte Stofeldt is married now. She and her husband are farming six or seven miles north of here." One corner of Barlow's mouth quirked toward a rare smile. "You won't need to walk. A few days ago, we arrested a horse thief in possession of half a dozen animals. We're trying to track down the owners, but the county is paying top dollar to a local livery. No one will mind if I board one here for a short time. I have a docile mare in mind."

The offer was both unexpected and welcome. "I would appreciate that," Hanneke assured him. She was quite capable of walking twelve miles in a day, perhaps catching a ride along the way, but reliable transportation in this weather would be most wonderful.

"You're comfortable riding alone?"

"*Ja.*" Hanneke had grown up on a farm.

"I'll bring her by later, then, and a saddle and grain and bedding as well. If anyone asks, just tell them you're doing me and the city treasury a favor by boarding her here." He got to his feet. "Your errand for me is not urgent. Give yourself time to…." He hesitated, as if groping for the right words. "Catch your breath."

Hanneke suspected he'd been about to say "calm yourself," but thought better of it. "I will." She walked him to the door before adding, "And if Hiram Aubuchon ever approaches again, I will be better prepared."

John paused with one hand on the latch. "Do not underestimate him, Hanneke. Or forget that he's not working alone." The deputy touched the brim of his hat and took his leave.

The caution chilled her anew, but she accepted his concern as a gift. She'd never told the deputy about the secret entrance in her grain barn, and she never would. Did he harbor suspicions? Quite possibly.

Once, at a desperate moment shortly after arriving in Watertown, Deputy John Barlow had been pulled into an unexpected mess involving two runaways. To his credit, he had chosen to ignore the Fugitive Slave Law and look the other way. They hadn't spoken of the incident since, but if the need for such a blind eye arose again, Hanneke did *not* assume that he would feel able to provide it. She sent up a prayer that neither one of them would ever find themselves in such a dangerous position again.

Then she considered what remained of the day. Above all else, she needed to keep busy and accomplish something useful.

The first thing to do was salvage her baking and set her kitchen to rights. She'd been raised in an area where wood was so scarce that half-timbered buildings had been mandatory, with black kitchens designed to let women bake, cook, and smoke meat with a single fire. Although seventy of her own eighty acres were wooded, she wasn't going to waste the blaze she'd kindled in the oven.

She fed a fresh batch of starter, mixed her dough, and separated it into eight round rye straw baskets to rise. Then, she heated water and began vigorously scrubbing her floors. Although the chore left her winded, achy-kneed, and raw-fingered, it was satisfying to scour away whatever trace of Aubuchon's boots had remained.

By midday, the loaves were ready to bake. In the *schwartze Küche*, she scraped the coals into the firepit before flipping the plump rounds, two at a time, onto the long-handled wooden peel she used to transfer the dough to the hot bricks.

Once the bread was baking, Hanneke retreated back to the parlor stove. After feeding it, she reached for a sweet little wooden bird carved with wings outstretched. The bird was a treasured talisman, left for her by an unknown soul who'd once sheltered in her grain barn. She squeezed it in her hand, wishing she didn't still feel agitated. *Aubuchon found nothing*, she reminded herself, *because I had prepared for just such a visit.*

Nonetheless, Hanneke could still feel the knot that had pulled tight in her chest. She'd been maintaining Fridolin's hidey-hole in the barn for almost a year, but since she'd never before actually encountered anyone seeking haven on her property, the risk had felt minimal. Aubuchon had brought the abomination of slavery into her parlor. Her resolve to help fugitive human beings had not wavered, but she felt as if someone had grabbed her hand and yanked her closer to a blazing fire.

Even worse, she hadn't known how to handle the wretched man. Hanneke set the bird aside and reached for her knitting, forcing herself to revisit the moment she'd allowed him to enter her home. Hanneke rarely got flustered, but the sad truth was that she'd done just that and let a bully overrule her instincts.

The realization was galling. Hanneke felt humbled…and achingly lonely. She wished she could have confided *everything* to John Barlow, starting with the moment the Negro woman had pounded on her door. Unless the Fugitive Slave Act was repealed, though, that would never be possible.

Hanneke closed her eyes and turned her face toward the ceiling. *Oh, Fridolin. Something horrid happened today. How I wish we could face these times together.*

Fridolin did not answer. He usually did not.

Hanneke exhaled slowly. Then, she purposefully straightened her spine. Very well. She would manage on her own. If ever confronted with such a despicable man again, she would not permit him to frighten her into abandoning her responsibility.

I just wish, she thought, that I knew how to better prepare for whatever ugliness I might next confront.

Chapter Three

That afternoon, Hanneke was just setting the last of her bread loaves to cool in the kitchen when, through the window, movement in the yard caught her eye. She tensed before recognizing John Barlow, who was leading a horse into her stable.

Hanneke pulled on her mittens and cloak. Before leaving the kitchen, she grabbed a carrot from the pantry. She felt compelled to pause briefly on the back porch, tipping her face up to catch a hint of warmth on her skin. Just as welcome was the *plop-plop-plop* of droplets falling from roof-hanging icicles, and the unmistakable murky scent of a thaw. Weeks had passed since the temperature last crept above freezing.

Then she went to meet her temporary mount. The mare was on the small side, perhaps fourteen hands high, with a glossy gray coat and a white streak on her nose. She showed no agitation when Hanneke stepped into the stall. *"Hallo, Schöne,"* Hanneke said softly, offering the treat on a flat palm. "You and I shall keep each other company until you can be returned to your own home."

John went back out to his wagon and returned with a saddle, blanket, and bridle. "I didn't have access to a sidesaddle. Can you manage?"

"I can indeed." Hanneke had been raised on a potato farm in Kreis Greifenburg, a district near the Baltic Sea in Prussia's Pomeranian region. When her only sibling, a brother, showed no interest in (or aptitude for) farming, Hanneke had gladly become her father's companion. When she was small, he often settled her before him on his horse while on an errand. She had loved leaning into his chest and feeling the mount's motion beneath her.

Later, during his final illness, she had often ridden alone when conducting farm or family business. "I believe I'll call her Cinder."

John patted the mare's withers. "I don't think you'll have any trouble with her."

"We'll do fine," Hanneke assured him. "Do you have time for a snack before you go?" He hesitated. "Still warm from the oven," she added. Attention caught, he followed her to the house.

After the morning's fuss, it pleased her inordinately to usher John into a tidy kitchen. She sliced away the hard, ashy bottom of one loaf and served the deputy two dark slices and a cup of coffee.

"Rye bread with caraway seeds," he murmured approvingly. "After marrying Ulricke, I quickly came to prefer such hearty bread." He polished off his first piece before refocusing the conversation. "Clara Steckelberg caught me at home earlier. She and Charles had also received a visit from Aubuchon."

Hanneke eyed him over the rim of her tin mug. The Steckelbergs were her closest neighbors, and Clara especially was a dear friend. "It's hard to imagine that she was not incensed," Hanneke observed.

"Well, she did want to share her opinions with me." Barlow's tone was sardonic. Clara was blunt on the best of days, and never let polite conventions get in the way of expressing her thoughts. "Evidently, Charles answered the knock. Once he understood Aubuchon's business, Charles launched into a lecture about the evils of slavery." The corners of his mouth quirked, just a little. "Charles was apparently quite fiery. When Clara caught on, however, she stepped onto the porch with a shotgun, fired over Aubuchon's head, and ran him off the place."

The image was satisfying, and the story confirmed Hanneke's unspoken suspicion that the Steckelbergs abhorred slavery as much as she did. Gracious! she thought with both ruefulness and admiration. Clara had handled the slaver much better than *she* had.

What, however, had happened when Aubuchon reached the next farm, and the one after that? Had another neighbor, motivated by personal beliefs or the prospect of a reward, been willing to offer assistance?

John drained his cup. "I must be on my way, but I'll let you know if I learn anything more about Aubuchon." He pushed back his chair and took his leave.

Alone again, Hanneke restlessly circled through her home. For most of the winter, she'd enjoyed the company of two good friends, Karoline Ketzler and her daughter Jacobine. They'd been in need of a safe space after the death of Karoline's husband, and Hanneke had delighted in their companionship through the frigid season's darkest days. Having helped Karoline through such a difficult period, and accepting custody of Jacobine while doing it, Hanneke loved them both. The Ketzlers had recently moved out, and although Hanneke was pleased about their new start, she did miss them.

So stop moping, she told herself, and do something useful. Deputy Barlow had asked for her help. Accomplishing that would lift her spirits more than scrubbing floors or baking more bread than she needed.

Stepping outside, she eyed the sky and concluded that with the mare, she still had time to visit Charlotte Stofeldt and return home before daylight faded. After quickly changing into her favorite green and brown plaid day dress, and bundling up, she saddled Cinder and was soon on her way. It felt good to get away from home. Besides, she hadn't had the opportunity to ride solo in a long time.

Savoring this unexpected bit of independence, Hanneke headed north. Having lived her first twenty-eight years in the Old World, she'd known only tired soil and largely treeless landscapes. Since emigrating last year, she had never ceased to marvel at southern Wisconsin's landscape of forests, prairies, and farms—some already prosperous, others fledgling, all fertile with promise even in winter. Deep woods were broken by open prairies, many with a few lone bur oak trees standing sentinel over the open space where coneflowers and Queen of the Prairie would bloom.

And the winter was waning, slowly but inexorably. A stack of buckets visible in a maple grove provided testament that sugaring season would soon be underway. Water dripped from melting icicles. She heard the growing chatter of redpolls well before she rounded a bend and saw several hundred of the small cherry-patched songbirds in a stubbled field. She paused to watch them bobbing about as they searched for seeds among the slushy snow.

The road was rough, but the mare proved deft and sure-footed, and Hanneke reached Charlotte Stofeldt's farm in less than an hour. Just one small field had been cleared, and she guessed that the farm had been established within the past two years.

A single large, rectangular two-story *fachwerk* building dominated the clearing. A housebarn, Hanneke realized, carefully situated on a hill with the slope allowing two stories on the east side. Such structures were intended to shelter livestock and people under a single roof. The practical style had been common in Pomerania, but she'd seen only a few in Wisconsin.

Today, smoke drifted a welcome from the chimney. A woman wearing a dark burgundy cape was hanging sheets from a line in the yard in the company of a small girl.

Hanneke nudged the gray mare up the drive and called, *"Guten Tag!"* as she drew close. "My name is Frau Bauer. Are you Frau Stofeldt?"

"I am." The mother made a *Stay here* gesture to her daughter before walking closer. She was a sturdy woman in her late thirties, Hanneke guessed, with a round face and a direct gaze that was neither warm nor concerned. "I don't believe we've met before. What is your business here?"

"I live south of here. Closer to Watertown." Hanneke dismounted and wrapped Cinder's reins around a fence post. "I assist Deputy Barlow upon occasion. He suggested my visit."

Frau Stofeldt snorted with annoyance. *"That* one."

Hanneke stifled a sigh. "The deputy's intentions are always good, but his manner can be…indelicate. Trust me, I know. The day I arrived in Watertown, he threatened me with arrest and ordered me to leave on the next stagecoach."

Frau Stofeldt's eyebrows pulled high with astonishment, but after a moment, her mouth curved in a smile. "Let's go inside where it's warm. You can bring your horse in also."

"May I help hang the rest of your laundry first?" Hanneke asked. Pegging heavy wet sheets on the line was not a pleasant task at this time of year.

"I'd be grateful." Frau Stofeldt led the way. "I do like hanging them in the fresh air, even if they come back inside half-frozen." She turned to the child—a pretty girl with dark curls framing her face, who looked to be about four years old. "Beatta, please run ahead and check on your brother."

The two women made short work of it. Then Hanneke fetched the mare, and they went inside the barn area, where six red Holstein cows were chewing their cuds and warming the space with their bulk. Frau Stofeldt pointed to the only empty stall. "My husband is away, so you can use that one."

Once Cinder was secure, Hanneke's hostess led her through a door in the wall that separated this area from the eastern half of the structure. They emerged into a smoky landing. A door standing slightly open revealed a large *schwartze Küche*, with a small fire still burning beneath the laundry cauldron. To close the chimney off or not, Hanneke thought, was ever the choice. In this house, letting some heat escape with the smoke had been deemed preferable to sealing inside both elements as she did at home.

Steps led both upstairs and down. A familiar smell drifted from below, and Hanneke heard bleating. Sheep. She started to ask a question, but reminded herself that chatting about animal husbandry did not fit the purview of Deputy Barlow's request.

Frau Stofeldt led Hanneke up the stairs to a main room, where Beatta was playing with a homemade doll near a baby sleeping in a cradle. Despite the presence of small children, the space was immaculate. The bed in one corner was draped with a woven coverlet. Bouquets of dried flowers sat on the table and a large desk. The sitting area was arranged on a thick wool carpet. Knitting needles poked from a basket on the floor. A small upright spinning wheel waited in one corner. The blue-and-white spongeware dishes displayed in a cupboard were lovely, as were several embroidered pictures gracing the walls. Nothing was fancy or expensive, but the room was welcoming.

Hanneke smiled. "What an inviting space."

The observation had been meant as a compliment, but it wasn't taken that way. "You may consider me a criminal," Frau Stofeldt said with quiet dignity, "but I am a law-abiding, respectable woman."

"That is indeed my impression," Hanneke said gently.

Some of the defensiveness seeped from the other woman's posture, and she nodded. Then she removed her quilted hood, revealing ginger hair captured in a braid and coiled behind her head. "I'm going to fetch some coals for the foot warmers. Make yourself comfortable."

"*Danke*, Frau Stofeldt."

She paused. "Please, call me Charlotte."

"And you must call me Hanneke."

In short order Charlotte had returned with a covered bucket and filled the two punched-tin warmers waiting on the carpet. Then, she took a chair where she could look directly at her guest. "Now. You're here about the summons. Let me make one thing very clear. I have no intention of returning to Pomerania. The deputy would have to drag me from my home in chains."

"I'm quite sure it won't come to that." Hanneke pulled a half-knit sock and thin needles from her pocket and began to work. She hoped that working on a sock might make the conversation feel more neighborly than confrontational. "Deputy Barlow wanted to hear your side of the story before responding to your former employer. Can you tell me why you chose to leave before fulfilling your service contract?"

Charlotte folded her hands in her lap. "I left because my employer, a married man, debased me."

Hanneke's jaw muscles tightened. Charlotte's voice was low and hard. Her gaze was intent and unblinking. Hanneke believed that the other woman was telling the truth.

A sheep's quiet *baa* drifted through cracks in the floor. Charlotte paused and drew in a long breath, as if willing herself to remain unemotional. Then she continued. "He was cruel in other ways as well. If I angered him, he denied me food or took my shoes. One whole January, I went about with nothing on my feet save a pair of stockings."

Hanneke well remembered how achingly cold Pomerania's winters could be. And now the wretched man wanted Charlotte returned to his farm?

"*Ja*. I did break my contract and run away." Charlotte lifted her chin. "But my employer broke his moral obligation to treat me with decency." She spoke with sudden vehemence. "*All* human beings deserve that."

Hanneke thought about the human beings who'd arrived at Safe Haven Farm in the dark. Too often, the line between slavery and indentured servitude blurred.

Before she managed to find a response, Beatta wandered close and held up her doll for Hanneke's inspection. "My *Mutti* made this for me."

"What a fine doll! Your *Mutti* must love you very much. *Danke* for showing me, Beatta."

Apparently satisfied, the child went back to her place by the cradle. Glancing up, Hanneke saw that Charlotte's expression had softened during the exchange. Now she spread her hands, then let them drop back into her lap. "So, Hanneke. You've heard my story. Are you going to tell that deputy to send me back to Pomerania?"

"*Nein*. I will simply share what you've told me. He will write a letter to your employer, which will likely end the matter. I am horrified by what you endured at the hands of your master, and I expect Deputy Barlow to be equally disgusted." She held the other woman's gaze. "I think you were quite brave."

Charlotte flicked one hand to wave that away. "I don't think of it that way. If I'd stayed, I would not have survived."

"I'm glad you've been able to make a new life for yourself." Hanneke tucked her knitting away and stood. "I couldn't agree more with what you said earlier. Every woman, man, and child, deserves to be treated with kindness and respect."

Charlotte studied her, head tipped, as if considering something. After a moment she said, "As you might imagine, I offer up prayers of thanks for my home and family here every day. I also grieve for everyone who is not able to exercise free will."

Hanneke nodded, unsure where this thought was going.

"I have been working to change the laws that allow slavery to exist in

America," Charlotte explained. "I am fortunate to live in an area where abolitionist sentiments run strong. Two other anti-slavery women and I meet regularly to write letters to our statesmen, hoping to convince them to do everything they can to abolish 'the institution,' as I've heard it called. Our next gathering is almost upon us." She gave Hanneke the meeting details. "Perhaps you would care to join us?"

Hanneke hesitated. The unexpected invitation was appealing, but if John took the mare back, she'd have to travel on foot. Besides, she made a habit of avoiding discussions about slavery.

"*Danke*, Charlotte," Hanneke said with true regret. "As much as I'd like to, I don't think I'll be able to come."

* * *

As she set out for home, Hanneke assessed her surroundings. Clouds had moved in. The descending sun was no more than a pale blur. The temperature had dropped as well, and she readjusted her wool scarf, so it covered her mouth and nose. "I'm fortunate to have you," she told her mount. "We'll be back at Safe Haven Farm before nightfall."

As they traveled south, Hanneke became aware of a growing fatigue. It had been a long and challenging day. She had accomplished John Barlow's task, though. That was good.

She was lost in thought when Cinder abruptly sidestepped and tossed her head. "What is it, girl?" Hanneke asked. When the mare whinnied, Hanneke dismounted. "Quiet down, now," she murmured soothingly. She studied her surroundings for evidence of whatever had spooked the placid horse, but the road was clear. A rodent scurrying underfoot might have caused momentary surprise, but Cinder was still anxious, shaking her head and snorting.

Hanneke widened her survey, studying the smudgy gray landscape. They'd just passed through two stump-riddled fields and were about to enter a wooded stretch. She didn't see anyone or anything unusual.

The mare pawed the ground impatiently. Tired and chilled, Hanneke was tempted to mount again and simply ride on…but *something* was troubling her mount. She wanted to know what it was.

She led Cinder toward a fence zigzagging along the edge of the field, planning to use the top rail as a hitching post. What had appeared to be flat ground, however, was actually a ditch filled with drifts of windblown snow. The bottom was wet with rivulets of water that had melted during the warmer afternoon hours.

Then Hanneke saw the black wool sleeve and gloved hand extending from the dwindling drift as if entreating someone, anyone, for help.

Chapter Four

"*Guter Gott!*" Hanneke gasped, pressing one hand over her chest. Had some poor soul frozen to death in a sudden storm? How long had the body been there, covered with snow? Imagining made her heartsick.

But…there was no time for that. She pressed one hand against the mare's flank and filled her lungs with bracingly cold air. There was work to do.

Hanneke led Cinder to a nearby sapling and secured the reins. Then she lifted her skirt and half-scrambled, half-slid into the gully. After pulling off one of her mittens, she wriggled two fingers beneath the glove's cuff. As she'd expected, no hint of life pulsed against her skin. The man—for it was certainly a man—was dead.

Planting her boots on either side of the small stream at the bottom of the gully, she began scooping sloppy snow away from the body. He'd fallen face down. Matted chestnut curls peeked beneath a fine fleece-lined fur hat.

I need to roll him over, Hanneke thought. She gripped one of his shoulders and tugged. He was so broad-chested that it took effort. He finally flipped over so abruptly that she staggered, lost her balance, and fell.

"Verdammt!" she muttered, because no one was there to hear. She staggered to her feet and slapped away globs of snow before her cloak soaked through. Then she leaned over the corpse.

Her jaw dropped in shock. This was no stranger. The man lying dead in the snow was Asa Hawkins.

…Wasn't it? The Asa Hawkins she'd known was perpetually angry, fierce by nature, and physically commanding. It was shocking to see him still now, waxy-skinned and diminished. There was no mistaking him, though. Although his wolfish smile was gone, she recognized the bad scars marring his left ear and cheek. He'd died wearing an expensive double-breasted frock coat of black wool, with two rows of gold buttons, typical of a man who'd reveled in his own accomplishments.

The wealthy Yankee was best known in Watertown as a successful businessman and sullen nativist. How had he come to die in a snowdrift on a rural road among farmsteads that mostly displayed European architecture? Had Hawkins been trying to help the Negro woman Hanneke had glimpsed at Safe Haven Farm? Finding Hawkins' body so soon after the colored woman had brought an injured white man to her back door was surely not a coincidence.

Hanneke's heart hurt to know that the presumably tiny handful of local Underground Railroad conductors had lost a vital link. What would happen now? Who could fill such a void? Hawkins had been a freight hauler and auctioneer. If every once in a while he'd hidden human beings among his other cargo, nobody had been the wiser.

Unless, Hanneke thought darkly, a slaver like Aubuchon had somehow realized what was happening. The previous spring, an abolitionist named Loomis had been killed in Watertown. And…what about the injured man who'd arrived with the Negro woman? Someone had, it appeared, tried to kill him. Now, Asa Hawkins was dead as well.

Had Hiram Aubuchon killed Hawkins?

With a shudder, Hanneke quickly glanced over both shoulders. The light was fading. No one was in sight. She was tempted to look for evidence of a stab or gunshot wound, but that could wait. She was cold, alone, and uneasy. *What I need to do, she concluded, is go fetch help.*

* * *

Full night had descended by the time Hanneke reached the Barlow farm. The sight of a lamp glowing softly in the front window helped ease the tight muscles in her neck. *"Danke,* girl," Hanneke whispered, patting Cinder's neck before dismounting. "You did a fine job."

When she knocked on the front door, John opened it so quickly that she suspected he'd heard her coming. "Frau Bauer!" Frowning, he gestured her inside. "What's wrong?"

The scent of fried sausage wafting from the kitchen made Hanneke's mouth water. "Asa Hawkins is dead."

John's eyes went wide for one stunned moment. Then he gestured her into a small sitting room, before asking, "When? How?"

Hanneke sidled close to a parlor stove and spread her fingers toward the heat. "I went to visit Charlotte Stofeldt this afternoon. On the way home, the mare suddenly startled. A man's gloved hand and lower arm were sticking out from a snowbank in a ditch. I dug him out enough to make the identification."

"Asa Hawkins." The deputy rubbed his jaw, clearly still absorbing the news. "Good Lord. Could you tell how he died?"

"*Nein.* I saw no obvious wound, but the gully was steep and running with snowmelt. Conditions were not ideal."

The deputy's mouth twisted unhappily to one side. Hanneke passed no judgment, assuming that he was imagining the task waiting for him. "I'll have to show you where the body is," she said, although she would *much* prefer to go home. "I doubt you could actually find it in the dark, otherwise."

Footsteps sounded in the hall before Ulricke Barlow appeared in the doorway. "Forgive me for interrupting."

Her husband popped to his feet. "Is there something you need?" Ulricke was a pretty blonde woman of delicate constitution. Hanneke had never seen her terse, impatient husband show her anything but genuine affection and care.

"*Nein,*" she assured him. "I'm wondering if there's anything *you* need." She glanced regretfully at Hanneke. "I assume this is not a social call."

"Sadly, a man has been killed," John told her. "Hanneke discovered his body and will return with me so I can find it easily. We'll need to leave at once."

"John!" Ulricke frowned. "Give the poor woman a chance to warm up."

She turned to Hanneke. "Have you had any supper? Stay here while my husband stables your horse and harnesses ours."

Ten minutes later, John and Hanneke drove from the yard in a wagon pulled by a Friesian draft horse. Hanneke felt somewhat revived by the warm sausage Ulricke had served on a thick slice of bread spread with a mustard sauce.

They traveled without speaking for a mile or so. It felt strange to be driving out at such an hour. Hanneke listened to the clip-clop of hooves, the sound brisk against the frozen earth and dulled by snow in sunless wooded areas. Barlow had hung a lantern near the seat. It seemed to anchor her.

Finally, the deputy spoke. "You're sure it was Hawkins." It was a flat statement, as if he wanted to believe she'd been wrong but knew otherwise.

She slid her hands beneath her cloak and tucked them into her armpits. "Quite sure."

John shook his head. "This is bad, you know."

"To say the least," Hanneke agreed grimly. They were choosing their words with care, but she understood exactly what he meant. Asa Hawkins had been a prominent man in Watertown. If he'd been murdered, his friends would demand hasty action to identify and punish the killer. John was the only lawman who knew of Hawkins' work with the Underground Railroad. That, Hanneke thought, presents a unique complication. Would the deputy feel compelled to speak to his boss about the incident last spring?

She couldn't refrain from asking. "John. Are you going to tell the sheriff what you know?"

He took a moment to respond. "Not if I can help it. If I reveal that I've known for almost a year that Hawkins was breaking the law...." His voice trailed away.

"Perhaps it won't need to come up?" Although dubious, she tried to sound hopeful. "I can't imagine that any of Hawkins' business associates or nativist friends knew about his...his clandestine activities."

"Pray that his participation in such activities is not ultimately revealed," John said morosely. "Public knowledge of that information could ignite a powder keg. People, including the sheriff, would demand to know who else was involved."

Hanneke had seen angry mobs marching through Watertown after dark with torches and weapons. She didn't want to see it again.

Then, with a sinking sensation in her belly, she remembered that—since she hadn't told him about her midnight visitors—the situation was even more snarled than John understood. She chewed her lower lip, unsure whether she should confide in him, or try to protect him by keeping her secret. There was no good choice, and no way to predict the implications of sharing what she knew.

John spoke from the gloom, startling her. "What's on your mind, Frau Bauer." He did not inflect the words as a question, and his tone was resigned.

I guess the decision is made, Hanneke thought. "There's something I haven't told you."

The sound of his weary sigh was so familiar that it actually steadied her. In a low voice, she said, "A colored woman brought a man I didn't recognize to my door early this morning, long before dawn. He'd been shot in the leg."

A low groan escaped his throat. "*Ach, um Gottes willen*, Hanneke! Why didn't you tell me this earlier?"

"Because I was trying to protect you," she hissed. "And the woman, who ran off immediately. And myself."

He held up one hand in grudging acknowledgment. "Did the man say who'd shot him?"

"He'd collapsed by the time I got to the door. I got him inside and tended—"

He jerked his head toward her. "A man you didn't even know?"

"The man was insensible. I couldn't leave him to bleed to death on my back steps."

A barred owl hooted from the forest: *Who cooks for you?* A few seconds later, a second owl, much farther away, responded. Wind whispered through bare branches.

John managed to stifle his irritation—again. "What happened?"

"I tended to his wound. It was a single shot straight through his calf. He also had a lump on his head. He appeared to still be unconscious when I went out for morning chores, but he disappeared before I returned to the house."

"You do realize that this stranger could have been a horse thief, or some deranged individual seeking to do harm."

Hanneke chose her words carefully. "I do not believe that was the case." She was confident he understood what she was getting at.

"Well, use more caution in the future," he grumbled, before changing the topic. "Are we getting close?"

"I believe so." She studied their surroundings for a few more minutes before pointing to a dead tree beside the road. "Just beyond that oak." She had noted a few landmarks near the body, and the skeletal trunk and remaining limbs were silhouetted black against the snow. "The body is down there."

Barlow set the brake, jumped down, and lit another lantern. "Here." He handed it over as she joined him. Then he pulled a coil of rope from the wagon bed and looped it over one shoulder.

Holding the lantern high, Hanneke watched as he sidestepped down to the body. After a quick look, he wrestled to get one end of the rope looped under Hawkins' body, just beneath his arms. Barlow muttered in both English and German. She was sorry he had to confront such a wretched task.

Once Hawkins was secured, the deputy made his way back and knotted the other end of the rope to the wagon. "I suggest you stand across the road," he told her. "I wish I had a better option, but I don't think I can drag him up the rise by myself."

John climbed back to the wagon seat and clucked to his horse. The Friesian was smaller than some breeds of workhorses, but capable. Hanneke turned away, listening to the wheels' slow grumble as the wagon inched forward. She looked at the heavens for reassurance, but saw only a few stars peeking through the clouds. This is horrid, she thought. Hot tears threatened.

Well, that simply would not do. Starch your spine, she told herself sternly. The night was not yet over.

Barlow didn't call out to her until he'd gotten the body into the wagon and wrapped it in a tarp. "What now?" Hanneke asked as she settled beside him on the seat. "Are you taking him to Dr. Rausch?" Hawkins would hate the idea of being tended by a German physician.

"*Ja*," John said tersely. "I trust Rausch. It won't make any difference to Hawkins at this point." He gave his attention to the horse for a few moments and they maneuvered a tight turnaround in the road. Once on their way, he returned to the conversation. "I can drop you at your place before I go to town."

"The detour would only slow you down," Hanneke observed. "I'll go to Watertown with you."

"That wouldn't be wise. After visiting the doctor, I'll have to stop at the sheriff's office. I'll need to give Hawkins' brother the news as well. I have no idea how long all that will take."

"I don't mind."

He turned his head to look at her. "That's a thoughtful gesture," he said skeptically, "but I suspect your kindness is prompted by curiosity."

"In this type of endeavor, curiosity is an asset," Hanneke responded pertly. Although tired, she did very much want to hear whatever Dr. Rausch had to say.

Once, the deputy would have given her orders, or at least argued. Tonight, he only nodded. Huddled against the wind, they drove on through the night.

* * *

"As you can see, the clothing is intact," Dr. Rausch told Deputy Barlow and Hanneke after a cursory examination of the dead man now lying on his examining table. Rausch was a dark-haired man with a narrow face and a sharp little beard. Hanneke had collaborated with him before and—after being initially treated with condescension—had managed to earn his respect.

John nodded. "He wasn't shot, or stabbed, or beaten."

"This, I think, caused Herr Hawkins' death." The physician held a lamp close to the patch of matted hair Hanneke had noticed earlier. "He received a single blow to the head."

Leaning closer for a better look, John frowned. "I see a little blood here, but not much. Perhaps he was thrown by his horse and hit his head when he landed."

Hanneke caught the faint trace of hope in his voice. *He wants to believe that Hawkins died by accident,* she thought, *instead of being killed by a slaver.* She wanted to believe that as well, but every instinct argued against it.

"I suspect that the blow did not kill him outright." Dr. Rausch stroked his beard, eyes narrowed with speculation. "He may have suffered *commotio cerebri.*"

John straightened. "What does that mean?"

"A commotion in the brain. Your dead man may have suffered a concussion. Many people who receive a blow to the head lose sensibility for a period of time, of course. Recovery depends upon the severity of the strike."

Hanneke nodded. She had observed such reactions herself.

"In rarer situations, the victim remains aware," Rausch continued, "complaining of nothing worse than a headache, only to suffer more acute symptoms later. A concussion can lead to confusion or other mental disability, and death."

"So it's possible that Hawkins was injured elsewhere and trying to ride home," Hanneke mused, "but became incapacitated and died along the road."

John rubbed his chin. "Or, he might have been attacked elsewhere and dumped from a vehicle—perhaps already dead, perhaps only insensible from the concussion."

Hanneke winced. She hadn't liked Asa Hawkins, but nobody deserved such a cold and lonely death.

"Since the body was frozen, it's hard to say how long he was in the snowbank." Dr. Rausch spread his hands. "I will do a full and proper examination later." He looked sternly at Hanneke over the spectacles pinched on his nose.

She understood that he wasn't willing to go any further with a woman present. Harboring no wish to see more, she nodded.

Satisfied, he turned to the deputy. "If I discover anything else, I'll get word to you. And someone will need to make burial arrangements. Promptly."

After thanking the doctor, John and Hanneke took their leave and returned to the wagon. "What do you think?" she asked.

"I think it will be no easy task to determine what truly happened." Barlow offered Hanneke a hand up and paused to offer words of praise to the Friesian before joining her on the seat.

Watertown had been settled on the site of an old French fur trade post only twenty years earlier, in 1836. An influx of Yankee settlers and European immigrants had prompted steady growth, however, and the town had incorporated as a city in 1853. Hanneke usually visited during the day, when Watertown buzzed with activity. The first railroad's arrival last fall had increased the number of dray wagons in the streets, and men involved in the construction trades remained busy.

Although she cherished no wish to move to the city, the streets in this area had become quite familiar. Dr. Rausch's home and office were located in what was sometimes called Watertown's "German Ward." Few vehicles were on the streets at this hour, although a number of men were striding along the walkways, probably heading home after enjoying camaraderie at a tavern or attending a social club.

John guided the horse around a corner. "I want you to wait at the tavern while I speak with Jerome Hawkins." He was referring to the Red Cockerel, a nearby establishment run by Hanneke's dearest friend, Angela Ziedler.

Hanneke frowned. "I had thought to accompany you."

"Jerome is a Know-Nothing."

Just hearing the common name for the secretive nativist group made Hanneke's stomach clench like a fist. Asa, Jerome, and their ilk were members of a political party created on a platform of hatred that sometimes spilled into violence. Know-Nothings despised European immigrants. She remembered Asa Hawkins' derisive sneers and seething malice. She remembered watching Know-Nothings parade in the street, hoping to terrify hardworking people and recruit other Yankees to their cause.

A part of her wanted to go to Jerome's anyway, and to look the man in the eye with a deputy sheriff present to bolster her courage. In truth, however, Jerome Hawkins was unlikely to speak about his brother if she were in the room. "My presence would likely only antagonize the man," she agreed, relieved she didn't have to decide for herself.

John dropped her off at the tavern and returned to the Red Cockerel less than an hour later. Angela offered him coffee, but he shook his head. "I'm eager to get home, and I suspect Frau Bauer is as well."

"Well?" Hanneke asked as they set out. "How did Jerome react to the news of his brother's death?"

"He appeared to be shocked." John tugged his hat lower on his head. "When I described the head wound, though, he flew into a rage. Threatened me and the entire sheriff's department with all sorts of trouble if whoever attacked his brother isn't swiftly brought to justice."

"That can't have been pleasant," Hanneke observed dryly, even more grateful that she'd stayed at the tavern. "Did Herr Hawkins share any insights about Asa's whereabouts in recent days?"

"Jerome informed me that he didn't keep track of his brother's schedule."

That was disappointing. "So, no help there. Are there any other family members in the vicinity?"

"Apparently not. I'll visit Asa's freight yard in the morning. Jerome did say his brother employed a man to oversee things there."

"What strikes me as curious," Hanneke mused, "is that Jerome assumed that Asa had been assaulted."

"Jerome's assumption gave me pause as well," Barlow conceded. "I didn't suggest that his brother might have been murdered, even though I think it's likely. We can't assume he didn't suffer an accident, and perhaps underestimate its severity."

Hanneke tucked one mitten cuff, which had slipped from her sleeve, back into place. "We both know that someone like Hiram Aubuchon would have a unique motivation for killing Hawkins," she murmured, "but having run afoul of Asa myself, it seems safe to say that he might have many enemies."

"I would guess that half of the foreign-born residents in the county have had some kind of altercation with him." John maneuvered the wagon to avoid a particularly deep rut. "I've seen him cross the street just to intimidate a newcomer. Frau Ziedler told me Hawkins had harassed her because of her brother's debts. Dozens of people may have wished him dead." He sighed. "For all I know, he and Jerome might have quarreled."

Where does one start an investigation, Hanneke wondered, with such an overwhelming number of possibilities? She wanted to ask John but decided against it. His need to withhold what might be critical information from his colleagues dreadfully complicated his approach. Had she helped John by sharing news of the colored woman and white man's nocturnal visit, or made things worse? She didn't know.

Hanneke had helped the deputy on murder cases twice before. Last spring, her efforts to understand her husband's "accidental" death had led to murder charges. In September, when her friend Karoline Ketzler's husband had been murdered, she'd helped identify the killer. Both times, personal relationships had compelled her to get involved.

For many reasons, this situation was completely different. She had absolutely no wish to involve herself any further.

Then she glanced at the man sitting hunched beside her. Even in the dark she sensed his gloom. It traveled with them like a dark cloud. Well, she thought, if John needs someone to talk with as he proceeds, I'll be glad to oblige.

And...and perhaps she might consider how—still staying on the periphery—she might be useful.

A small dog burst from the shadows by a brick home, barking frantically until they'd moved on. They passed two men on a street corner, arguing in a language Hanneke couldn't identify. She wished her fingers were warm enough to knit, for it would have been a comfort.

Chapter Five

The next morning, before full dawn, Hanneke bundled up and slipped to the grain barn. In order to reduce the chance of being spotted by an unexpected visitor, she always checked the hiding spot early. Now, the need for stealth felt more urgent. She had returned her supply box, but as usual, there was no indication that anyone had crept recently into the hiding spot.

In the stable, Hanneke was surprised but delighted to find that John Barlow had returned Cinder. *"Guten Morgen, mein Freund!"* she exclaimed. Charlotte Stofeldt's situation had slipped from her mind after finding Asa Hawkins' body, and John hadn't asked for details. Nonetheless, since the visit was complete, Hanneke hadn't expected to see the horse again.

Well, she was glad to care for the mount until her rightful owner could be found. John must have brought her back *very* early that morning. She was sorry she'd missed him.

Hanneke let her geese and chickens outside before entering the sheep pen. "I wouldn't mind sharing a roof with you," she murmured, remembering how the comforting snuffles and bleats had drifted through the floor inside the Stofeldt housebarn. Although she dreamed of adding a second breed to her stock one day, she was quite fond of this small flock she'd inherited from Fridolin. With luck, the afternoon would warm up enough to let them out to pasture. Their wool was several inches long now, but she was cautious. In the meantime, Hanneke decided, I will take advantage of having the mare to go visiting after breakfast.

Her first stop was a couple's small log home several miles away. She'd been summoned a few days earlier when young Frau König had been struggling to deliver her first baby. This morning, Herr König, who must have seen her approach through a window, hurried outside with an equally panicked expression. "Thank God you've come," he said in a low voice. "She won't stop crying."

"The baby?"

"My wife!"

Ah. This was not the first time Hanneke had tended to an exhausted and overwhelmed new mother who felt unequal to the task. "Try not to worry," she murmured. "I'll see to them both."

Inside the cabin, the smell of soiled linens hung thick and sour in the room. Hanneke spent some time reassuring the young woman, and eventually received a wan smile. "I didn't realize how tired I'd be," the new mother admitted, "but I'm still overjoyed that God answered our prayers."

"*Danke schön*," Herr König added hoarsely, his eyes glistening.

Hanneke tidied the cabin, washed the baby's soiled linens, and left with a large packet of dried rhubarb. She'd used the last of her own weeks ago, and anticipation made her stomach growl. When called to help an ill or injured neighbor, she was always gifted some such token of gratitude. Most of the European farm families settling this area survived on a barter economy, trading what they produced and pitching in when someone needed help. Hanneke often traded warm stockings or scarves for milk and butter, harvest labor, or store merchandise she couldn't afford.

She was reflecting on blessings when a sudden flapping sound near a crossroads caught her attention. Someone had nailed a broadside to an ancient oak facing the junction. Large block print across the top read *Runaway — $300 Reward.*

Hanneke felt frost crystals form in her sternum. She'd never seen such a notice posted in her rural area before. Dismounting, she found her feet unwilling to walk closer. Several minutes passed before she could force herself close enough to read the rest of the message.

Absconded from her owner's Arkansas home, the negro girl Celia, aged about twenty; has very black skin; speaks poorly due to several missing teeth. She possesses a violent disposition and must be approached with caution. If apprehended, deliver the girl to jail directly. The reward will be paid by Mr. Hiram Aubuchon, currently residing at the Planters' Hotel.

"Mein Gott," Hanneke whispered. This Celia was almost certainly the woman who'd stopped at Safe Haven Farm. Hanneke remembered the faint whistle behind her desperate plea: *Please, you got to help him.* Missing teeth could cause such an impairment.

Hanneke pinched her lips together. Was the rhetoric "violent disposition" designed only to make local people less inclined to help Celia, and more likely to help capture her? Or…had something happened that pushed the poor soul beyond endurance, and she lashed out? If Celia had actually done violence, why would her so-called "owner" hire a kidnapper and offer a hefty reward to bring her back?

The obvious answer to that question made moisture pool sour on Hanneke's tongue. The man or woman with legal authority over Celia didn't expect the return of a now-docile servant. They wanted revenge, and it would surely be brutal.

Grimly, Hanneke studied the heavy parchment nailed to the tree. The broadside must have been posted recently, for it showed no sign of weathering. She had assumed that Celia, after leaving the wounded man behind, had kept running north and was miles away by now. Aubuchon, however, must have reason to believe otherwise.

I thought you were gone! Hanneke moaned silently to Celia, and offered up a prayer for the runaway's safety.

Dismounting, she took a moment to study her surroundings. Then, with her heart suddenly thumping, she strode to the tree and ripped the broadside down. She crumpled it as best as she could before stuffing it into her saddlebag, planning to burn it as soon as she got home.

There. She felt a little breathless as she swung back into the saddle, but satisfied as well.

* * *

Half an hour later, Hanneke arrived at the Muehlhauser place. Gerda Muehlhauser was a special friend who'd done Fridolin a great kindness before he died. Hanneke would forever be grateful.

She was almost there when she saw Gerda's husband Oscar walking down the road, hands thrust in pockets. Oscar was a small man with stringy gray hair who made his own beer and was drunk more often than not.

Hanneke was not inclined to pause for conversation. The difficulties in Gerda's life were largely due to Oscar. He was not a violent or purposefully unkind man, but he was also not a good provider. Other than raising a couple of Saddleback hogs, he spent his time growing barley and hops to brew into beer. The couple largely existed on produce from Gerda's garden, and profits from the parcels of land Oscar periodically sold off to pay bills.

"Herr Muehlhauser," Hanneke said politely. Oscar touched his slouch hat as he passed. Hanneke was glad to see that he appeared to be walking without difficulty today.

Hanneke found Gerda sitting beside a window, darning a sock. Her wrinkled face brightened when she recognized her company. "Hanneke! It's good to see—" Her sentence ended in a paroxysm of coughing. She snatched a handkerchief, clutching it over her mouth.

"I'm sorry to see that you're no better." Hanneke frowned. "I stopped by to leave a tonic that should ease your throat." She provided her friend with a dose of the syrup she brewed with mint, thyme, grated ginger, and honey. Next, she cut a slice of the rye loaf she'd brought. At the end of their visit she asked, "I passed Oscar as I arrived. Was he going to town?"

Gerda shared an unexpected smile. "He was going to work."

Hanneke tried to hide her surprise. "What is he doing?"

"Someone hired him to do some odd jobs. The labor won't take more than several days, but he did come home yesterday with a few coins." Gerda's expression held hope. "I'm grateful."

"Perhaps this will lead to other opportunities for him." Hanneke squeezed her friend's hand. "I'll stop back soon and see how you're coming along."

The Muehlhausers lived just north of Clara and Charles Steckelberg. Although they were Hanneke's closest neighbors, she and Clara hadn't sat down to chat and sip coffee since before the last snowstorm. There was time for one more stop.

Clara must have spotted Hanneke's approach, for she stepped onto her back porch. "I'm not used to seeing you arrive on horseback," she observed as Hanneke dismounted. Clara was not one to waste words on pleasantries.

"John Barlow asked if I'd be willing to board her. She was stolen, and I'm saving the city treasury boarding fees while the deputies track down her owner."

Clara's wooden clogs thumped against the floorboards as she led Hanneke inside. Older than Hanneke by at least a decade, she was a stocky, slightly stooped woman with a lined face. She was responsible for most of the farm's management, wore clothing from another era, and was one of the most capable people Hanneke had ever met.

"I can't stay long," Hanneke explained as she sank into a chair at the table. "I'm on my way home from Gerda's place."

Clara poured two cups of steaming coffee. "How did you find her? She was sickly when I stopped by last week."

"Her cough was no better," Hanneke allowed, "but I'm optimistic that the syrup I left will help."

"Was Oscar there?"

"Gerda said he'd found work. He's doing odd jobs for someone."

"That man," Clara said flatly. Hanneke nodded. She wanted to believe that Gerda's husband might become a better partner, but she also had doubts.

As the conversation moved on to companionable topics, the unease caused by recent events eased a bit. It was pleasant to speak of church news and flower seeds and the disappointment of finding spoiled potatoes in the root cellar. The familiar kitchen smelled of woodsmoke, vinegar, and the mustiness emanating from a heap of shriveled turnips that her friend had been chopping. Hanneke was glad she'd stopped.

Clara walked outside to see her off. "Hanneke, Charles is taking the wagon to town tomorrow. If you need to shop for anything bulkier than what a saddlebag will hold, he'd be happy to pick you up."

Hanneke considered as she swung back to the saddle, then shook her head. "I'm grateful for the offer, but I can't think of anything I need."

The milky sun was high overhead when Hanneke emerged from the woods into her own yard. She stifled a sigh as she looked at her smokeless chimney. It's odd, she thought, what triggers grief. She'd been living alone for ten months, but the miserable loneliness of coming home to a cold, dark, and empty home never abated.

One day, she promised herself, I *will* somehow come home to see smoke curling from the chimney.

For now, indulging in gloomy thoughts accomplished nothing. After getting Cinder settled and releasing her sheep to their pen, she gathered an armload of firewood and went inside.

In short order, Hanneke had a kettle of leftover potato soup heating in the cooking niche. She decided to light the parlor stove as well. With her errands complete, it would be pleasant to spend the afternoon knitting. The money she earned knitting warm utilitarian items was always welcome.

Her greatest joy, however, came from designing and creating fine lacework. She'd spent much of the winter spinning, designing, and knitting to create a gossamer shawl featuring intricate circular motifs. When she'd worn this Rolling Wheels wrap to church recently, an elderly woman took one look and commissioned something similar for herself. Hanneke was eager to get started.

After kindling a blaze and adjusting the stove damper, she started to circle to the workroom where she stored her sketchbook—only to stop abruptly in the front entry. A folded piece of paper lay on the floor. Someone had pushed it beneath her front door.

Hanneke scooped it up and peered at the inked script. *Frau Bauer, your carded wool must be picked up tomorrow.*

Bewilderment wrinkled her nose. She sometimes sold excess fleece at Reichmann's Carding Mill in Watertown, but she hadn't been there in months. If the message hadn't included her name, she would have assumed it had been delivered to the wrong house. And…even if she had left fleece at the mill, she couldn't imagine anyone driving to her farm to deliver the note. Especially without signing it.

Then a prickling sensation crawled over Hanneke's skin. *Oh.* This note was not what it seemed. Although she didn't understand the intent of the cryptic missive, she knew in her bones that it had nothing to do with wool.

It had, she believed, something to do with the Underground Railroad.

Was Herr Reichmann an abolitionist? He'd always been cordial, but Hanneke didn't know him well. Even if he *did* help runaways, she couldn't imagine why he would suddenly reach out to her. Perhaps Aubuchon's appearance had set something in motion…?

Hanneke's eyes narrowed as she remembered Hiram Aubuchon's oily smile. This message could be part of a trap. Had Asa Hawkins been drawn from his home by some equally mysterious communication? Aubuchon wouldn't think twice about employing lies or other tricks to get what he wanted. A warning twisted uneasily in her gut.

Then she took a deep breath. Unless he'd seen her rip the broadside off the tree, which seemed unlikely, she'd done nothing since Aubuchon's visit that would raise his suspicions. Besides, she lived alone on a farm surrounded by forests. Even if Aubuchon did suspect her of getting in his way and wished to harm her, there'd be no need to lure her to a carding mill in Watertown. It seemed far more likely that Herr Reichmann wanted or needed to speak with her.

Well, there was only one way to find out. Hanneke did have several sacks of unprocessed wool that she could take along. If this summons turned out to be a misunderstanding or prank, she'd still have legitimate business to conduct at the mill.

Hanneke returned to the kitchen and tossed the note into the dying fire. Then she bundled herself back into her heavy cloak and hood. She needed to go tell Clara that she'd changed her mind and would greatly appreciate a ride to Watertown in the morning.

* * *

After a restless night, Hanneke made quick work of morning chores and returned to her bedroom to tidy up. My Sunday dress for the trip to town, she decided. She would present a dignified impression when she walked into a situation at the carding mill that she didn't yet understand. Tucking the Rolling Wheels lace shawl around her shoulders bolstered her spirits even more. Hanneke wasn't a particularly prideful woman, but wrapping herself in this spider's web of a shawl made her feel accomplished.

She was waiting on her front porch, frowning at the pale gray clouds building overhead, when Charles Steckelberg's wagon turned into her drive. "Guten Morgen!" he called cheerfully as he climbed down.

Clara's husband was a kind man and a generous neighbor. He'd once been a professor of classic literature in Bavaria. Dreaming of a unified Germany, he'd involved himself with a quickly quelled uprising. Fearing reprisals, Charles had fled his homeland and made his way to Watertown with dozens of other revolutionaries. These "Latin Farmers" still gathered frequently to discuss and debate philosophy and politics. He was ill-suited for farm work, but—unlike most of his friends—he doggedly stayed with it for Clara's sake.

Before joining Hanneke, Charles gathered a large armful of straw from the wagon bed. "Clara sent this over," he explained. "She has all she needs. I'll load those—" he nodded at the heavy burlap sacks of wool—"while you tuck that inside."

"*Danke!*" Hanneke exclaimed. She hadn't grown rye the previous summer, and some of her bread-rising baskets needed to be replaced. She wanted to make coiled-straw bee skeps as well.

Once the straw was stashed in her workroom, Hanneke locked the house and climbed up to the wagon seat. "As always, I'm grateful for the ride."

"I'm happy to have the company," Charles assured her as he released the brake. "However, I do wonder why you don't simply take all your fleeces to the mill at once after spring shearing, as I do."

"I don't mind picking and cleaning some of my own fleeces over the winter," she assured him. "The lanolin is good for my hands. It's also preferable to card and spin my own wool as needed for various knitting projects. The work is done to my own specifications, and I save money. The fleeces I have today are surplus, so I'll sell them directly."

"Ah." He nodded with approval. "I see that you have reasoned through the situation with thoughtful care. As the great philosopher Emmanuel Kant once wrote, 'All our knowledge begins with the senses, proceeds then to the understanding, and ends with reason. There is nothing higher than reason.'"

Hanneke sensed that her friend was on the edge of launching into a full lecture on intellect and free will. Since she knew from experience that the monologue could easily last the entire trip, she decided to change the subject. "Are you preparing for planting season?"

"We are." Charles nodded in affirmation, although after a moment, he cleared his throat. "That is to say," he conceded, "Clara's taken charge." They exchanged a knowing smile and passed the remainder of the trip in companionable conversation.

An oxbow turn in the Rock River bisected Watertown, and residential communities and shops were growing on each side. The shores were lined with flour mills, lumber mills, and tanning mills. Tucked among them were smaller enterprises. One was Reichmann's Carding Mill. The sounds of buzzing saw blades drifted from the nearby lumber mill. A heavy wagon loaded with new-cut logs rumbled into the yard as another piled high with planks rumbled out, presumably bound for the train station.

Charles pulled into the drive beside the carding mill and deposited Hanneke's fleeces on the designated delivery platform. "Your errand won't take long. Shall I wait, and then drop you off at the Red Cockerel?"

Hanneke usually visited Angela when in town. Today, though, she shook her head. "*Nein, danke.* I'll walk home."

After Charles had driven away, Hanneke approached the red frame structure. A sign on the wall by the door assured customers that Herr Reichmann was prepared to card wool of all qualities, up to the finest Merino and Saxony; that spinning wheels and other tools were available for sale; and that although money was never refused, most types of country produce would be taken in exchange.

That was all well and good, Hanneke thought, but I am here on other business. A sensation of fluttering moths emerged in her belly. Something about the quiet and solitude was making her uneasy.

Perhaps she should have asked Charles to come inside with her after all.

Well, it was too late for that. Besides, if her suspicions were correct, she'd been summoned to a conversation that would not take place if she wasn't alone. Hanneke set her shoulders, drew in a deep breath, and went inside.

Chapter Six

Hanneke was met with the familiar display of wheels for spinning flax and wool, hand carders and combs, niddy-noddies, and other items useful for home textile work. Near the right wall, where business transactions were conducted, an inkwell and a huge account book were ready for use.

Two counters separated the customer area from the long workspace. Herr Reichmann was nowhere in sight. Hanneke could hear the mechanical rumble of a carding mill, where a spinning drum and rollers teased out tangled fibers.

"Hallo?" she called, expecting the proprietor to stop his machine and hurry to greet her.

Moments passed. Hanneke concluded that Herr Reichmann must not have heard her. Slipping through the gap between counters, she walked into the workroom.

The cold space smelled faintly of grease, dust, and wool. A mound of fleeces waited by the picking machine, which removed the largest bits of dirt and debris caught among the fibers. During the busy season, after spring shearing, seasonal workers kept multiple machines going day and night. Today, the factory felt gloomy and unnaturally quiet.

Hanneke spotted Herr Reichmann working alone at the far end of the room with his back to her. He was adding picked wool to the wooden tray that fed the carding machine.

Except…it wasn't Herr Reichmann. The worker's shoulders were too broad, and he wore the scuffed boots and heavy clothes of a manual laborer.

She'd never seen Reichmann without at least a proper businessman's shirt and vest, even when working the machines.

Hanneke suddenly had no more patience for mysteries. *"Guten tag!"*

Jerking upright, the man finally did what was needed to shut off the machine. Then he turned to face her.

Her mouth dropped open. "You!" She'd last seen this man by candlelight, lying on her kitchen floor, apparently unconscious and bleeding from a gunshot wound. Her mind struggled to connect that image with the seemingly vigorous man in front of her, but his features were familiar: tawny hair falling over his forehead, the prominent cheekbones, and thin nose. Only his eyes, an unusual shade of gray, had gone unnoticed during their first encounter. Those eyes were disconcertingly intense. "What—"

"We must speak quickly," he said in English.

The need to conduct this conversation in that tongue further frayed Hanneke's nerves, for she was not fluent. "Who *are* you?" she demanded. "Where is Herr Reichmann?"

"He has gone to Milwaukee and asked me to fill in for him today. My name doesn't matter. What does matter is your demonstrated sympathy for certain individuals."

People on the run, he meant. People like Celia from Arkansas, whose legal owner had placed a bounty of $300 on her head.

The man folded his arms and leaned against the machine, ankles crossed. By all appearances, he was chatting about nothing more than the weather. Still, Hanneke sensed troubled currents beneath the calm demeanor. "At the moment, the situation in this county is particularly perilous. Several slave catchers are on the prowl in this vicinity. One of them tried to kill me. Now Asa Hawkins is dead."

Hanneke reached inside her cloak and adjusted her shawl.

"Hawkins' freight business was the backbone of local efforts. It will not be easily replaced. In the meantime, there is cargo in desperate need of transportation."

Celia? Hanneke wondered, knowing better than to ask. She moistened her lips with her tongue. This was a mighty leap from leaving crackers in her barn. John Barlow could retrieve the stolen mare at any moment. Her own sphere was limited, and she wasn't familiar with the countryside north of here.

"You won't be alone," he added, as if sensing her thoughts. "I will drive a wagon to our destination. I'm asking you to accompany me."

Her eyebrows pulled high. "You want me to share your wagon seat after someone just tried to *kill* you?"

"The shooter knew what I was doing that night, but not who I was. He never saw my face."

Hanneke did not feel reassured.

"Any kidnappers on the lookout will be more likely to overlook a vehicle carrying a couple than a lone man." His low voice held an urgent edge. "However, I can't promise that we won't encounter a problem along the way."

No, you can't, Hanneke thought. If he had made such a promise, she would have shut down the conversation.

"The punishment for helping a runaway is up to six months in prison," he continued. "And a one thousand dollar fine."

Hanneke swallowed a bubble of inappropriate laughter. For someone who rarely had more than ten dollars to her name, finding that kind of money was unimaginable.

The man's gaze did not waver. "Are you willing?"

Hanneke wanted to tell him that she needed more time to consider; that she needed to go home and settle down with her knitting by the parlor stove and think this proposal through properly. She already knew, however, that he wouldn't permit her that. Instead, she asked, "Where would we be going?"

His mouth tightened with impatience. "I'm taking a huge risk by even speaking to you. Before I say more, you must swear your willingness to help, and to remain silent about it."

Hanneke looked away. This stranger was asking her to put her life in his hands. It did not suit her nature to make a momentous decision without understanding all pertinent details. Also, she could not pretend that recent events had not affected her. The prospect of this dangerous and illegal task made her queasy.

At the same time, though…she also felt a seedling of aspiration quiver to life inside. She'd spent almost a year passively leaving supplies for a very few, unseen runaways. How many times had she longed to become more involved with abolitionist work? To be more useful? She knew the risks, but in truth, there was nothing to consider. This request was exactly what she'd been yearning for.

She met the man's stare. "I want to help. I swear to my willingness, and to my absolute silence."

Relief flashed in his eyes. "Start walking east from your place at dawn the day after tomorrow."

Saturday. Hanneke wondered if he thought the roads might be quieter on the weekend.

"Bring food that can withstand the journey," he continued. "Wear that same shawl."

"Wear—this one?" she stammered, fingering her Rolling Wheels wrap. "Why?"

He ignored her question. "You will need to make arrangements for your livestock. We'll have four long days of travel to reach our destination and return."

"Four *days*?" A trip of such duration had not occurred to her.

"Four days."

She tried to consider the ramifications of the journey. "And…what type of accommodations can I expect?"

"Safe ones." He held her gaze. "I am good at this, Frau Bauer. I will do everything in my power to protect those in my care from harm."

Hanneke believed he meant what he said. In any event, she'd already made her commitment. "I'll make the necessary arrangements, and I will do my best to be helpful." Then, perhaps to salvage a bit of her own sense of agency, she folded her arms. "However, I will not come without knowing your name."

His lips twitched, as if struggling with the unexpected urge to smile. "Very well. You may call me Gideon."

"Thank you." Although Hanneke suspected that he'd simply grabbed that name from the air to satisfy her request, she felt better for asserting herself anyway. "I must say, I'm surprised that you turned to me for assistance. Surely someone more experienced…."

"Your inexperience, in this case, fills a need. The other shepherds in this area are being watched."

Shepherd. As a devoted sheep farmer, the word had special meaning for her.

The front door opened. Hanneke startled, but Gideon's composure didn't waver. "Good morning, madam!" he called. "I'll be right with you."

Hanneke watched as he went to greet the customer. If she hadn't known better, she would never have guessed that Gideon had recently suffered a nasty injury. The double calf wound must have been painful, but although his gait might have been slower than normal, he did not limp. His self-control was extraordinary. Although, if we encounter any problems, she thought, he will not be at his best.

He sold the customer two pairs of hand carders and ushered her out the door. Once he'd returned, Hanneke couldn't help fixing him with a pointed look. "You shouldn't even be out of bed. Is this trip wise?"

"This trip is necessary."

Ja, Hanneke thought, of course, it is. She remembered the terror she'd heard in Celia's voice. When Gideon had been shot, Celia could easily have abandoned him and kept running north. And yet, she'd taken the precious time needed to drag her wounded guide to Hanneke's back door.

Well, she thought, it was good to be cognizant of Gideon's gunshot wound. Surprisingly, however, that knowledge didn't cause undue alarm. She knew very little about Gideon, but she did believe that when serving as a shepherd, he was not a man to cross.

She turned to leave, then paused. "Oh—I did bring three sacks of raw wool to have processed. They're on the loading dock."

"I'll take care of them."

She was unable to quell one last question. "If there's some way I can prepare myself for…." She spread her hands. Secrecy and veiled communication were absolutely essential, but quite irksome nonetheless.

"You can't prepare," Gideon told her. "Each encounter is unique." Then he turned back to the machine.

* * *

Hanneke walked back to Safe Haven Farm in record time. Stray thoughts and questions shot through her head like marbles. With every step, the enormity of what she'd agreed to do felt heavier.

You are a capable woman, she reminded herself, and this is something you can *do*. Still, she did wish that she didn't have to wait until the day after tomorrow to leave on the journey with Gideon.

As she approached the house, the sight of another piece of paper, this time pinned to her front porch by a stone, made her clench her teeth. What *now*?

She snatched it up and recognized Jacobine Ketzler's handwriting. *William and I came to visit. We'll try again late this afternoon.*

Hanneke's shoulders relaxed. What serendipitous timing! She was pleased with the prospect of seeing her dear young friend Jacobine and the girl's beau, William. It was especially timely because she'd already decided to ask William to care for her livestock while she traveled with Gideon. And with any luck, they'd be able to stay for supper.

After a midday meal of barley soup, Hanneke settled down in the parlor to knit. All of her fine lace shawls were unique, and the delicate patterns required more concentration than any other task. She'd made good progress with the commissioned shawl by the time she heard Jacobine and William at the back door.

She hurried to greet them. "Welcome!" she exclaimed. "I'm very glad to see you both." Jacobine had become like a daughter during the last fall and winter, when she and her mother had lived with Hanneke at Safe Haven Farm.

"I've missed you!" Jacobine said earnestly. She was a shy, sweet girl of fifteen, with a faint sprinkling of freckles on her nose and flaxen braids pinned in a circlet around her head. "*Mutti* sends her love."

"I'll stop to visit next chance I have," Hanneke promised. Karoline Ketzler was a tinsmith who'd once had a shop on her farm nearby. After recovering from a family tragedy, she'd found a tiny two-story building for rent in Watertown, with a shop below and a private room above. Hanneke knew that both of the Ketzlers missed their former, rural life, but a fresh start was just what Karoline had needed.

Then Hanneke turned to Jacobine's fiancé. "You look well, William. How is your family?"

As he hitched out of his heavy coat, William smiled. "Everyone is fine."

William Bluewing was a young Ho-Chunk man. His people, despite horrific treatment by the U.S. government, had helped some of the first Pomeranian immigrants survive their inaugural winter in the area—on land that the Ho-Chunk had occupied for generations. Many members of the tribe had been force-marched to reservations west of Wisconsin. William's parents had refused to leave and managed to evade the soldiers. Now, William, his mother, and his two younger sisters often camped in a secluded glade on land that, by United States law, Hanneke owned.

The more she got to know the Bluewings, the more she liked them. William was a scholar who spoke several languages, wanted to go to college, and hoped to become a teacher. He was also a man of integrity, steady in hard times, and utterly devoted to Jacobine.

Now, Jacobine's expression faded to chagrin. "Frau Bauer, do you have time to look at my knitting? I tried to fix a mistake, and I made everything worse."

"Of course. Let's go into the parlor."

The three of them clustered near the stove. William had brought a book to read. Jacobine removed a half-completed waistcoat from her carrying basket and showed Hanneke where she'd run into trouble. "I've already put hours and *hours* into it! I truly don't want to rip it all out and start over."

Hanneke peered at the work. "That won't be necessary, *Liebchen*. You lost too many stitches while doing decreases for the waist. See? You only need to undo a couple of rows." She handed the knitting back to Jacobine and guided her through the necessary repairs. "That's it. Now, start again at row forty-three. Considering that this is your first fitted garment, you're doing wonderfully well."

William and Jacobine stayed for an early supper of beans and sauerkraut. As they settled at the table, William paused before picking up his fork. "I have a favor to ask, Frau Bauer. I'm hoping you will grant permission to tap maple trees in the woods."

"Of course! As many as you'd like. I'd be glad to help, actually. I've been wanting to learn how to tap trees, if you're willing to show me." Weather in the Old Country was not suitable for growing maples.

He looked pleased. "Of course! The best time to tap is when daytime temperatures are above freezing and nighttime temperatures below freezing. That nice thaw two days ago got the sap running." He spread goose grease on a slice of bread before adding, "I'll let you know when the time is right. I think another snowstorm is coming."

Hanneke sincerely hoped that winter wouldn't roar back through southern Wisconsin while she and Gideon were on the road.

"I wouldn't mind if we get another big snow," Jacobine told William, "if you and your friends organize another snow snake contest!"

"The one you held last month was fascinating to watch," Hanneke agreed. William and some of his Ho-Chunk friends had constructed a long, winding track. Men and boys hurled decorated spears down the track, hoping that their own went the farthest.

As soon as the meal concluded, William cocked his head toward the door. "I wish we could stay longer, Frau Bauer, but I promised to get Jacobine back home in a timely fashion. I do not want to anger Frau Ketzler."

Jacobine began collecting dirty plates and carrying them to the dry sink. "Actually," she confided, "*Mutti* is growing more fond of William, all the time. I'm hoping she'll change her mind about the wedding date, and not make us wait until I'm sixteen." She looked pleadingly at Hanneke. "Perhaps you might speak to her…?"

"Absolutely not," Hanneke said firmly, not for the first time. "That's between you and your mother."

When Jacobine had slipped away to use the outhouse, Hanneke caught

William's eye. "I have a favor to ask. I'm leaving, day after tomorrow for a trip. I expect to be gone for four days. Would you be able to care for my animals?" She held his gaze for an extra moment. If there was anyone she trusted to tend her sheep and poultry—and to hold his tongue about the request—it was William.

He didn't ask questions. "I'm glad to."

When Jacobine returned, Hanneke embraced them both. "Can you manage some bread? I baked extra." She handed them two loaves wrapped in linen towels. "Now, you best be on your way before the temperature drops any farther."

Standing on the porch, Hanneke watched them walk away in the twilight. She missed their company already. She mused that perhaps she should go to Charlotte Stofeldt's gathering, planned for the next day, after all. She'd had good reasons to decline the invitation…but spending an afternoon with abolitionists sounded appealing just now. Besides, the travel and visit would occupy a fair chunk of the day.

Hanneke felt a sudden stab of longing for Fridolin. *Husband, I'm trying to do the right thing, and will endeavor to make you proud. Please watch over me.* Clouds hid the stars he'd so loved, and that she turned to for solace in difficult moments. A coyote howled from some distance away. Others joined in, yipping and baying, then abruptly fell silent. Hanneke felt lonesome.

Then she thought about Celia and felt an instant twinge of shame. I, Hanneke thought, can't *begin* to imagine the profound loneliness of a woman being hunted down as she fled through unfamiliar terrain by herself.

Chapter Seven

The next afternoon, Hanneke was the first guest to arrive at Charlotte Stofeldt's place. Her hostess—after a moment of surprise—looked pleased to see her. "Why, Hanneke! I didn't think you were coming."

"My schedule shifted unexpectedly," Hanneke told her contritely. She didn't want to appear indecisive. "I hope you don't mind."

"Of course not!" Charlotte assured her. "I'm glad to see you."

After settling the mare in the barn, they emerged onto the inner landing. Charlotte turned to the steps leading up to the living space, but Hanneke couldn't keep from looking down to the lower animal shelter. "You keep sheep?"

Charlotte frowned, perhaps wondering if the question was an oblique reference to the smell drifting up the stairs. "We do."

"I'm a sheep farmer, you see," Hanneke explained quickly. "I'm always curious about other people's flocks. What breed do you keep?"

"Rambouillet."

Hanneke caught her breath. "Rambouillet?" Sometimes called French Merinos, Rambouillets were the largest of the fine wool sheep. Hanneke was quite fond of her own Cotswolds, but she longed to improve her flock with Merinos.

Charlotte's face relaxed. "Would you like to see them?"

The two women enjoyed a quick but quite pleasant visit to the housebarn's lowest level. Hanneke admired the ewes' heavy fleeces, and Charlotte willingly answered questions about yarn quality and lambing rates. "The wool is a pleasure to spin," she concluded. "The fibers are longer than most Merino, nice and dense, with a well-defined crimp."

Hanneke wriggled her fingers through the closest animal's cream-colored wool with a sigh. "Lovely." As they went upstairs, she reflected that after meeting Charlotte on Deputy Barlow's business, it was most pleasant to discover a strong common bond.

In the main room, baby Henni lay in his cradle, kicking his legs and drooling on a wooden teething ring. Charlotte's daughter Beatta was practicing spinning with a drop spindle. "How nice to see you again, Beatta!" Hanneke said. "You appear to be doing very well with your spindle."

"I don't like spinning," Beatta admitted glumly. "My yarn breaks over and over."

"Mine did as well, when I was first learning," Hanneke confided. "I had to practice a lot."

She was helping Beatta when the other guests arrived. Sisters Berta and Erna Pohl, both likely in their fifties, arrived from the nearby village of Clyman's Corners wearing matching dresses of honey-colored wool. Hanneke suspected that the bolt had been marked down on shopping day. That example of thrift, and the genuine warmth in their greetings, made her feel welcome.

The four women gathered around the table. Charlotte was well prepared with paper, quills, ink, and the names and addresses of their representatives in Congress. "And for President Pierce as well!" Hanneke murmured. Gracious! She hadn't imagined writing to the president of the United States. Although, she mused with some chagrin, I don't know why not.

"I've read that his secretaries open all mail," Charlotte explained, "and keep tallies of opinions expressed. It is *essential* that he hear from people who are outraged by the Fugitive Slave Act."

"I am glad for the chance to contribute," Hanneke told her companions. "And I shall endeavor not to blot the ink."

Berta Pohl waved that notion aside. "We are grateful to you for swelling our diminutive ranks today, Frau Bauer." She reached for a piece of paper, but instead of picking it up, her fingers curled into a fist. "I admit, it's discouraging to gather week after week for the same task. Wisconsin was a *free* state before that abominable act became law. Some of the kidnappers' victims have lived respectable lives here for many years after fleeing slavery. Others were brought here by masters, and later freed, but targeted anyway."

Erna nodded. She was a plump woman who wore spectacles and winked frequently, apparently due to a tic. "Can you picture yourself as a hardworking soul settling here, finding work, perhaps starting a family— only to have a group of armed slave catchers burst into your home and drag you south in shackles?"

"I suspect that such terror is unimaginable except to those who've lived it," Hanneke murmured. On clear nights, she often gazed toward the Big Dipper and wondered who might be following its brightest star north—perhaps to her own grain barn. Her mind struggled to conceive what that fugitive might have experienced, and what they might be experiencing right this moment…but she knew she never would.

"That's what happened to Joshua Glover." Charlotte glanced to Hanneke. "Do you know that story?"

Hanneke shook her head. "When did it happen? I arrived in Wisconsin only last spring."

"He was born a slave in Missouri. After running away, he settled in Racine and got a good job at a sawmill. Two years later, in 1854, a friend betrayed him."

A friend betrayed him. Hanneke winced.

"The poor man was captured," Charlotte continued, "and locked up in the Milwaukee jail."

Erna leaned forward and spoke in a hushed whisper. "Many Milwaukee citizens oppose slavery, though. A mob of thousands formed and broke into the jail—"

"That was unacceptable," Charlotte muttered.

"—and freed Herr Glover!" Erna finished triumphantly.

"Don't forget that woman," Berta put in. "She lived in Kenosha, I believe. She was so fair that she passed as white for years, but the slavers still caught her and took her south. They had sworn that they would have her, dead or alive."

Hanneke took a deep breath. The specific stories these women were sharing made abstract ideas much more real, just as Aubuchon's appearance had.

At the same time, this gathering made Hanneke realize how hungry she was for such conversation. She never attended abolitionist gatherings in Watertown, never spoke of the Fugitive Slave Act with even her closest friends. *I am sitting,* Hanneke marveled, *with three women who know much more about anti-slavery history and efforts in Wisconsin than I do.*

When they'd all completed their missives, Charlotte collected the letters and promised to mail them. "Well done, ladies. I'll set out refreshments."

She served cheese, rye crackers, and the doughnuts Hanneke had contributed. Then she picked up Henni, who'd started to fret, and brought him back to the table to nurse discretely beneath a small blanket. *Very nicely knit,* Hanneke noted approvingly. Twisted stitches and bobbles created texture within a geometric pattern.

While nibbling, the women chatted about everyday matters. When Berta mentioned that the sisters' brother Felix, who did carpentry work, sometimes suffered from rheumatism, Hanneke reflected on home remedies she'd found most successful. Charlotte mentioned reading in a lady's magazine that women's skirts were getting more voluminous, and they all lamented the expense of even more fabric. "Not to mention," Hanneke added sardonically, "the additional annoyance for farm women who regularly engage in heavy labor." While she took care to present herself well, as behooved a widow and businesswoman, she had no intention of discarding practicality as a guiding principle.

Then Erna leaned forward. "Charlotte, have you heard anything more about that unfortunate man who was recently found dead in a gully?"

The question startled Hanneke. She should have expected it, actually, but she'd been too distracted by her upcoming trip with Gideon to think ahead. She set her plate aside and pulled her knitting from her pocket.

Charlotte kissed the top of Henni's downy head before responding. "I have not."

"It happened not far from here," Erna told them, with a wink that made her report seem clandestine. "I don't know if the authorities have even identified the poor soul."

Hanneke decided there was no point in staying silent on the basic details. Presumably, an account would be shared in the newspaper's next edition. She drew in a long breath and released it slowly. "Actually, I'm the one who found him."

Charlotte clapped one hand over her mouth, staring at Hanneke with horror. Finally, she stammered, "Did you—that is, you're not local. Did you see the body when you were riding home from here the other day?"

"I did."

Berta reached to pat Hanneke's hand. "You poor dear! That must have been dreadful."

"It was a shock," Hanneke allowed, stifling a shudder. "I fetched one of my neighbors, who is a deputy sheriff."

"What had *happened*?" Erna asked, her eyes still wide. "Was the victim a traveler passing through?"

"The authorities don't know how he came to be in the gully. The man was identified as a Watertown businessman named Asa Hawkins."

"That's not a name I know," Berta said, frowning thoughtfully.

"I'm quite sure we never met," Erna agreed, and Charlotte shook her head.

Soon after that, the Pohl sisters said their goodbyes and departed. "I'm *very* close to finishing this sock," Hanneke told her hostess. "Do you mind if I linger for a few minutes?"

"Of course not!" Charlotte flapped a hand at the question. "I'm glad of the company—oof!" She shook her head at Beatta, who was trying to climb into her mother's lap. "*Liebchen*, I can't hold you right now. I'm busy with the baby."

"I'm getting cold!" Beatta protested.

Charlotte's voice remained calm. "You'll have to be patient until I've got Henni back down in the cradle. I'll build up the fire then." She shifted her son from one side to the other and adjusted the blanket. "Perhaps you might *politely* ask Frau Bauer if you may sit with her. I don't imagine she'd mind."

Hanneke put her work aside as, without hesitation, Beatta approached. Only after she'd clambered onto Hanneke's lap did she whisper, "May I please sit with you?"

"Of course you may," Hanneke told her. Beatta's trust was welcome, as was her heavy, warm weight. She smelled faintly of smoke, but something sweeter as well. Hanneke's heart melted like beeswax as she wrapped her arms around the child. Her longing for a family of her own had not died with Fridolin.

"I hope you don't mind," Charlotte said uncertainly, nodding at Beatta.

"Not at all," Hanneke assured her softly. "Your daughter is a dear."

Charlotte's expression softened. "Beatta is one of my rewards for having summoned the courage to escape my servitude."

"If I might ask…how did you manage to get away?"

Charlotte didn't speak at once—not out of reticence, Hanneke thought, but to give herself a moment to turn her focus inward and confront dark memories she probably tried hard to avoid. Finally, she said, "One night, the master came home drunk. When he passed out, I simply stole away in the dark." She made a helpless gesture with her free hand. "I didn't have a plan. I just knew I would rather die than stay at that wretched place for one more day. Emigration seemed like the best option, so I began making my way toward Hamburg." She met Hanneke's gaze directly. "I traveled at night and hid during the day and snatched whatever bite of food I could find. It was a—a difficult journey."

"I don't doubt that." The words felt inadequate.

"The day after I finally arrived at the port, I saw Beatta's father wandering through the crowds. He was clutching her in his arms and approaching lone women. His wife had died the night before, and he had tickets for two adults to make the crossing. He was as frantic for a helpmeet as I was to leave the Old Country behind. The ship captain married us that night, after we were on board."

At least I had several days to get to know my husband, Hanneke thought, gratefully and without judgment.

"I've never had a moment's regret." Charlotte's tone was barely above a whisper, but she raised her chin with a touch of pride. "My husband is a good, kind man. He worked hard and was able to buy this property two years ago. I couldn't love Beatta any more than I do, and now we have Henni as well."

Hanneke's throat felt thick. "You've been blessed." She gently displaced Beatta. "I'm sorry," she told the child. "I have chores waiting at home."

"Will you come visit again?" the girl asked.

Hanneke chose her words carefully. "If I can, I will." Barlow might retrieve the mare at any time. Besides, her pending trip with Gideon eclipsed all other planning for the moment.

"You'd be welcome." Charlotte's voice was wistful. "Perhaps we could share a wool workday. I've been admiring your shawl all afternoon."

Hanneke laughed. "As I've been admiring your blanket! I would enjoy another visit very much."

A few minutes later, she was riding Cinder down the Stofeldts' drive. Something felt different, and she realized that the convivial gathering had lifted her spirits. She wondered what Deputy John Barlow would think of her budding friendship with the lawbreaker he'd sent her to question and almost laughed out loud to imagine it.

The temperature was dropping. Hanneke kept the mare to a walk, not wanting to risk hitting any new ice slicks. Half an hour or so later, they approached the gully where she'd found Asa Hawkins' body. She'd kept her gaze on the road when they'd passed earlier, but this time, she decided to stop.

She wished she knew if John Barlow had found something helpful among Hawkins' business records. If the man died of some freak accident while simply delivering goods to a customer, there presumably was a record of his trip. *Not* finding such a record would add credence to the theory that Hawkins had been on secret abolitionist business and met trouble.

Well, Hanneke thought, studying the area more closely wouldn't do any harm. Whatever had brought Hawkins here on a cold night, she wanted to understand how Hawkins had ended up down in the ditch. If he'd been thrown from a horse, he must have landed either right on the gully's edge, or on the slope itself, before tumbling down to the bottom. How had he suffered the head wound that Dr. Rausch had discovered?

She spent several moments brushing through the snow on the narrow bank with one boot, searching for a stone or other protrusion that might have met Hawkins' skull. Nothing. It seemed unlikely that such a fall would lead to a deadly commotion in the brain, as Dr. Rausch had called it. Especially since Hawkins had still been wearing a fleece-lined fur hat when she'd found him at the bottom of the ditch.

She frowned, stamping her feet absently to keep the blood circulating as she scrutinized the likely trajectory of Hawkins' descent into the gully. Months of snow had crushed dead grasses along the slope, and both her efforts and John's had trampled them further. It was at least possible that something had slipped from a pocket as Hawkins had tumbled. That warranted a closer look—if, Hanneke thought, I can do so without breaking my neck.

A nearby dead tree offered a low branch that Hanneke was able to break into a rough walking staff. Sidestepping gingerly, she began searching the slope for any hidden small objects. The stick helped her balance as she crouched, using her hands to shove away snow and tear apart rotting mats of plant material. The half-frozen, half-soggy muck sent cold needles of pain into her fingers. She neared the bottom without discovering anything, much less some remnant that might miraculously explain Hawkins' death.

Then she surveyed the gully itself. The snowbank that had concealed Hawkins was diminished, and more water was running through the ditch than she remembered. Hanneke didn't see anything in the shallow water. A small item might have disappeared in the mud below, but she couldn't proceed without immersing her leather boots in the snowmelt. With some reluctance, she abandoned the idea of searching further. This far from home, that would be most unwise.

Finally, her gaze rose to the gully's far side. The snow appeared to be undisturbed.

There's nothing else I can do here, Hanneke thought. Her failure to find some overlooked tidbit was disappointing, even if not surprising. She hoped that Deputy Barlow's day had been more productive. Or perhaps one of Hawkins' acquaintances in Watertown would provide some new insight. Those interviews with Know-Nothings and other well-to-do Yankees must, of course, be left to John....

With a sudden start, she thought, Or perhaps not. She knew one possible informant that the deputy did not: Gideon. He had already concluded that Asa Hawkins had tangled with a slaver. During their upcoming drive, she would ask if he had any actual knowledge about Hawkins' death, or helpful observations about the man and his local role.

The afternoon was growing late. Rising stiffly from her crouch, she cautiously made her way back to Cinder. "Let's head home, girl," she murmured. She settled herself in the saddle.

As they set off, Hanneke noticed idly that the steep-sided gully diminished as soon as they entered the woods. The farmer who'd hacked the small field behind her from the ancient forest must have deepened a natural feature to provide better drainage from the hard-won plot.

Several deer abruptly bounded across the road, down into the ditch, and up again into the woods. She watched their white tails flash as they quickly melted into the shadows. Her forehead furrowed as she spotted something unexpected on the far slope. Something had churned a channel of snow on the gentle rise beyond the low ground.

That was no deer, she thought. Had a bear lumbered through? Or a human hunter? That seemed the most likely explanation...and yet, this was an odd spot for someone to enter or exit the woods.

Even odder, the snow beside the road on *this* side had not been disturbed. What under heaven had happened here?

Hanneke set her jaw. Wet boots or not, she was unwilling to ride home without taking a closer look.

She made her way to the low ground where several inches of icy water had pooled. After eyeing the most likely route, she clutched up her skirts, and quickly splashed through. She leapt onto the rise and managed to catch her balance by grabbing the trunk of a sturdy red twig dogwood. Clinging to it, she stamped each foot until she felt steady.

Then she took a good look at the agitated patch that had first caught her attention. Melting snow had blurred whatever distinct marks had been made earlier. However, she was certain that the scuffle marks visible had been made by shoes, not paws. Staggered oval indentations, each the size of a human foot, were now visible leading into the forest. A larger hollow in the snow had been flattened a few feet away.

Hanneke edged closer to the depression. The person fell, she thought, and by the look of things, had scrambled mightily to get back on their way. Crouching, she placed one mittened palm on the flattened snow.

Slowly, a feasible possibility began to emerge. *Nein.* Not a possibility. The only logical explanation.

A scolding squirrel scampered up a nearby tree, pulling her from her thoughts. I must get back on the road, Hanneke thought. Time was passing, and although her boots had held up better than she'd feared, a bit of water had seeped in between soles and uppers.

She stood, but before she could turn away, a tiny spot of color caught her attention. Her breath hitched when she saw a spot of blood staining the snow.

Except…it was not blood. Hanneke used her teeth to pull off one mitten before carefully exploring with her fingers. What she'd mistaken for blood was actually the tip of a piece of yarn. Lifting her palm had apparently disturbed just enough flakes to reveal it.

She brushed away more snow to reveal a small tangle of wool yarn, stained a lovely but unusual red hue. As she gently pulled it free, something else rose with it. Hanneke placed the find on one palm, then sat back on her heels. What under heaven was this?

Chapter Eight

When Hanneke rode into the Barlows' drive, John emerged from the stable and strode to meet her. "Frau Bauer?" As he offered a hand to help her dismount, his expression was wary. "I beg you to assure me that you haven't discovered another dead body."

"I have not." She paused to shake out her skirt. "I can also assure you that Asa Hawkins was not conducting commercial business when he died."

John arched one eyebrow as he took that in. A woodpecker drilled at a nearby tree with astonishing speed. The scent of woodsmoke drifted through the clearing. After a moment, he said, "I just got here myself. Come into the stable while I see to the horses."

As John tended to chores, Hanneke told him about searching without success for something Asa Hawkins might have left behind and the unusual disruption and tracks she'd found down the road. "And when I pulled the yarn from the snow," she concluded, "I found this." She held out her palm, revealing something glossy as porcelain, perhaps half an inch long, cream-colored with darker spots. It was a pretty thing, roughly egg-shaped and humped.

John paused, curry comb in one hand. "What is that?"

"I believe it's a seashell." Hanneke turned it over to reveal a narrow split with fine-toothed edges.

"That doesn't look like any shell I've ever seen."

"A *sea*shell," Hanneke repeated patiently. "Not from local waters." The clam and mussel shells she'd seen near the Rock River were clumsy things compared to this delicate beauty. "See this little hole?" She pointed to one end. "I believe the person who left the faint footprints was wearing this shell—probably around the neck—when the yarn broke."

The deputy looked like he was getting a headache.

"I've had more time to consider this find," Hanneke said consolingly. She wrapped the yarn and shell back into a handkerchief and tucked it away in a pocket. "Did you visit Hawkins' freight yard? Was a wagon missing?"

He appeared ready to protest this seemingly abrupt turn in the conversation, but stopped himself. "I did visit. His assistant said one wagon and one horse are missing. God knows how far the horse bolted, or who finally found him." He shook his head. "Anyway, the man hadn't seen Hawkins in four days, and believed he'd ridden to Milwaukee to inspect possible cargo."

Hanneke began pacing back and forth in the aisle to both stay warm and to give herself a chance to consider this new information. The details fit perfectly into place.

Then she turned back to Barlow, still in the stall with his black Morgan. "Since Hawkins died north of here, nowhere near Milwaukee, we know he lied to his own yard manager." She instinctively glanced over her shoulder and lowered her voice. "That implies that he was engaged in his secret work at the time."

John applied the curry comb to his gelding's withers in slow, circular strokes. "I agree."

"I've seen the broadside regarding a fugitive named Celia, who was almost certainly the same woman who came to my house. For whatever reason, she didn't escape north after all. I believe Hawkins had Celia with him when he was accosted."

"They must have been traveling well after dark," the deputy muttered. "And she must have been well hidden. Anyone in these parts would pay careful attention to an unknown black woman traveling with a Yankee man."

"Indeed." The rural Pomeranian community could be clannish, preferring to keep company with friends and family from the Old World, or members of their own church congregation. She took a deep breath. "Hawkins most likely died just before, or during, the last big storm. Somehow, Celia managed to get away."

"You think Celia ran through the gully to avoid leaving tracks by Hawkins' body."

The image made Hanneke wince, for she doubted that the runaway had boots as sturdy as her own. "I do."

"How far down did you find that shell?"

"About a quarter mile."

John's mouth twisted sideways. "You realize that there's no way to prove this theory."

"Of course, I realize that!" She struggled against a surge of impatience. "Given that the tracks emerged from the water, can you think of any more plausible explanation? A newly-arrived European hunter wearing an exotic shell bracelet, perhaps?"

The deputy blew out an equally exasperated sigh and handed her the curry comb. "Hang this on the nail, will you? I'm going to haul water for these beasts so we can go inside."

They walked into the kitchen just as Ulricke was lifting an iron kettle from the counter. John leapt to take it from her and placed it on the small cookstove. "Are you well, my dear?"

"I'm fine." Ulricke smiled over his shoulder. "It's nice to see you again, Hanneke. I hope you'll stay for supper. I'm heating up some soup."

The room smelled deliciously of potatoes and rosemary, but Hanneke spoke apologetically. "*Nein, danke schön.*" There were shadows beneath Ulricke's eyes, and in the dim light, her cheeks looked flushed. Hanneke had long wished that Ulricke would give her a chance to offer whatever relief she could.

Ulricke, though, was a private person, and their friendship was growing slowly. "I'd be grateful to warm myself for a few moments," Hanneke added, "but then I need to be on my way."

Ulricke did not argue. "The other fire is burning as well," she told Hanneke. "I expect you and John have things to discuss."

In the parlor, Hanneke hitched a chair up to the stove and removed her boots. "Forgive my liberty," she said to John, "but I wasn't able to stay completely dry this afternoon."

He waved a hand. "By all means."

She positioned her footwear as near to the stove as she dared, then settled herself and pushed her feet forward until the heat baked through her thick stockings. It felt wonderful. "Much better."

"Let me see that shell again." He leaned forward, arm outstretched, and she dropped it onto his palm. He held it close to an oil lamp before shaking his head. "I still don't know what to make of this."

She spread her palms. "I don't either. The only information I can add is about the yarn itself. I was surprised by the hue, which almost certainly was dyed with cochineal—"

"Is this important?"

Hanneke knew that John was tired, and eager to return to the kitchen, but she did have a point to make. "Cochineal comes from an insect that is common in South America. Even if I could get it here, it would be very expensive. And while at first glance it seems unlikely that someone bound in chattel slavery would have access to it…."

"A wealthy owner might."

Hanneke nodded. She suspected that such a pretty scrap of yarn would not be easy to come by in the slaves' quarters. It was not hard to picture a defiant woman taking a bit of yarn, fashioning a necklace of sorts, and wearing it beneath her dress.

She gave John a sidelong glance. "Did you speak of the Underground Railroad to the sheriff?"

"I did not." He sighed. "I very much wanted to somehow prove that a thief came upon Hawkins on a dark night, struck the blow, and stole his horse." His tone was sardonic. "I'm less hopeful of that outcome now."

"It's better if you don't have that necklace." Hanneke extended her palm to receive the yarn and shell. That would have been true of any item suspected of belonging to a runaway, but inexplicably, it seemed especially important that the shell stay with her.

John surrendered it willingly. "I brought home something you'll want to see as well." He picked up his saddlebag, which he'd brought into the parlor. The first item removed was a leather-bound ledger, which he set aside. Then, he extracted a small drawstring pouch made from black satin.

The item it contained was so tiny that when he displayed it, Hanneke first thought that his palm was empty. She needed a few seconds to discern the irregular earth-toned sliver. "What is that?"

"It's hard to say for sure," John conceded, "but Dr. Rausch removed it from Hawkins' head wound." He used one fingernail to turn the bit over, revealing a dark, glossy sheen. "Our best guess is that it's a shard of glazed pottery. It looks black now, but in sunlight, it's deep blue."

An image of a killer galloping down a dark road with a pot in one hand appeared in her mind. Hanneke forced it away. "So…Hawkins died after being hit in the head with a crock? Or perhaps a small butter churn?"

The deputy gave a weary shrug. "I have no idea, but I figured you'd want to know."

"*Danke.*" Hanneke accepted that statement as the gift it was as she reached for her boots. "I need to tend my animals, and let you enjoy your supper. Please give my warm regards to Ulricke. Oh—shall I leave the horse? I can walk from here."

"No one has reported a missing gray mare," John told her, "so you might as well keep her for now."

Hanneke nodded gratefully. Then, as they both rose, the ledger caught her attention. "What's that?"

"The records Asa Hawkins kept regarding his freight and auction business. I don't expect to learn anything important from it, especially now, but…." He made a rueful gesture. "I have to try."

"I'd be glad to study it, if you like," Hanneke offered. She hated to think of him spending his evening hours squinting at figures instead of being good company for Ulricke. Besides, she'd be grateful for a task that would pass her own evening hours—*oh*. "If it's not urgent," she added. "I'll be away from home for a few days."

John's gaze sharpened. "Where are you going?"

"Just visiting a friend." Annoyed with herself, Hanneke fussed to arrange her scarf and hood.

"What friend is that?"

Hanneke wanted to shriek at him to stop. His voice was low and flat, but she'd been subjected to his disapproval too many times to miss it. "No one you know."

"I just—" he began, but some second thought caused his mouth to clamp into a tight line, as if afraid his words might yet escape. He needed a moment to subdue his protest. "Do you have someone to help with your stock?"

"William Bluewing," she said, and that seemed to satisfy him. "So. As I said, I'd be happy to study the ledger for you if I might keep it until I return."

"That would be fine," he said stiffly. "I'm obliged." He handed her the book, and she tucked it carefully beneath one arm.

He walked her to the front door. "I regret the dangerous nature of your journey," he muttered as she stepped out to the porch. "For the love of God, woman, keep firm hold of your wits." Then the door closed behind her.

Trust John Barlow, Hanneke thought, to instantly understand the deeper meaning behind her passing comment about being gone for a few days. He'd grasped the nature of her trip, even though he knew nothing of the specifics. His acuity was both impressive and irritating.

As she walked toward the stable, she tried to decipher the heart of John Barlow's parting comments. I don't believe he disapproves of my efforts, she decided, but he does worry about my safety. She couldn't decide if that made her feel better or worse.

John had not unsaddled the gray. Hanneke secured the ledger, led the mare outside, and swung to the saddle. She glanced at the modest *fachwerk* home where John and Ulricke were no doubt sharing supper and news of the day. Lamplight glowed behind lace curtains. Smoke drifted from the chimneys. Two different chimneys for two different stoves.

Then she startled, mortified. I must indeed be overtired, she thought. Lifting her chin, she clucked lightly to Cinder. "Come along, my good friend. Let's go home."

* * *

After supper, Hanneke packed spare clothing in a recently purchased carpetbag featuring pleasant shades of green, brown, and red, made up in a pattern of cabbage roses. Presenting herself well helped earn respect when she conducted business with merchants or customers in Watertown. At first light, she'd set out to meet Gideon. She wanted to make the same impression—capable, respectable—while traveling with him.

Next, Hanneke filled a large basket with bread, cheese, dried fish, fruit leather, and a few other items that should stand up to travel. She also threaded the shell she'd found on a sturdy length of her own heavy Cotswold wool. She'd spun it with high-twist singles and a high-twist ply, and the tight nature of the finished yarn made it much sturdier than the red piece that had broken. She hoped to return the necklace to its rightful owner if, as she suspected, Celia was both the person who'd lost the shell *and* the person she'd be helping to freedom on the Underground Railroad.

That done, Hanneke tried to occupy herself with Hawkins' accounts book. After struggling for a time, she slammed it closed. Squinting at columns of names and numbers and trying to decipher an unfamiliar accounting system would require more mental capacity than she could muster at the moment. Good thing John had said it could wait until she returned. It would make much more sense to go to bed early and get a good night's sleep.

Once in bed, though, she found herself listening to every sigh of wind against the windowpanes. Her pillowcase felt suddenly scratchy against her cheek. The air held an unfamiliar heaviness. She thought about embarking on an illegal journey with strangers. She thought about allowing Aubuchon into her home, letting him get the best of her. She thought about the grim set to John Barlow's face as he tried to communicate things he dared not shape into words.

Enough, Hanneke told herself. It was too late to second-guess herself about the wisdom of the coming excursion, even if she wanted to. Which she did not.

She reached out and curled her fingers around the pretty little seashell she'd found, which she'd left on her bedside table. She liked how one side was smooth and glossy, while tiny points lined the split on the other.

Without knowing why—and despite her long-held impatience with any notion of mysticism or spiritualism—she found the shell compelling. After all, its appearance that day was nothing short of fantastical. What had compelled her to place her palm *exactly* over its hiding place in the snow? It was inexplicable. Impossible, even.

And yet…it had happened.

Still clutching the shell, she curled into a tight ball beneath the blankets and finally drifted into a fitful sleep.

* * *

Hanneke blessed the cardinal who sang a greeting as she left her home the next morning. The sky was troubled with clouds, and the air was cold and damp against her cheeks. Several inches of snow had fallen overnight. She felt tingly inside but wasn't sure if she was nervous or merely resolved.

She'd dressed in her warmest layers, and now carried her carpetbag in one hand, the food basket in the other, and a circular water bottle formed of brown glass around one forearm. Turning east, she strode purposefully through the new powder toward the thin flush of pink struggling to brighten an overcast sky. She was determined to present herself with assurance.

Perhaps half a mile later, she rounded a bend to find Gideon waiting for her with his hands in his pockets beneath the arching limbs of white oaks and black cherry trees so ancient their branches touched over the road. He wore dark clothes again—black hat and wool coat, sturdy brown trousers, high and well-worn work boots.

He stood beside a dark blue wagon with a big bay roan in harness. The cargo was covered with heavy canvas, lashed down well with cord. A small gap between the tarpaulin and the wagon's tailgate revealed the cut ends of neatly sawn planks.

There is a human being hidden somewhere in there, she thought—presumably Celia. Her surety about this outing faltered as she confronted Gideon's wagon bed. How could a young woman bear hiding for two days in some cramped space among the lumber? When had she last eaten? How would she relieve herself? Did she have warm clothes? Was her hiding space well-padded? Although the wagon had a spring seat up front, there was nothing to spare living cargo from brutal jouncing on the rutted roads. It would be a wretched trip.

Gideon caught her attention by motioning with one hand. She realized he'd been watching her. Those gray eyes don't miss much, Hanneke reminded herself, and made a conscious effort to make her expression equally devoid of emotion.

After sliding her bag and basket beneath the seat, he extended a hand. "Let's go," he said quietly. Lifting her skirts with her free hand, she climbed up and settled on the seat's left side so he could handle the wagon brake with his right hand.

Gideon settled beside her and picked up the lines. "Get up, Arion," he called to the roan. The wagon lurched forward.

"Oh!" Hanneke grabbed the seat as one iron-rimmed wheel banged into a deep, now-frozen rut in the mud. She looked over her shoulder, fearful that some of the stacked planks might have banged onto their hidden traveler.

"Don't," Gideon said quietly. "Never, *ever* look behind you. The lamb is fine."

Their living cargo, he meant. Hanneke clenched her teeth. Irritating as it was, she understood why he'd corrected her. The fugitive is trusting Gideon with his or her life, she thought. I must do the same.

She sent up a prayer asking God to keep them all safe. Then, she settled in for a long ride. For better or worse, they were on their way.

Chapter Nine

After his muted admonishment, Gideon subsided into his own thoughts. Hanneke had wondered whether he would be at least minimally sociable or keep his focus entirely on the task at hand. Apparently, he truly required nothing more from her than her presence. That had been the arrangement, after all, Hanneke reminded herself.

Nonetheless, as time passed, she grew restless in the silence. This simply would not do. She couldn't spend four days with someone without at least desultory conversation.

Besides, there were *so* many things she wanted to know.

Stifling the questions she most wanted to ask, she cast about for a safe topic and cleared her throat. "Is this your wagon?"

"It is. I use it for my work."

Hanneke felt chagrined. She'd been so focused on this job that it hadn't occurred to her to wonder what Gideon did to actually earn a living. "Are you a farmer?" His vehicle was heavy, but shorter than most farm wagons.

"A farrier."

That explained the man's muscular arms and shoulders, Hanneke mused, for shoeing draft horses and oxen required a great deal of strength. She wondered if he had a shop in Watertown but decided that was too personal a question to ask. Perhaps Gideon traveled where he was needed, hauling tools and a portable forge in the wagon. If he worked alone, no one would notice if he took time off for more clandestine activities when the need arose.

Gideon appeared at ease on the seat, driving with his forearms resting on his knees. As the miles passed, however, Hanneke became acutely attuned to his constant vigilance. He might look like a sleepy farmer, but when she darted quick sidelong glances his way, his gray eyes were watchful, constantly scanning their surroundings.

They had passed into unfamiliar territory, but the rolling landscape felt comfortable. The woodlands and fertile prairies were dotted with a few large farmhouses of brick or frame, but mostly smaller log and *fachwerk* homes. The sound of axe blades on hardwood drifted to her ears as men and women split firewood to fill their wood boxes for the day. They passed a few young children trudging to school with tin lunch buckets. Hanneke wondered if their mother had tucked baked potatoes into their pockets, as her own had done on cold mornings when she was a child.

She was indulging in a moment of nostalgia when a welcome shaft of sunshine abruptly poked through the clouds. She considered the landscape, the sky. Then she turned to Gideon. "We're driving southwest."

"We are."

His affirmation perplexed her. "I assumed we'd be heading north."

Gideon finally shot her a look, one side of his mouth crooked in the tiniest hint of a smile. "All the newspaper articles about the Underground Railroad make it sound as if it operates as a regular train does and moves north like an arrow. People imagine scheduled stops with a conductor waiting at each to guide fugitives along the next segment."

"And it's not." Hanneke had never had the opportunity to learn anything specific about the system's logistics, but she understood his point.

"No." Gideon's gaze shifted to a flock of wild turkeys in a field, but only for an instant. "There are lots of gaps where travelers are on their own. People get lost. They wander in circles or run for days in the wrong direction. Sometimes, people zigzag and swerve to avoid slave catchers."

Images flickered through Hanneke's mind. She pressed her lips into a tight line.

Gideon shifted his weight. "The very few people who make it to Canada have probably run twice the distance you'd think by looking at a map."

That "very few" comment was distressing. This man—this stranger—was clearly not a novice at his business. "How long have you been doing this work?" she dared ask.

"A long time." His voice scraped over the words.

This man's soul is weary, Hanneke thought. Things he knew, things he'd experienced, had scorched his heart.

She knew better than to ask a personal question, so she presented a more innocuous one. "Why did you want me to wear this?" She plucked an edge of the Rolling Wheels lace wrap from beneath the heavy wool shawl and cloak she'd draped over it. "It does little to keep me warm."

"Because it's distinctive." Gideon shrugged. "I sent word ahead. If we get separated, and you have to make your way to our final destination alone, a shepherd there will recognize you by it."

Hanneke's eyebrows arched high. She turned that unanticipated scenario over and over in her mind, as she might study an unusual rock from all sides. They were passing a small farm, and she turned her gaze to a man stretching a deer hide out on one side of his log home in preparation of tanning. Finally, she said, "That being the case, perhaps you'll be so kind as to tell me what our final destination is."

"Nope," Gideon said without hesitation. "Tonight will be time enough."

* * *

Hanneke had vaguely imagined traveling on seldom-used lanes, but Gideon did not avoid busier roads. It does make sense, she mused, as he edged their wagon to the right so a man hauling a load of hogshead barrels could pass unimpeded. They were less noticeable on a route frequently used by those traveling for commerce. Residents of tiny hamlets unused to such traffic would be much more likely to take note of strangers rattling through.

They stopped at midday along a huge marsh. When Gideon led his horse to drink, an indignant, ruddy duck exploded from the dense cattails near shore, his bright blue bill gleaming in the sun. Hanneke succumbed to a moment of longing for a slice of roasted duck, steaming hot from a Dutch oven nestled among coals.

Instead, she and Gideon stood beside the wagon and unwrapped sand-wiches. As he held out an open pouch of dried apples, she tipped her head toward the wagon.

He shook his head.

"Have mercy!" she hissed. "Surely a bit of food—"

"Not in daylight. *Never* in daylight." Muscles worked in his jaw. "Do you know that the Fugitive Slave Act allows a slave catcher to drag in any colored person they wish? The courts rely only on the slaver's word that the individual is indeed a slave. The soul in chains is not permitted to speak. There are no jury trials in such cases. Whoever makes final judgment gets paid a small amount if he frees the accused, but twice as much if he declares the prisoner a slave."

Hanneke pursed her lips with disgust. It was despicable. No wonder Gideon was unyielding about his "never in daylight" decree. It would not do for anyone to see that they were traveling with a Negro.

His voice softened. "You, however, need to eat."

Knowing that he was right did not keep her first bite of rye bread and smoked ham from turning into sawdust in her throat. Looking away from the wagon did nothing to soften the knowledge that someone hungry and cold was huddled just a few feet away, no doubt listening to every hushed word.

It was intolerable.

"Think of the prize," Gideon counseled quietly, once again apparently hearing her thoughts. "That's how fugitives survive. Anything can be endured in the moment when freedom beckons on the horizon."

Hanneke nodded. It occurred to her that Gideon was quite well-spoken for a farrier, but she knew better than to say so. Instead, she changed the subject. "You knew Asa Hawkins."

Surprise flickered in his eyes, and perhaps wariness as well. He chewed a leathery ring of dried fruit before responding. "We'd met."

She chose her words with care. "Do you believe he died while engaged in his secret line of business?"

"Yes."

He has no doubts, Hanneke thought. She nodded slowly before her eyes narrowed with speculation. "What do you know that I do not?"

Gideon pulled the apple bag's drawstring and tucked it back into his pocket. "What I know is that when I'm doing this type of work, the only thing that matters, the only thing to *think* about, is getting the lamb to a shepherd. Everything else can wait."

Hanneke stifled a grudging sigh. "Very well," she conceded. However, she added silently, as soon as our primary goal is achieved, we shall return to the question.

After munching their simple meal, they proceeded on their journey. For a while Hanneke managed to pass time with some stiff-fingered knitting, even if she did have to pause frequently to warm her hands. It was a godsend, truly, for she feared she might have gone mad without distraction on this long drive.

Sadly, predictably, in late afternoon, the temperature sank with the sun. Hanneke tucked her project away with regret. At least she could reclaim her mittens.

"There's a farmhouse on the left, just beyond the bend. We'll stop there."

Hanneke startled, for it was the first thing Gideon had said in hours. It was welcome news, though. Her body quivered with the need to stretch stiff muscles, sit by a fire, and—if she was lucky—drink something steaming hot. Her own longing shamed her, for she'd had food and water, and comfort stops along the way. She couldn't begin to imagine how cold, stiff, and hungry their lamb must be.

Hanneke watched the terrain intently as Gideon guided Arion, the roan, around a wooded curve in the road. She glimpsed buildings through the trees before a fair-sized farm emerged in a clearing. Yankee, she suspected. The gleaming white house boasted frame construction and a front lawn. Most Europeans considered lawns a shocking waste of fertile ground.

The air smelled of hickory smoke. A small red cart filled with firewood sat near the front step, a vivid crimson splash against the backdrop of snow and white paint. A spotted dog of indiscriminate origin trotted from one of the outbuildings but raised only one half-hearted bark. Hanneke gripped the wagon seat in anticipation of the turn.

Gideon drove past the farm drive without so much as turning his head.

Hanneke's brow furrowed, and she clenched her teeth to keep from protesting. Why were they traveling on? Had she misunderstood what he'd told her about stopping for the night?

Nein. Most decidedly not.

For several minutes, only the muffled clip-clop of the horse's hooves broke the stillness. Finally, Hanneke could no longer abide Gideon's silence. "Why did—"

"It wasn't safe."

Hanneke swallowed hard. That could only mean one thing: slavers were in the area.

"I know another place where we should be all right." He hunched over, elbows on knees. "Getting there will take us well out of our way, though."

"I see." Her words were clipped with the effort to maintain her composure. She glanced compulsively over both shoulders but saw no one. "How did you know?"

He hesitated, as if debating whether to respond. Finally, he said, "The red cart was a sign."

Hanneke sent a silent message to their hidden passenger: *I'm so very sorry we can't stop yet.* Then she closed her eyes for a moment, drew in a slow breath, dug in her carpetbag for an extra wool scarf, and adjusted her expectations.

Hanneke was half-dozing on the wagon seat by the time she realized that Gideon was setting the brake. She was cold, hungry, achy, and so stiff that she stumbled while climbing from the wagon. Gideon grabbed her forearm to steady her. The night was dark. If there hadn't been several inches of reflective snow on the ground, she might not have been able to discern that he had parked behind a two-story log farmhouse. Instead of providing comfort, the sight of the house only highlighted her awareness of their precarious situation.

We would not have stopped here if Gideon didn't believe it was safe, she reminded herself. Looking up, she glimpsed a few stars between the moving clouds. Fridolin was up there, keeping an eye on her. In this moment of not knowing where she was or who she was with, that thought was reassuring.

"Wait here," Gideon murmured. "Since we're not expected, I need to explain."

As he spoke, two figures emerged silently from the back door—one wearing pants, one wearing a skirt. Hanneke watched them huddle with Gideon, but she couldn't hear their low-pitched conversation. After only a few moments, the woman hurried over, grasped Hanneke's free hand, and towed her into the house.

A single taper burned in the kitchen. The tantalizing smell of roast venison and rosemary lingered among the shadows, but Hanneke saw little.

"Upstairs," the woman murmured in English. She was of stocky build, and her voice suggested someone of advanced years, but she did not remove her cape or the large hood hiding her face. She lit a candle lantern and led the way up a steep, narrow staircase.

"You may sleep here tonight." The farm wife led Hanneke into a small chamber furnished with a bed, a chair, and a nightstand just big enough for the lantern beside a ewer and pitcher. "You can rest here for a bit."

"Thank you."

"When your companion is ready, the two of you can eat some supper downstairs by the fire." The woman turned to leave.

"Wait, please." Hanneke stepped closer. "What about—"

"All is being seen to." The woman left, shutting the door behind her.

So dismissed, Hanneke sank onto the bed. She'd imagined that her help might be needed at this juncture, especially if the runaway being transported was indeed a woman. Yes, Gideon had asked for nothing beyond her presence. Still, as a capable and willing woman who prized being useful above all else, the situation was vexing.

Then Hanneke frowned again, this time at her own spurt of petulance. Gideon barely knew her. This farm couple didn't know her at all. A fugitive's life was at stake. It would take time to gain the trust of these people who'd already risked their own safety and security by working for the Underground Railroad. Hanneke starched her resolve to prove herself a willing and able shepherd.

She had made herself somewhat more presentable by the time she was summoned back downstairs. The only light in the small sitting room came from the fire crackling in the fireplace. Gideon was already seated, and two bowls waited on a small table. A low murmur suggested that their host and hostess were in the kitchen.

Hanneke crouched on the outer hearthstones, tucked her skirts out of harm's way, and held her palms toward the blessed flames. Gideon picked up his spoon and began to eat. Only when Hanneke's cheeks began to feel scorched did she settle in the other chair to enjoy her own portion of venison stew and dumplings.

After a few much-savored bites, she realized that Gideon might well disappear without a word if she didn't speak up. She dabbed her mouth with a napkin, strove for a neutral tone, and spoke just above a whisper. "How did our passenger fare today?"

"Lambs do what they must. Ours is now warm and fed."

His statements might have been meant to reassure, but even in the flickering firelight, Hanneke saw the fleeting grimace that tightened Gideon's mouth. *Even though he's doing what he has to,* she thought, *he's worried about the runaway.*

Pursuing that thought would accomplish nothing, however. She changed the subject. "May I show you something?" He didn't object, so she gently pulled the shell she'd found near Asa Hawkins' murder site from beneath her bodice. Concealing the find beneath her dress had seemed the safest way to carry it, and in truth, she liked the feel of it against her skin. Now, she slipped the yarn loop over her head and handed the necklace to Gideon.

His eyebrows rose as he studied it on his palm—for Gideon, a rare break in his composure. "Where did you get this?"

Hanneke explained. "Based on what I observed in the landscape, I feel fairly certain that whoever lost this shell had been traveling with Asa Hawkins. When whatever happened to him *happened,* the shell's owner fled. Do you know what it is?"

"It's a cowrie shell." He rubbed it with his thumb. "In Africa, I'm told, they've been used for centuries as currency."

Now, Hanneke blinked in surprise. "As *currency*?" The unusual affinity she'd felt for the small shell had not suggested anything so mercenary.

Gideon gestured with one hand, dismissing her unspoken and simplistic conclusion. "Many people also prize cowrie shells for spiritual reasons. They protect those who carry them by warding away evil."

Hanneke pulled her knitting from her pocket as she took in that revelation. Her sensibility, and her Lutheran upbringing, rejected outright the notion that a seashell could keep evil at bay…and yet, she had indeed received an intangible sense of comfort from the cowrie.

In any event, she thought, the cowrie shell had other and more useful stories to tell. "I feel an urgent need to get this back to its rightful owner," she told Gideon. "I admit, my primary motivation involved connecting with the only person who might be able to tell me something about Asa Hawkins. After what you've said, though, I understand that the person who lost the cowrie may be especially anxious for its return." She hesitated, debating whether to be more specific. "Is there any chance that…." She let the question dangle.

He stretched out his legs, crossed them at the ankles, and tented his fingers over his mouth. A log popped in the dwindling fire, sending a cascade of sparks over the hearthstones. The faint scent of cherrywood tobacco drifted from the kitchen. The farmer must have lit his pipe.

Finally Gideon leaned closer, letting the shell dangle from its yarn string until she took it from him. "You will have the opportunity to return it." His low tones were almost inaudible. "When the moment is right."

Hanneke had to content herself with that. Nonetheless, Gideon's confirmation of her suspicions prompted a bit of satisfaction inside. She thought back, piecing moments together. Gideon had been helping Celia toward Canada when Hiram Aubuchon or one of his employees got close enough to shoot. After leaving Gideon at Safe Haven Farm, Celia had somehow connected with Asa Hawkins. *He* had been trying to help Celia when he died. During her frantic rush from the gully, she'd lost this cowrie shell. Somehow, Celia had reconnected with Gideon, and here they all were.

Reflecting on what Celia had already endured, both as a slave and on the run, was painful. Hanneke's fingers clenched the knitting needles. She and Gideon absolutely *must* keep the woman safe.

"Frau Bauer."

Lost in thought, Hanneke startled. "Yes?"

"For your own safety, I've told you as little as possible about this undertaking. However, this is probably the best time for me to share some details you need to know."

Hanneke sat up very straight.

"The detour tonight will delay us tomorrow, but by early evening, we should reach our destination. Are you familiar with Milton?"

"I am not." She'd traveled by coach from Milwaukee to Watertown upon her arrival in Wisconsin, but once settled at her own farm, she hadn't been farther than Charlotte Stofeldt's place.

"It's a small town with an uncommon number of abolitionists. We will stop for the night at a stagecoach inn called The Milton House, where new shepherds will take responsibility for our companion." He reached into one pocket and extracted a small piece of paper, folded once. "Here. Take a look at this."

Accepting it, Hanneke found a rough hand-drawn map. She didn't know why he was suddenly sharing such information, but after his previous silence, it bolstered her spirits to know where they were going.

Gideon folded his arms and leaned closer. "If anything happens before we get there, if we are set upon, your sole duty is to take the lamb and run."

Hanneke's eyes widened. *This* was why he was showing her the map. She willed her voice to stay as calm as his. "Do you think that is likely to happen?"

"No. However, I did not think it likely that the red cart would be out at the farm where I had planned to spend the night. Slavers are in the area."

"Aubuchon?"

"I can't say for sure, but…." He lifted one palm, let it drop again. "It's likely. The point is, in this business, things can change in an instant. We must be prepared to adapt."

"Of course."

In the firelight, Gideon's intense gaze held a hint of something sharper, something fierce. "I am well armed and will do everything in my power to stop Aubuchon or any other slaver from following you. Whatever. Is. Necessary. Do you comprehend what I'm saying?"

Lieber Gott. Hanneke licked her lips, suddenly gone dry, before nodding.

"Do not turn back. Do not even *look* back. Do you understand? All that matters is keeping our charge safe."

The image of him confronting an attacker to protect her and Celia made the venison stew curdle in Hanneke's stomach. It took effort to keep from protesting, but since his scrutiny was unwavering, she swallowed the words. Instead, she asked, "How will I know where to go?"

"If we're still outside of town, head for the closest woods. Look for marshy ground or a stream you can walk in, at least for a while. It throws off your scent."

It throws off your scent.

Hanneke finally understood in a visceral way exactly what she might have to confront as a shepherd on the Underground Railroad. She knew with sudden clarity that she would never forget this moment. The fire popped and sizzled, the shadows wavered, the smell of meat and smoke and tobacco lingered in the cold air, and every fine hair on the back of her neck prickled.

"Make your way to The Milton House," Gideon was saying. "It's a two-story hexagonal building, attached to a commercial block with shops below and rooms to rent above. It's right on the town square, see?" Leaning over, he tapped an **X**. "You can't miss it. The whole structure is made of grout."

"Grout?" Hanneke repeated, trying to imagine such a thing.

"Your best landmark is the tall windmill that pumps water for the railroad station just across the road from The Milton House." He tapped another spot on the map. "Commit this to memory."

Hanneke angled the paper toward the fire and squinted at the map in the gloom. Although not detailed, it clearly showed The Milton House, the railroad station, and the town square. Lines indicated smaller streets branching out, and a bit of the surrounding countryside. After a couple of minutes, she sat up straight and silently returned the map to him.

He crumpled it into a ball and tossed it into the flames. "Leave the lamb nearby, well hidden. Go inside and ask for Nancy or Joseph Goodrich, the proprietors. They know exactly what they're doing."

That's good, Hanneke thought, for I clearly do not.

Chapter Ten

The next day, as dusk was descending, Gideon told Hanneke that they were about two miles from Milton. "I've circled around. Do you know the direction we're heading?"

The simple question annoyed her until she realized that he was testing her awareness. "We're approaching from the east." They'd needed to skirt around a lake with marshy shores, but now were driving due west.

He ended the conversation with a single nod.

Hanneke shifted her weight on the seat in a vain effort to find a more comfortable position. It had been another long day, for they'd left their farmhouse lodgings before dawn. The woman there had sent them on their way with two cold sausages and two warm biscuits, all wrapped in a linen napkin. "Thank you," Hanneke had murmured, hoping their hostess understood that her gratitude extended beyond the food to the refuge she and her husband had provided. The woman pressed her hand. "Go with God," she whispered before scurrying away.

The temperature had dropped overnight. Hanneke had not been able to knit for more than ten minutes at a time before her fingers grew too numb to hold the needles. That left her with nothing to do but study their surroundings and listen to the wheels crunch on packed snow. When she spotted the tip of a church steeple in the distance, she felt a flush of relief.

Gideon made a sudden clucking sound. "Get up, Arion."

Hanneke braced her feet to steady herself as the roan broke into a trot. Her heartbeat seemed to speed up as well. Something was wrong. This was the first time Gideon had abruptly quickened their pace like this.

Hanneke slid a sidelong glance at her companion. Anyone watching might have sworn that his posture and demeanor didn't shift, but after two days on the seat beside him, Hanneke perceived the change. The narrow space between them vibrated with sudden tension. His jaw was tight.

"What's the matter?" she asked in a low tone.

"There are two riders coming up behind—*no*. Do not turn around."

Hanneke had already suppressed the instinctive urge to look over her shoulder. Beneath her many layers, a sudden sheen of sweat dampened her skin.

Gideon slapped the lines lightly against Arion's broad back, and the tired horse obliged with a brisker gait. "They're still a ways back, but closing the gap. If there's going to be a confrontation, it will come soon."

Hanneke tucked her hands into her armpits. "So close to town, are you sure the riders mean trouble?"

"Can't swear to it. I'm pretty sure, though." He called another command to his horse, and they abruptly veered into a narrow, wooded lane.

The turn allowed Hanneke a quick glimpse of the horses trotting behind them. Their riders were well bundled against the chill, with hats pulled low. She opened her mouth to say that leaving the main road in favor of something more rural and isolated did not seem like a good idea, then clamped it closed. For better or worse, Gideon was in charge.

He repositioned his boots against the footboard. "I know what I'm about. Just remember everything I told you last night."

Frost crystals formed in Hanneke's marrow. You must stay steady, she told herself. That's what Gideon and Celia both needed. "Are they still following?

"Yes."

"Should we try to hide? Is there another safe place nearby?"

"I want to get to Milton. Lots of people there will come to our aid if things get ugly."

That reassurance did little to quell Hanneke's mounting anxiety. It was hard to grasp that the situation had truly come to this. The thought of watching Celia dragged away by slavers made bile rise in the back of her throat.

Gideon barked a command to Arion. The wagon pitched forward. Hanneke grabbed the seat, fighting to keep from tumbling. As they bounced and lurched, she felt a tightening sensation beneath her ribs, as if someone was over-winding a pocket watch. Her hands ached with the effort of hanging on. *Lieber Gott*, how Celia must be suffering in the wagon bed.

That image sparked a flame of pure and welcome rage inside, burning away her fear and tempering her resolve. If Hiram Aubuchon or any of his ilk thought they could—

A gunshot shattered the evening.

Time fractured. Stray images whirled through Hanneke's awareness, as if she was inside a kaleidoscope. The wagon swerved to the left. One wheel went off the road and banged into a pothole. The roan whinnied with wild alarm. Two shrieking ravens flew up from a tree. "Arion, whoa!" Gideon shouted.

The seat tipped to a dangerous angle. Hanneke clutched and clawed to stay in the vehicle, but the pitch was too extreme. As she lost her grip, she glimpsed Gideon, snatching a long-barreled gun from beneath the seat.

Pain shot through one hip as gravity forced Hanneke's body over the side of the wagon seat. She slammed into the ground. Crystalline snow felt gritty and cold against her face. One shoulder throbbed. Her lungs groped for oxygen. Her brain strained to grasp what was happening.

Clarity returned as the sound of wood creaking and groaning above her pierced the fog. Arion shrieked. Crab-like, Hanneke scrabbled sideways until free of the wagon's trajectory. She thought it was going to roll, but after a moment, it came to rest at a dangerous angle.

Celia! Hanneke screamed silently, praying that the woman had not been crushed.

Lumber clattered from beneath the tarp Gideon had lashed in place over his load. Hanneke scrambled to her feet and stumbled to the wagon.

Hoofbeats thudded on the packed snow. The riders were upon them.

A flash caught Hanneke's eye a second before another shot exploded. A whiff of burned gunpowder reached her nostrils. Gideon stood by the wagon, reloading his smoking gun.

More lumber banged from the space between the tarp and the side of the wagon. The gap seemed bigger than it had just seconds ago. Then, two feet in worn brogans with pegged soles poked through the opening. A woman—*nein*, a girl, really—slid through the opening, briefly revealing bare black legs before her skirt and navy blue cape settled in place. She fell to her hands and knees, but at once was up again and struggling to find footing among the scattered planks. A faded turban-like kerchief covered her hair.

Hot tears of relief pricked Hanneke's eyes as she grabbed the other woman's elbow to steady her. "Celia? *Gott sei dank—*"

Two more shots fired in close succession. An unearthly howl rent the air. Gideon, bellowing like a demon, was running toward the two mounted men.

Nein. Not two. One man lay crumpled in the lane as his horse galloped away. His companion, still astride, was struggling to calm his own horse. Hanneke's pulse pounded in her ears. The kaleidoscope fragments whirled faster. Focus! she commanded herself.

Celia. She must get Celia away from here.

A pistol fired. Hanneke looked over her shoulder just in time to see Gideon stagger two steps and sink to his knees in the road. *"Gideon!"* she cried, feeling a wave of panic. Celia and Gideon both needed her help—

Celia grabbed Hanneke's hand with an oaken grip and jerked her into the woods. *"Mistress, run!"* she hissed.

Hanneke ran. A final shot rang out behind them as they stumbled blindly into the woods. She didn't look back.

Celia took the lead. Hanneke assumed that the young woman's strategy involved simply putting as much distance between themselves and the surviving slaver as possible. Hanneke could think of no better option. A child could follow their tracks with ease, but there was nothing to do but keep going. Gasping for breath, straining to hear a shout or gunfire, she and Celia dodged skeletal thickets, tripped over shadowed roots, crawled over fallen logs, and skidded on icy patches.

She was acutely aware that every single step took them farther from Gideon. Was he alive? Wounded? Dead? Would she have been able to save him if she'd stayed behind? The wondering gnawed at her heart.

Remembering that horrid moment of indecision made her feel dizzy. Then she realized that her pace had slowed, and Celia was waiting for her up ahead. You must, Hanneke told herself, set aside all thoughts of Gideon. The decision to leave him behind could not be undone. He was no longer with them. That meant she *had* to cling to her wits and find a way to deliver Celia safely to The Milton House.

Himmel, hilf uns, Hanneke prayed, as she scrambled forward. *Der Himmel helfe uns allen*. Heaven help us all.

Soon, the full blue-black shades of night descended. A barred owl sitting on a branch overhead stared at them with its unblinking yellow eyes. Tree limbs whispered in the light wind as if urging them on. This is not a dream, Hanneke told herself. I am truly plunging ever deeper into a pathless forest with a freedom-seeker, running from a slaver.

To Hanneke's chagrin, Celia had to stop several more times to wait for her. The last time, Hanneke found her crouching beside a dense, shrubby clump of common ninebark. Hanneke bent over with hands on her knees to catch her breath. "You must have…the eyes…of a cat."

Celia, who was shivering violently, had almost disappeared into her cape. "I got practice. Run at night, hide by day."

Between Celia's dialect and the whistling sound within her speech, Hanneke had to both listen and think to make meaning. Still, she caught a barely discernible tremble in Celia's tone. It worried her. She also didn't like the way Celia had pressed both arms over the front of her body, as if willing herself strength.

We must find a place to rest, Hanneke thought. Soon. She was physically exhausted and emotionally drained, and Celia was surely in even worse shape. Hanneke sorely wished that she had her carpetbag and food basket. They'd been under the seat when the slavers attacked and must have stayed there when the wagon tipped.

How much time had passed since they bolted into the woods? How far had they traveled? She didn't know. It was not a feeling she relished. Had they lost themselves in an endless forest?

Well. She must manage. "We need to find some kind of shelter," she murmured, hoping her quavers stayed in her stomach instead of reaching her voice.

The dark silhouette that was Celia shifted. "You know where we are?"

"No," Hanneke admitted. "However, I have some acquaintance with the stars. If we can find an open space, I can get my bearings." Stars glittered among the black lace of tree branches overhead.

Celia rose to her feet. "I know the Big Dipper and the North Star."

"I imagine you do." Hanneke stamped her feet, which were aching with cold inside her boots. "May we walk together? I don't think I can run anymore, and we can help each other stay warm." Receiving no objection, she took Celia's arm and pressed close.

Sometime later, Hanneke sensed a thinning among the leafless trees. At the same moment, Celia held up one hand, signaling caution. Creeping forward, they came upon a clearing studded with stumps. There was no sign of fallen timber, but moonlight revealed oxen hoofprints and a clear double trail churned in the snow. Whoever owned these woods had taken advantage of winter weather to cut timber and skid it out by sled.

Looking up, Hanneke felt a bit of comfort. This sky was familiar, even if this place was not. *Fridolin, please watch over us.*

As much as she loved the stars, however, a clear sky meant that the temperature was likely to continue dropping. Keeping to the shadows, Hanneke considered. "Let's follow the tracks and see what we can find."

Trudging forward, the two women soon came to the back of a farm lot. Hanneke studied the landscape from the tree line. The modest home was of *fachwerk* construction, its pale clay nogging showing clear. The Pomeranian half-timbered style made Hanneke long to seek shelter there, but only for an instant. Being Pomeranian did *not* mean the residents would be sympathetic. Perhaps they would report her and Celia to the closest authority and pocket their reward.

A burned-out barn stood at the back of the yard. "Wait here," Hanneke whispered. Celia nodded and crouched at the base of a white oak tree. Hanneke gingerly crept forward, bracing herself for discovery.

No barking dog reported an intruder as he raced toward her from his night watch. No honking, hissing geese appeared to slap their wings and raise an angry alarm.

Hanneke slipped through the barn's door space and surveyed her surroundings. There was nothing left inside. Hardly surprising, but disappointing. She'd hoped to find a scorched horse blanket or a bit of straw to rest upon. Nonetheless, although the roof was gone, the lower stone walls—about four feet tall—would provide a little shelter from the wind. Since no one was making any use of the space, they wouldn't have to worry about someone making a midnight trek from the house to check on a sick cow or to chase a coyote or skunk from frantic hens. This will be adequate, Hanneke decided.

Moments later, she felt doubt nibbling her confidence with sharp little teeth. She pressed her hands to her temples. In truth, it had been easier when they'd been blindly running. She was confronting another potentially life-and-death decision. *Was* this ruin a safe place for Celia to hide, perhaps for many hours? What if Aubuchon or another slaver was following their tracks right now? What if Celia became seriously ill?

Then Hanneke gritted her teeth. This was no time to wallow in what-ifs. Lifting her chin, she forced numb appendages to move and went to fetch Celia.

When they were both inside, Hanneke chose a dark corner where they could huddle together. Celia slid down the wall, as if support was required to sit down on the stone floor. She had shown enormous resilience earlier, but the nocturnal run had clearly taken a toll. "Celia, do you feel unwell?"

Celia shrugged. Hanneke didn't like the way the woman was shuddering. Fumbling stiff-fingered, she wrestled off one of her own flannel petticoats and one of the three shawls she'd worn for the journey. She planned to set off for Milton by herself, and brisk walking would warm her up. Sitting here alone, Celia would only get more chilled.

"Here," Hanneke said. "Put these on." She helped Celia secure the extra garments in place.

Then Hanneke huddled down beside her and hugged her close, inhaling stale sweat and something she couldn't identify. "May I see if you have a fever?" she asked, even as she pressed the back of her hand against Celia's forehead. The skin felt hot.

Hanneke maintained her composure, but as a healer with no medicinals to offer, she wanted to shriek with frustration. "I'm sorry I wasn't able to grab any supplies when the wagon crashed," she said. "I'll see if I can at least find some water." While running, both of them had consumed a handful of snow from time to time. It had done little more than wet their tongues, though, and Hanneke feared that larger quantities might do more harm than good.

Celia struggled to produce from the folds of her own cape a battered tin cup packed with snow. She wedged the cup between them. Hanneke understood she was trying to let the snow melt. Then Celia revealed a pale bag with a strap she'd worn over one shoulder. It might have been fashioned from a pillowcase. Reaching inside, she retrieved one big square biscuit so hard it took effort to break it in half. She held out one piece in wordless offering.

Hot tears stung Hanneke's eyes as she accepted the gift. "I'm going to do everything I can to keep you safe," she promised, quietly and fiercely. After abandoning Gideon, she was desperate to deliver her lamb to the Underground Railroad station in Milton.

Celia hitched her shoulders in a small, fatalistic shrug before gnawing off one corner of the biscuit.

"We can rest here together for a bit," Hanneke said after a few minutes, "but I need to go find the next safe spot." She started to bite her lower lip but stopped at once; it was too wind-cracked and tender for such callous treatment. "I am worried about how easy it would be for someone to follow our tracks."

To her surprise, Celia shook her head. "Those bounty hunters were too stupid to bring dogs. One tracker was down when we lit off. If the other had been able to follow, he'd have found us already. Maybe your man killed him."

Hanneke started to clarify that Gideon wasn't "her man," but she swallowed the words as irrelevant. "Still, I hate to leave you alone."

An abrupt coughing fit made Celia stop before saying, "This place be fine."

She paused before adding, "And I got me a knife."

"You have…a knife?" It had never occurred to Hanneke that Celia might be traveling armed. Had she stolen it? Or had one of the Underground Railroad shepherds given it to her? Too much violence had been done already, and Hanneke struggled to find an appropriate response. "I fervently hope that you never need to use your knife on a slave catcher."

"Well, I hope I *do*." Celia shifted her weight. "And if I fail, I'll use it on myself." Her voice had taken on a new timbre, hollow and resigned, as if the idea of her own death had been accepted long ago.

It took every ounce of self-control that Hanneke possessed to swallow a shocked gasp and instinctive objection. What had Celia endured that would lead her to such a resolute conviction? Hanneke had read plenty about the horrors of slavery. How very different it was to actually sit beside a survivor. In the silence that followed, the faint sound of a distant train whistle drifted through the night. She tipped her head back against the stone wall so she could better see the glimmering stars.

After a moment, Celia added, "My only chance be to get to that safe house."

Celia was right, of course. If a slaver tracked them to the barn, Hanneke knew she wouldn't be able to stop him. She hugged Celia extra close for a moment, trying to impart as much body warmth as she could. Then she eased away and got to her feet. "I'll bring back help," she promised, "as soon as I can."

Celia handed Hanneke the tin cup. Only a bit of the snow had melted, but she sipped it gratefully. After returning the cup, she turned her back and left Celia alone.

Chapter Eleven

Once outside, Hanneke slipped back into the trees and crept through the shadows, paralleling the farmyard, skirting a stump-studded field. The only sounds were the slow crunch of her footfalls in the snow, the occasional snap of a breaking stick, and the huge flap of a great horned owl displeased by her approach. You can do this, she told herself. You are a capable woman.

It seemed to take forever, but finally, she reached the lane in front of the farm. Keeping to the forest edge, she paused, pressing one hand over her chest. Her heart was thumping. Her breathing was too quick. Until now, all of her attention had been fixed on the moment, on Celia's immediate welfare. Being alone provided space to worry about Gideon.

Space as well to worry about the slaver who had shot him and, most likely, killed Asa Hawkins. Had the man she'd last seen on horseback escaped? Had the man lying on the ground survived to bind his wounds? For the first time, Hanneke felt capable of thoughtfully considering the bounty hunters' attack. The assessment didn't take long, and the results were alarming.

First, the vile and violent men they'd encountered earlier had known where to find them. If some informant had set Hiram Aubuchon or his ilk on the trail of Gideon's rescue mission, did he or she also know that one Hanneke Bauer was a willing participant? Hanneke shuddered and wrapped her arms across her chest. Aubuchon knew where she lived. She would not be safe even after she got home.

Second, the slavers' first shot had come from a distance. Had they assumed that the woman riding beside Gideon was Celia, hiding in plain sight? Why, though, did they shoot in the first place? If their goal was to capture Celia, why not just approach the wagon with guns drawn and make their ugly demands? Had they already decided to kill Celia outright? Ending her life might be kinder than dragging her back to a furious master...but men like Hiram Aubuchon were not kind.

A burst of wind startled Hanneke from her dire thoughts, and she set her shoulders. Well. Such speculations wouldn't help anyone. Celia's safety was still her priority, and she couldn't be *too* far from Milton. So, Hanneke counseled herself, stop worrying and make haste.

The clearing allowed an unimpeded glimpse of the heavens. She oriented herself before carefully reviewing her memory of Gideon's map. Then, with a determined nod, she set out. She hadn't yet eaten the hard biscuit Celia had shared, and she gnawed that as she strode along. In the starlight, her breath puffed foggy.

She paused often to listen, straining to hear hoofbeats or the faint crunch of a footfall on snow. After two days of dodging buggies and wagons, phaetons, and carts, the late hour and absence of other travelers prompted Hanneke to leave the rougher terrain and follow the lane. She did keep to the edge, though, ready to plunge into cover if needed. If anyone spotted her, she'd have a difficult time explaining why she was walking alone in the middle of the night through a community unknown to her.

Eventually, the road dead-ended at a three-way crossroads. A clutch of panic seized Hanneke when she realized that no option seemed to lead east. "I don't know which way to go!" she whispered. The prospect of trudging in the wrong direction while Celia shivered in the roofless barn was horrid. *Please guide me*, she entreated the night sky, not even sure if she was asking Fridolin for help, or God.

Perhaps one of them responded, for after a moment, she chose one of the forks in the road and kept going. Her gut thrummed with the fear that Celia might not survive the night on her own. She wanted to pick up her skirts and run...but cold, fatigue, hunger, fear, and the shock of the slavers' attack made such an energetic pace impossible.

Hanneke tried to avoid icy spots and the deep gouges made by iron-rimmed wheels during muddy periods. Nonetheless, sometime later, she stumbled and fell, landing on her knees. A few moments later, she was surprised to realize that she hadn't risen. *I only need a moment of rest,* she told herself. *Just a few moments.*

She'd fallen beside a stand of pussy willows, and she reached out to finger a branch. The shrubs had already produced their furry catkins. Their appearance was one of the first signs of spring. When Hanneke was a child, she had dearly loved gathering such branches with her mother to brighten the house after a gloomy winter. They displayed them in a big blue vase. Hanneke's mother had not been an overtly demonstrative woman, but the display always pleased her. "Well done, Hanneke," she'd say quietly. "Well done indeed."

Well done, Hanneke.

The echo of her sweet mother's voice was a gift. The memory of spring's promise was a gift. Hanneke rose unsteadily to her feet.

When she studied her surroundings, she realized that the forest had thinned. Pushing past the willows, she saw that the road had curved to the edge of a large lake, its marshy edges stippled with the silhouettes of dormant bullrushes and sausage-shaped cattails.

Her shoulders sagged with relief. There were plenty of wetlands in the area, but Gideon's map had shown only one lake east of Milton. If this was indeed that lake, then she had a good sense of where she was.

Hanneke picked her way along the shoreline until it began to veer south. Frowning, she considered. She needed to leave the lake, but she wasn't sure exactly where to turn. When she instinctively lifted her head to orient herself, she discerned an odd horizontal wedge of—of *something*—peeking pale above the treetops.

What under heaven was that?

Then, just as quickly, she realized she was seeing the edge of a windmill blade. *Your best landmark,* Gideon had said, *is the tall windmill that pumps water for the railroad station just across the road from The Milton House.*

Hanneke didn't know whether to laugh or cry. She had not gotten lost and wandered frantic through the county. Her aching feet and quivery muscles had not stopped functioning. Her courage had not deserted her. In just a few minutes, she'd find the good-hearted souls who would provide aid and comfort.

* * *

As promised, The Milton House was unmistakable. The grout building, a two-story hexagonal hotel attached to a continuous block of shops, was pale in the murky light. Hanneke leaned against the trunk of a primeval oak to establish her bearings. She almost leapt from her skin when the door of a nearby stable banged open, and a quartet of men emerged. It took a few moments to realize that instead of being ambushed by bounty hunters, she'd happened upon a group of drunk men who were probably heading home from a clandestine card game. She pressed one hand over her ribs as the men lurched away.

A few lights were burning around the town square, including one at the hotel's door, but no one else was in sight. Hanneke adjusted her cloak so a bit of her Rolling Wheels shawl was visible and scurried toward The Milton House.

Raised voices drifted through the window as she approached. Hanneke wanted nothing more than to burst inside and shriek for help, but she resisted. That would not do! Not when a slaver might be inside. Besides, a lone woman presenting herself at midnight was sure to attract attention from anyone still up. She must not let her inner frenzy override decorum.

Praying that Nancy or Joseph Goodrich was on duty, Hanneke let herself inside the lobby. Her first sensation was a wave of blessed heat thrown by a barrel stove. The air smelled of pipe smoke and beeswax. With the light from only one candle that burned from a wall-mounted sconce, Hanneke's quick scan of the room revealed a tall secretary desk, books and a globe, and maps pinned to the walls.

No one else was present except two elderly men almost hidden in one corner who'd apparently been playing a boisterous game of draughts. One had frozen with his hand hovering above the checkered board, still holding one of the small wooden disks. Both were silent now, staring with wide eyes. Was that because of her bedraggled appearance, or because respectable women normally wouldn't dream of entering such a male domain? Probably both.

Hanneke wasn't sure what to do next. "Mr. Goodrich?" she asked hopefully, looking from one to the other.

Both men shook their heads, but one stood, reached for a bell waiting on the desk, and gave the striker a firm blow. In the silence that followed the bell's ring, he shifted his weight, nervously fingering his bushy white beard. "Ma'am, you should wait in there." He pointed toward a doorway.

Before Hanneke could respond, a woman perhaps thirty years her senior strode into the room. Despite the late hour, she was attired in a deep blue dress dotted with small tan paisleys. Beneath her white cap, a precise center part bisected smooth, dark hair. Her gaze dipped ever so briefly to the Rolling Wheels shawl. "My dear," Nancy Goodrich said calmly. "It's so good to see you." She slipped one arm through Hanneke's.

In that instant, Hanneke felt the weight of an anvil slip from her shoulders.

"Let me show you where you can rest." As they left the room, Mrs. Goodrich looked over her shoulder. "Jim, Leo, please end your game before you fall asleep on the floor. I don't want to find you down here in the morning."

They passed a staircase leading to the second floor as Mrs. Goodrich briskly guided Hanneke through a dining area where a table was already set for breakfast, and on through a genteel parlor clearly intended for traveling ladies to rest.

Then Mrs. Goodrich opened another door and led Hanneke back outside. Hanneke blinked with new confusion. "What—"

"Don't speak," the older woman murmured.

They emerged in the yard behind the hotel. Hanneke didn't realize they were approaching a small log cabin until it loomed from the shadows. As the two women reached the door, it swung open silently on well-oiled iron hinges. A firm hand circled Hanneke's wrist and pulled her inside.

"I need help!" she gasped.

"Blessings be to God that you found us," muttered a large man with brown hair, mustache, and beard—Joseph Goodrich, she assumed.

At the same moment, a familiar voice demanded, "Where is the lamb?"

Hanneke whirled toward the corner with a gasp. Gideon sat on a heavy three-legged stool by the hearth, where a low fire crackled. His posture was stiff. "Tell us quickly!" he barked.

Hanneke moistened her lips. "The lamb is hiding in a burned-out barn perhaps three miles from here. She has a fever. I can show you the way." At least, she hoped she could.

Joseph Goodrich waved that offer aside. "There's only one such barn in the vicinity. I know exactly where it is."

"I'll go with you." Gideon began struggling to his feet. "I'm the one she knows."

"*You* will stay right here," Mrs. Goodrich informed him. "And *you*—" she fixed Hanneke with an equally implacable stare—"also need to warm up, eat, and rest. I will go with my husband and provide a woman's comfort."

Before Hanneke could do more than blink, the couple left the cabin, pulling on their wraps as they went.

Hanneke stared after them for a moment before curiosity, savory aromas, and the beguiling promise of warmth pulled her to the fireplace. She found roasted potatoes in a Dutch oven and a basket of gingerbread on the table. *This cabin must be where food is prepared for guests,* she concluded, noting flour barrels and kegs of beans, labeled pouches holding herbs, and a wedge of cheese wrapped in cloth.

Right this moment, she could have contented herself with shoe leather. Plate in hand, she dropped onto another three-legged stool beside the hearth, close to Gideon. "I am immensely grateful to see you alive. Do you have wounds needing attention?" She forked up a bite of potato, roasted in lard. It tasted so good she almost swooned.

"No." He made a dismissive gesture with one hand. "What happened?"

She most wanted to hear *his* tale, but after forking up another bite, she obediently focused on her own. "After my charge and I ran into the woods, we—"

"*No*. What happened to you when we were attacked?"

Hanneke frowned slightly, struggling to parse his intent. "Well, I fell to the ground when the wagon tipped over. Then I realized that our passenger was crawling from the fallen lumber. I was running to help extricate her when I heard another shot, and saw you fall to your knees in the road. Then we ran."

"The girl had to prompt you to flee." Gideon's voice held an unmistakable edge of anger. "My instructions were succinct and clear, but you failed to follow them."

Hanneke put down the piece of gingerbread she'd been holding, incredulous that despite everything she *had* accomplished since the attack, he'd chosen to greet her with accusations. "I only hesitated for a second or two."

"You faltered. Such indecision can get a shepherd or lamb killed."

"You might have been grievously injured!"

"That would not have mattered."

Embers were beginning to smolder within Hanneke's ribcage. "*Mein Gott!* For all I knew, you might have been bleeding to death in the road. Doesn't your life matter, too?"

He stared at the writhing flames for a moment before using one foot to shove another log into the coals. "I need to get some rest," he muttered, and leaned against the wall behind him. "There's a daybed over there." He jerked one thumb toward the other side of the room and closed his eyes.

Hanneke felt as if she'd been hit in the face with a plank.

You failed. You faltered.

Precious food remained on the plate, but she set it aside on the table. Her appetite had disappeared.

You failed. You faltered.

She wanted to protest his condemnation more strenuously. It was difficult to imagine that any new helper on the Underground Railroad wouldn't have reacted exactly as she had in such a moment! But sadly, she could not. Gideon's instructions had indeed been clear.

She rose and crept through the gloomy room to the narrow cot that had been shoved against the far wall. The bed frame was narrow, and the feather tick lumpy. It didn't matter. She wrapped her cloak about her and spread out a wool blanket that had been left folded on the bed. Then she lay down and curled into a tight ball, facing the wall.

Weary as Hanneke was, echoes of Gideon's denunciations buzzed in her mind like angry hornets. While she hadn't expected or wanted praise for what she'd done to keep Celia safe, it had not occurred to her that Gideon would be critical.

Hanneke pinched her lips together. Would she have taken the lead a second later if Celia hadn't been quicker? She wanted to believe it.

In truth, though, she would never know.

A hearthstone's weight settled on her chest. She had so very much wanted to succeed in this endeavor. She'd wanted to take a more active role in the local efforts to help the occasional freedom-seeker clawing their way north. When the opportunity arose, she'd believed she could rise to meet the need.

But by Gideon's standards, she had not succeeded.

That knowledge left an acrid taste in her mouth. Hanneke was not a boastful woman, but she did take quiet satisfaction from being industrious, solving problems, and meeting challenges.

Hanneke balled the blanket in her fists. Given the flat assessment and finality she'd heard in Gideon's voice, it was hard to imagine that she'd be given a second chance. He needed someone he could rely upon to follow his guidelines exactly.

A hard lump rose in Hanneke's throat. She pulled the blanket over her head so Gideon couldn't hear her cry.

Chapter Twelve

Hanneke jerked upright when a door banged open. Where was she…? Ah, *ja*. The Goodriches' cabin. The room was still shrouded in shadows, but they weren't quite as deep as before.

Nancy and Joseph Goodrich came inside, half-carrying Celia between them. Gideon lurched to his feet.

"We need to get this poor girl settled." Nancy glanced at Hanneke. "I need your help."

Hanneke hurried forward to take Joseph's place, linking one arm through one of Celia's. She seemed much worse off than when Hanneke had left her in the ruined barn, as if the extra hours of cold and hunger had broken her will. She clearly would have fallen without support, and her chin drooped toward her chest.

Hanneke fretted her lower lip. She didn't think she could bear it if Celia died now. A sheen of new tears made her blink. Had she failed after all?

"We must get her settled at once!" Nancy hissed again. "I think she's in pain."

Hanneke shoved her self-doubts aside to meet the moment. Gideon walked stiffly to a braided rug and toed it aside, revealing a trapdoor in the floor. The setup was not dissimilar to a trapdoor in Hanneke's own pantry, which led to a root cellar. However, instead of a staircase, a rope ladder dangled from the trap door before continuing on in sheer blackness.

Hanneke eyed the arrangement with trepidation. Gracious! That was a complication.

Gideon stayed in the cabin proper. Joseph, holding a lantern, descended first to light the way. Hanneke and Nancy Goodrich managed to get Celia down the swinging ladder to a dank, subterranean space with dirt floor, and walls, but it was a struggle. Hanneke's knees were trembling by the time they reached the root cellar, and she made a show of considering the crates and barrels lining the walls until she felt steady. The space smelled of musty apples. *At least there's room to make a pallet for Celia on the floor,* she thought, but there was no hint of accommodation—not a quilt, not a spare candle.

Nancy seemed to read her thoughts. "Not here," she murmured. "This spot is too exposed."

Joseph raised the lantern to illuminate a low door she hadn't noticed in the gloom. "This way. You'll need to either stoop or crawl to get through the passage."

Stoop or crawl? The *passage?* Hanneke cast a stricken look at Celia. "I don't think that—"

"With our help, she will manage." Nancy's resolute tone forestalled further discussion.

The rough-dug tunnel they entered was perhaps four feet high, earthen, except for an occasional beam wedged in place to stabilize the ceiling. Joseph walked with his back hunched, holding the light to help illuminate the passage for the others. Awkward as it was, Hanneke also crouched low as she scrabbled through so she could help bring Celia along behind her. Nancy brought up the rear.

Celia required frequent pauses. After what seemed like an interminable journey, they crawled through a brick-lined portal and emerged into another root cellar. Smoked hams and sausages hung from the heavy wooden beams that supported a plank ceiling overhead. Barrels and kegs suggested long-term food storage. Best of all, a straw-filled mattress lay on the floor.

Joseph lit two lanterns sitting on the shelf over the tunnel entrance while Hanneke and Nancy eased Celia onto the mattress. "The public dining room is directly overhead, so we must keep our voices down," Nancy whispered. "If you can stay with her for a few minutes, Joseph and I will go back up and fetch extra blankets and hot food."

Hanneke crouched beside Celia. "I have experience as a healer," she assured the Goodriches over her shoulder. "I'll see to her needs."

After the innkeepers went on their way, Hanneke unhooked the clasps on Celia's cloak and began a gentle examination. "We're in a safe place now," she murmured. She touched Celia's forehead with the back of one hand. The girl's skin felt hot as a glowing coal, and it was damp.

"I'm gonna die," Celia mumbled.

"You most certainly are not!" Hanneke took a breath and spoke more gently. "Not if I can help it, and Mrs. Goodrich as well. All you must do now is rest and recover your strength."

Celia responded to the encouragement not with acceptance, but with what Hanneke perceived as a profound weariness. The girl's eyes drifted closed.

"You may not give up!" Hanneke murmured fiercely.

Then she caught her breath. Bloodstains blotched Celia's skirt.

Hanneke's heart dropped like a stone in a pond. Suddenly, she understood why this strong young woman had given up hope. Celia was pregnant, and if she hadn't miscarried already, she was in danger of doing so.

* * *

By the time Nancy returned, dragging a basket behind her, Hanneke knew what there was to know about Celia's condition. She waited while Nancy tucked two patchwork quilts around the barely responsive girl. Nancy also managed to slide two spoonfuls of well-mashed potatoes into Celia's mouth and give her sips of the hot tea she'd brought in a bottle.

Frostbite was a distinct possibility, and Hanneke carefully inspected the young woman's fingers and toes. She'd never assessed colored skin for frostbite before, but she did her best. Hanneke was relieved to see that Celia's feet were unblistered, at least, and felt warm. That's encouraging, she mused, using the moment to replace Celia's worn stockings with a thick new pair.

When Nancy rose, the look she gave Hanneke was grave. The two caregivers retreated toward the far corner of the cellar.

Hanneke shared her news. "I believe our lamb is about three months with child. Both of them are in danger."

Lips moving in silent prayer, Nancy closed her eyes for a moment. Her face was composed when she met Hanneke's gaze again. "Is she losing the child now?"

"I feared she had already lost the babe," Hanneke admitted. "However, I found no evidence of tissue. No clotted blood. I suspect the problem stems not from the placenta, but from the ongoing rigors of her journey." She understood the girl's silence, but she did wish that Celia hadn't kept both the pregnancy and the blood loss to herself. The rusty stains had been hidden by her cape, and Hanneke might have missed them now if the wheat-colored garment had been constructed of darker fabric.

Nancy considered. "You have cared for a woman in such distress before?"

"I have," Hanneke told her. "More than once. There is no need to consider a doctor." Bringing in anyone else to examine Celia would be both dangerous and pointless. "What she needs most is rest and nourishment. She is not fit to travel." Hanneke clasped her hands, waiting to hear the innkeeper's response. Obviously, the Goodriches were experienced and committed conductors on the Underground Railroad. That did not mean, however, that they would be comfortable hiding an ill runaway for an indeterminant period of time.

To her relief, Nancy immediately put that fear to rest. "Of *course*, she must stay here." Then she took one of Hanneke's hands in both of her own. "I assure you my husband and I will do everything in our power to ease her struggles of all kinds. We will pray to God that both mother and child might be spared."

The older woman's gentle words provided a measure of comfort. Nancy, Hanneke thought, is a woman of admirable morals. Compassion and resolve as well.

"I best go explain the situation to the gentlemen," Nancy was saying. "Then I'll brew some bone broth for both of you. It's restorative. I'll bake some cornbread as well. I've yet to meet a Negro who doesn't appreciate cornbread."

Hanneke nodded, then glanced toward Celia, who had curled into a ball beneath the quilts. Most likely, she was struggling with cramps, but she made no whimper or moan. "We will need more clean cloths and water. Warm, if possible."

"I'll see to that. And there's apple cider vinegar in that jug." Nancy stepped sideways and tapped an earthenware vessel. Then she scuttled back into the tunnel and disappeared.

Hanneke returned to the mattress and pulled a low stool close. Who was the father of Celia's unborn baby? Was the infant the result of rape, or had Celia left behind a husband or companion she loved dearly—perhaps for the sake of the child?

She coaxed Celia to sip some water from a bottle that Nancy had brought. Then she soaked a small cloth, added a few drops of vinegar, and dabbed Celia's forehead. "This will help draw out your fever."

"It don't matter," Celia mumbled.

Hanneke frowned with concern. Celia's air of defeat simply would not do. She wouldn't regain her strength if she didn't want to.

It occurred to Hanneke that if Celia died now, the girl would never have a chance to share whatever knowledge she might have about Asa Hawkins' murder. In truth, though, right this moment that mattered not at all. Hawkins was dead, and Deputy Barlow was very far away from this dank, musty root cellar in Milton.

All I want, Hanneke thought, is for Celia to find freedom, deliver a healthy child, and live a peaceful life. Celia's courage, displayed in her dangerous attempt to attain those things, was inspiring. It would be a bitter blow if after coming so far, Celia became one of the majority of runaways who didn't reach Canada.

A new ache bloomed in Hanneke's heart. If there was one thing she couldn't abide, it was feeling useless. There must be something else I can do, she thought. Something that went beyond bone broth and cider vinegar. Something that would rouse Celia from her despair.

The obvious answer presented itself at once, as if whispered in her ear. Hanneke didn't know if Fridolin had given her the insight, or perhaps one of Celia's ancestors. It didn't matter.

Hanneke scrabbled at the cord around her neck. Her fingers trembled as she lifted free the necklace hidden beneath her own bodice and pulled it carefully over her head. "Celia."

The young woman did not rouse.

Hanneke glanced at the ceiling and raised her voice as much as she dared. "Celia! I have something to show you."

Still no response.

Hanneke placed the glossy cowrie in one of Celia's hands and curled her own hand on top, fisting Celia's hand tight around the shell. "I think this might belong to you."

For a few seconds, Celia did not stir. Then, her body stiffened. Her eyes fluttered open. She began to finger the shell, a growing look of disbelief nudging away her blank expression. Hanneke brought the lantern closer.

Celia held the shell before her face for a better look. "Where...." she began hoarsely.

Hanneke explained where and how she had found the shell. "It was threaded on a frayed piece of red yarn. Does that sound familiar?"

In the dim light, Celia's eyes turned glassy with tears.

Hanneke leaned closer. "Does the shell belong to you?"

Celia slowly pressed the fist holding the shell against her chest. Several moments passed before she managed to quaver, "I believed...this was gone... forever."

"I made a sturdier cord to protect it," Hanneke explained softly. "May I slip it over your head?" It took a few moments, but she managed to ease the necklace over the runaway's head and tuck the shell beneath Celia's collar, so it lay next to her skin. "You rest now."

Hanneke was starting to rise when she felt Celia clasp her hand. The dark fingers, calloused and chapped, clung to hers for a few moments. Hanneke felt a surge of something visceral and deep flow between them, forming an unshakeable bond.

Heavy footsteps overhead broke the spell. Celia pulled her fingers free, curled on one side, and let her eyes drift closed.

Hanneke sat back on her stool. I may have failed Gideon, she thought, but in finding the shell necklace and returning it to Celia, I did do *something* good. That knowledge helped a bit to soothe the raw spot that Gideon's condemnation had rasped in her heart.

* * *

"Mrs. Bauer."

The whispered words—and the gentle hand on Hanneke's shoulder—were enough to startle her awake. Blinking, she realized that she had dozed off on the stool with one cheek resting against the cold wall.

Nancy Goodrich stood over her. "Your patient appears to be sleeping peacefully."

She does indeed, Hanneke observed. Relief made her feel wobbly.

"Now it is time for you to do the same," Nancy murmured. "I brought the broth and cornbread and more bedding. You're beyond exhausted, my dear."

The notion of sleeping horizontally was immensely appealing. In short order Hanneke had nourished herself, used the bucket that served as a chamber pot, and was ready to settle down on the pallet Nancy created for her. "You're very kind."

Nancy waved that away. "I wish I could settle you in a guest room upstairs, but it's best that no one sees you." She sighed. "I do need to report that Gideon wants the two of you to leave as soon as possible. Don't worry, I bought you some time." She unfolded the last blanket and spread it out. "I insisted that you get the time *you* need to recover from your ordeal before setting out on your two-day journey home."

Hanneke had seen Gideon walk normally with two bullet wounds in one calf, and somehow make his way here—apparently after getting shot *again*. She doubted very much that he would have too much sympathy for her weariness. "And he agreed?"

The corners of Nancy's mouth hinted at a smile. "I think he's a little afraid of me."

That provoked a quickly tamped bubble of laughter as Hanneke stretched out on her makeshift bed.

"Also, I left something of yours in the tunnel. I'll go fetch it."

Hanneke was too bleary to even imagine what that something might be, so it was a happy surprise to see Nancy scrambling back into the cellar with Hanneke's carpetbag. "How...."

"An axle snapped when the wagon went off the road, but Gideon managed to hide your bag," Nancy explained. "Joseph repaired the axle and was able to fetch it for you."

"Please give him my heartfelt thanks," Hanneke murmured. She had been dreading the prospect of journeying home without her extra woolens. Even worse, her favorite knitting needles were in that bag.

"This can wait." Nancy set the carpetbag aside. Before she had even crawled from the room, Hanneke was sound asleep.

When she woke sometime later, Hanneke had no idea what time it was. The darkness was disorienting. She was used to feeling acutely attuned to the earth's rhythms and cycles, but in the windowless cellar, she had no way to sense whether it was even day or night. She felt groggy and grubby. Nonetheless, she could tell that the sleep had done her good.

She lit a new taper, and saw that Celia was awake. "How are you feeling?" Hanneke hurried to join her.

"Some better."

"I'm relieved to hear it." Hanneke tipped her head. Until now, the urgent demands of the moment had kept her from getting a good look at her charge. Celia was hard-muscled but painfully thin. Her headscarf had slipped off in the night, revealing the black braids it had concealed. She had a scar near her mouth, and speaking revealed her missing front teeth. Even now, though, Celia's oval face held a guarded expression. Caution, Hanneke realized, must be a lifelong habit for someone born into slavery.

Well. Hanneke wasn't sure how long she'd be able to stay with the girl, and she needed to make the most of it. "Any backaches or cramps this morning? Let me take a look at you."

A few minutes later, she was pleased to announce, "The bleeding has stopped, which means the baby is likely well. It's still essential, though, that you continue to rest and gather your strength."

Celia nodded. Then she pulled the shell free of her clothes and stroked it with her fingers. "We'll be all right now."

Hanneke moved closer. "If I may ask, where did you get such a shell?"

Celia hesitated. Hanneke wasn't sure if she had asked too personal a question or if Celia had been taught at a young age not to converse with white people. Slowly, haltingly, Celia explained that the necklace had belonged to her mother, and her grandmother before her. The shell's value wasn't just familial, however. This type of shell protected the spirit of those who wore them.

At this junction, the younger woman looked uneasy, as if unsure of how such a statement would be received. Hanneke nodded and whispered, "In that case, I can see why the shell means so much to you. How very special."

The night Gideon had said something similar she'd instinctively rejected that idea. She believed that a holy cross was the only protection a person needed. As she saw the unwavering belief in Celia's eyes, her doubt seemed self-righteous. As a child, she'd been taught to fear Catholics—and the religious medals they carried—but the few she'd met since coming to Wisconsin had been truly kind people. Her friend William Bluewing carried something special in a little leather pouch. Hanneke didn't know what it was, but she knew it was important to him. And, in truth, most pious Pomeranian Lutherans had a strong superstitious streak, believing in talismans and old Norse practices. Many different people, it seemed, wore or carried tokens of faith.

Celia paused again, as if the decision to share more of her story remained challenging. "The night I whispered to my mama that I was gonna run, she done took off the necklace straight away and fixed it on me."

Hanneke's heart squeezed as she imagined Celia's mother in that moment. "She obviously loved you very much. It must have been awful when you realized it was missing."

"Like someone done cut my heart out." Celia turned her head away, as if the memory of the moment she'd realized the necklace was gone was too painful to share.

That loss, Hanneke understood, was why the girl had given up hope. Why she believed that the complications of her pregnancy would be fatal. This time, she took Celia's hand in hers, trying to impart strength. "I think I must have been meant to find it for you."

Celia added, "I couldn't birth my baby without it. These shells are special for that." She pulled the necklace free and let it dangle. "See? It's shaped like a woman gone with child."

Hanneke's mouth quirked toward a smile. "I had not noticed that before." Then she hesitated. She didn't want to tire Celia further…and yet, this might be the best chance she got to ask an important question. "Celia, can you tell me about the day you lost it? I don't want to bring up bad memories, but whatever you can tell me might be very helpful."

Celia crumpled the quilt with her free hand, but after a moment, she nodded. "Yes, ma'am."

"Please, call me Hanneke." It was an impulsive revelation. Hanneke knew that Gideon would be unhappy with her for sharing her name. "At least when we're alone," she amended, but in truth, she didn't care. She wouldn't dream of sharing anyone else's name, and Gideon was already unhappy with her. If she was able to call her lamb by name, it felt inappropriate and rude to keep her own name a secret.

Celia's eyes had widened slightly at the personal invitation. Then she stopped, perhaps trying to decide where to begin. A burst of female laughter drifted through the ceiling. It must be mealtime of some sort.

Hanneke tried to encourage Celia without pressing too hard. "How did you come to show up at my door that night?"

"Well, I come up the Rock River to Watertown. Maybe a week ago."

Hanneke imagined a moonless night, the current's hushed murmurs, a pregnant girl not yet twenty years old. And, Hanneke hoped, a rowboat or a makeshift raft.

"Someone in Illinois told me that Aubuchon was nosing around up here." Celia nodded slowly, as if going back to the moment in her mind. "Right then, I knew I was in bad trouble. I disappeared out of there quick and started running. In circles, I figure, because I didn't dare wait for the conductor I was 'sposed to meet."

Had that been Gideon, Hanneke wondered, or someone else?

"After a few days on my own, your man started helping me. He done risked his life to save me from the slavers."

"How did—" Hanneke began, wondering how the two had connected, but immediately shook her head. "No. That is none of my concern."

Apparently, Celia agreed. "Anyway, we was heading toward your barn when he got shot."

"Did you see the person who fired the gun?" Hanneke pinched her skirt into accordion pleats. Surely she wasn't breaking any rules by asking who tried to kill Gideon that night…was she?

"No, ma'am, but we was on the run." Celia flicked the air with her fingers. "It was surely them slavers tracking us."

This is maddening, Hanneke thought. She understood the need for brevity and opaque description, but it was still a struggle for her to understand so little about how the Underground Railroad actually worked. "It was quite courageous of you to bring him to my house instead of running off. That kind of selflessness would make anyone's mama proud."

"*Oh.*" Celia licked her lips, as if unused to praise. "After that, I was on my own. Before he got shot, your man done told me to wait near a certain ole dead tree near a road if we got separated. It's got two rows of woodpecker holes running up the trunk, neat as your mama's hem stitches, so I knew it when I found it. I stayed out of sight in the woods until a big man came and got me and hid me in his wagon."

A big man? Hanneke's jaw muscles went taut. That was likely Asa Hawkins.

"Can I have some water?" Celia whispered. After several sips, she continued. "He was haulin' potatoes, and he covered me up with sacks."

Hanneke suppressed a shudder. *Mein Gott*, that sounded even worse than Gideon's scheme.

"I don't like travelin' during the day, but everything was all messed up, what with your man getting shot and all," Celia said. "We drove for a while. Then we stopped somewhere. The big man left me in the wagon while he went to talk to someone. I prayed I might get taken in overnight, but the big man was in a putrid mood when he got back to the wagon. He didn't say nothing to me, but I could hear him cursing and muttering."

That most certainly sounds like Asa Hawkins, Hanneke thought.

"After a while, he settled down. Got quiet. We jounced along for a while. Suddenly I felt the wagon slide and start to tip, like one wheel went off the road."

It happened to Celia *twice*, Hanneke thought. Unbelievable. She tried to imagine being crammed into a wagon bed like cargo and feeling it go off the road.

"Potatoes were bouncing all around me, and the horse started putting up a fuss and making noise. I ended up on the bank of a snowy ditch and rolled into the water." Celia's voice was emotionless. "It weren't too deep."

Nein, Hanneke thought, but the snowmelt in the gully had been icy. "You're fortunate you didn't end up with a fever and pneumonitis." In her experience, the lung problem that some called "Old Man's Friend" was a leading cause of death.

Honestly, it was a miracle that Celia and her unborn child had survived the ordeal.

As if reading her mind, Celia admitted, "All I thought on was protecting this baby in my belly."

"What a terrible shock that must of have been."

"When I got up the big man was lying in the snow. I did try to rouse him"—she sent a sideways glance at Hanneke—"but I promise you, that man was *dead*. The horse had bolted, takin' the wagon with him."

Hanneke grimaced, imagining the moment.

There weren't nobody in sight, but I knew a slaver might come around the bend any second. I took off, heading on down that gully for a piece to hide my tracks before heading back into the woods."

"Which is where you lost your necklace." Hanneke watched a centipede race along the wall with lightning speed as she sorted all of that through. She was convinced that Celia had been with Hawkins when he died. As soon as she returned home, she would share that information with John Barlow.

Still, Celia's memories did not include details about Hawkins' final encounter with whoever had struck the blow to the head that had, it seemed, caused his death sometime later.

That individual had somehow struck Hawkins a deadly blow…and Hanneke had no idea how she or Deputy Barlow could ever track the killer down.

Chapter Thirteen

As the day passed, Hanneke marked time by the sounds of guests gathering for meals overhead—chairs scraping, indistinct conversations, even the occasional faint clink of china. Sometimes a muffled *clang* announced a train steaming down the tracks to stop in front of The Milton House. Stagecoaches came and went as well.

The cellar felt like a different world. Nancy Goodrich brought extra candles, and some bread and hard cheese to nibble. Celia dozed. Hanneke passed time by knitting. Hiding in the dark wasn't comfortable, she mused as she stretched out a kink in her back, and yet it was restful in an odd way. She also appreciated the respite from men's company.

That evening, Nancy brought down a small kettle filled with stew. With her first whiff of chicken and rosemary, saliva pooled in Hanneke's mouth. "After you eat," her hostess murmured, "Gideon would like to speak with you upstairs."

"Of course." Hanneke had been expecting the summons, but she sighed anyway.

Nancy offered to sit with Celia, so after savoring her meal, Hanneke navigated the tunnel by herself. She clenched the lantern with one hand, held her skirts high with the other, and dreamed of her own home, with two sets of stairs boasting handrails and well-cut risers.

The rope ladder was more challenging, but she coped. *Gott sei dank* for sensible clothing, Hanneke thought. She'd seen wealthy women in Watertown wearing wide skirts hemmed so ridiculously low that they swept the walkways.

The little room was dim. Several clean iron kettles were arrayed on the table, tipped upside-down to prevent rust. Nancy had confirmed that meals for inn guests were prepared here.

Joseph was nowhere in sight, but Gideon was once again sitting by the fire. She was still angry with him. *If you want a ride home,* she reminded herself, *you best be cordial.* Nonetheless, she remained silent as she perched nearby and met his gaze.

Gideon's face wore its customary mask of composure, but his opening gambit was unexpected. "Frau Bauer, I must apologize for the way I spoke to you. It was inappropriate."

Hanneke felt her eyebrows rise. He was not apologizing for what he said, only the way he said it. *You failed. You faltered.* The words still scalded her heart.

He paused, as if expecting a response. A few moments passed before he continued. "Have you recovered your strength?"

"I have, yes."

"Then we will leave first thing in the morning."

Hanneke drew in a deep breath and lifted her chin. "I am hoping our departure can be delayed."

He regarded her with those piercing eyes. "Aren't you worried about your livestock?"

"Not at all," Hanneke informed him coolly. "The friend looking after them won't stop until he's sure I'm home." That was true. She had faith in William Bluewing. "I'm worried about our lamb. She has improved, but the danger isn't past. I'd like to see to her care for another day or two."

"Mrs. Goodrich will attend her."

"Celia trusts me. I've had more experience with such conditions than Mrs. Goodrich has."

Gideon nudged a log deeper into the fire. "We leave in the morning. I know you'd prefer to take care of her yourself for a few days longer if you could—"

"If I could, I'd take her all the way to Canada!" Hanneke retorted, stung by his indifference.

"You've let this become personal."

Hanneke folded her arms. "After all that's happened, how could I not?"

"It's not a matter of how," he told her. "It's simply what must be. It's how the system works." He spoke quietly, patiently, as if instructing a child.

Hanneke felt a muscle twitch below her left eye. "I insist, sir, that you refrain from patronizing me. If 'the system' has no room for flexibility and compassion, it needs improvement."

He didn't move. In her heart, Hanneke knew her accusation was unfair. The Underground Railroad was constructed from abolitionists' compassion, and people like Gideon and the Goodriches risked *everything* in its service.

Nonetheless, she couldn't bring herself to apologize. My general point has merit, she thought. She realized that Gideon might have pressing business waiting for him in Watertown, but if that was the case, why didn't he just say so?

Because, of course, Gideon was not a man to share even innocuous information lightly. I presume, Hanneke thought darkly, that I'm an even bigger failure in his eyes now. She shook her head, completely at a loss. "How can you bear it? How can you help pass runaways along without wondering how they fare? How dare you judge me harshly for a moment of compassion?"

He shifted in his seat. "Frau Bauer. Are you always so forthright?"

"I am indeed. Anything less is a waste of time."

The rattle of ironclad wagon wheels drifted through the window. In the distance—perhaps the train station—a man shouted. A half-burned log settled in the fireplace, sending a spray of sparks toward the ceiling.

Gideon finally spoke. "We will leave at dawn."

Although his evasion didn't surprise Hanneke, she realized that it disappointed her. There was nothing for it, though. "Very well." She rose to her feet, and he did also. Suddenly, however, she thought of something she'd put out of her mind while caring for Celia in the cellar. "Are *you* ready for the rigors of travel?"

"Why wouldn't I be?"

Hanneke refrained from stamping one foot, but only with effort. Honestly, the man could be most vexing. "Because you were shot when the slavers attacked us?"

"Ah." He nodded. "I had assumed that Mrs. Goodrich had told the tale. I wasn't shot, Frau Bauer. I only pretended to be in order to draw them closer. I fight best with a knife."

I fight best with a knife.

Incredulous, Hanneke stared at him. What kind of plan was *that*? Wouldn't the slave catchers have been much more likely to simply shoot him from a distance? Did the man harbor a secret wish for death?

She opened her mouth to ask, but instead inhaled slowly. That was too personal a question. Getting back to the issue of his wellness, she observed, "You must have been injured. When I arrived here at the cabin, you were moving with difficulty."

"One of the horses kicked me. I suspect I have a couple of cracked ribs." He shrugged. "They're bound now and will heal up in time. I also have a gash in one arm. Joseph stitched that up for me. I assure you, driving home will present no difficulties."

Hanneke was still mentally grappling with Gideon's choices during the attack. "When you noticed the men following us, why did you turn into such a lonely lane? Were you already trying to lure them closer?"

"I am under no obligation to explain my decisions to you," Gideon told her blandly. "I can assure you, however, that my primary goal was to protect you and the lamb."

Hanneke started to turn toward the trap door, then stopped. "Was Hiram Aubuchon one of the men who attacked us?"

"He was not."

"Do you think they were working for him?"

"Almost certainly."

Hanneke eyed Gideon. The change in his voice was almost imperceptible, but she caught the faint edge of something dark in his tone. "Did you recognize them?"

"I've run into one of them before."

"Oh?" Hanneke's brows rose toward her hairline, for she hadn't considered that possibility. "Who was it? What happened?"

"Levi Cox." Gideon spat the name and muttered something unintelligible. "Let's just say I am a chestnut burr in his shoe. We've tangled before." He held up one palm. "You don't need to know anymore."

"As someone who maintains a rest stop in my barn for those in need," she observed sharply, "I do indeed deserve to know more about anyone involved in the vile business of chasing runaways."

He responded only with one more of his fatalistic shrugs.

She stood tall and straight, and put steel into her gaze. "I also deserve to know the fates of those two men who attacked us. I will not leave this house without knowing what kind of danger we may still face."

After a moment, Gideon lifted one palm in apparent acquiescence. "One of them is dead."

Hanneke's lips pressed into a tight line, chilled by Gideon's precise summary. Was this the first time he'd killed someone, or had he done it before?

"Cox was wounded but escaped." He picked up a piece of tinder and twiddled it in his fingers. "It's unlikely that he'll trouble you further, but…." He spread his palms. "You would be wise to remain vigilant."

That advice did nothing to reassure her. I will be profoundly grateful, Hanneke thought, when my agreement with this brooding man is fulfilled. With a nod of acknowledgement, she left him alone.

Celia was still sleeping when Hanneke returned to the cellar, so Nancy and Hanneke retired to two chairs at the other end of the small room. "We're leaving in the morning."

"Gideon told me as much." Nancy cocked her head with a look of sympathy. "I can see that the situation is troubling you. This is your first experience as a conductor, yes?"

Hanneke snorted a bitter laugh. "First and last."

"Why do you say that? You've done so well. That young lady"—she gestured toward the pallet—"almost certainly would be dead without your efforts."

To Hanneke's horror, the unexpected praise and kindness brought tears to her eyes. She quickly swiped them away. "Gideon doesn't agree. He called me a failure because I hesitated when I thought he'd been shot."

"I see." Nancy looked away, fingering the cross worn on a gold chain at her throat. Then she patted Hanneke's arm. "Our friend Gideon has unreasonably high standards, but I assure you, Joseph and I trust him completely. He's devoted his life to the cause."

"And risked it as well." Hanneke hadn't decided whether Gideon's defiant approach to danger was a help or a hindrance.

"Yes," Nancy conceded. "I know very little about him, but we all must answer our consciences as we see fit and try to do the right thing—and God's will—in the face of such a monstrous evil."

"Well, in any event, I don't expect Gideon to ask for my help again." Hanneke reached for her knitting, craving the solace of wool in her fingers. Then she looked up at the older woman's kind face, shadowed by candlelight. "I probably shouldn't ask, but…how long have you and Joseph been doing… what you do here?"

Nancy smiled. "No, you shouldn't ask. Perhaps the best thing to say is that we brought our convictions with us when we settled here in 1839. We're Seventh Day Baptists, you see."

Hanneke nodded. She'd never heard of Seventh Day Baptists before. If all of them were like Nancy and Joseph, she thought, they must be a mighty force in the world.

"God will bless you for your efforts," Nancy assured her quietly. "If you wish to continue this work, my best advice is to let your own heart guide you. Don't allow one man's harsh and hasty words deprive you of the chance to serve." She rose to her feet. "I need to go up."

The next morning, Hanneke said goodbye to Celia in the hushed and dim cellar. "I made a few things," Hanneke whispered, placing a small stack of knitted goods in the girl's hands as she lay on her mattress. "The item on top is for your journey."

Celia lifted a winter hood Hanneke had knit in thick-spun, milk-colored yarn. "It should be spacious enough to cover your kerchief, if you bind up your hair," Hanneke explained, "but if you pull on the drawstrings, it will snug up tight around your face."

A faint smile appeared before Celia schooled her expression back to her customary impassive bearing. "You knit this just for me?"

"I did. It's cold where you're going." Hanneke patted her other offerings. "There's a small blanket for the baby when it comes, and a cap and booties."

Celia held each piece up to study more closely, her eyes shining. "Thank you. These be just what we need."

"I wish I'd had time to do more," Hanneke murmured.

"These'll suit us just fine." Celia ran a finger along one edge of the blanket where Hanneke had added a bit of openwork along the hem. "You even made this fancy."

Hanneke was gratified to see that Celia was pleased by the simple design. "May I put these away in your sack for you? That's the cleanest place." Celia slept with the cotton sack, and her presence would also deter any mice looking for nesting material.

"Yes, please."

Hanneke had no trouble fitting the woolens into Celia's travel sack. It was discouraging to see how few things the girl had with which to start a new life—a carved wooden spoon, a tin cup, a spare kerchief, an extra pair of socks, and…what was this? Hanneke's fingers found something small and round. Curious, she pulled it free and regarded a one-inch disk carved from bone. Four dark, incised lines bisected the disk in the center, effectively marking the piece like a pie cut for serving.

This must be another precious token from Africa, Hanneke surmised. The simple pattern fascinated her, and she wanted very much to learn something of its story; of the meaning inherent in the design. When she glanced at Celia, however, she saw that her patient's eyes had already closed.

This is not your concern anyway, Hanneke reminded herself, and tucked the disk back into the sack. Celia had almost nothing to cling to. If the bone circle—like the seashell—brought the girl comfort or evoked her ancestors' wisdom, Hanneke would not intrude.

She gently put a hand on Celia's shoulder to rouse her. "It's time to say goodbye," Hanneke whispered. "I wish you the very best in life, and will pray that you reach Canada and have a safe delivery."

When Celia once again grasped her fingers, Hanneke imagined that she felt every muscle and bone in the girl's chapped hand. I've only had Celia's company for a short time, she thought, but she has indeed become dear to me.

A lump rose in her throat, and she forced herself to rise. "May God bless you on your journey," she whispered, softly touching Celia's cheek.

Then Hanneke left the cellar, scrabbled through the tunnel, and climbed the rope ladder for the last time. The morning was still painted in shades of deep blue and gray. Gideon, who'd already harnessed the horses, was waiting for her. After accepting a light hug from Nancy Goodrich, Hanneke climbed into the wagon. With no sound but the soft thudding of Arion's hooves, they were on their way.

* * *

After two long and almost silent days of travel, Gideon stopped his wagon on a narrow farm lane a mile or so from Safe Haven Farm. A strand of silky hair had fallen over his forehead, and he shoved it away before turning those unusually piercing gray eyes to her. "You can make your way from here?"

"Of course I can." Hanneke was already holding her carpetbag. The basket she'd brought was gone for good.

Gideon dropped the lines long enough to offer a hand as she descended. Once she was safely down, he touched two fingers to the brim of his hat. "Thank you for agreeing to help."

"You are welcome." Hanneke nodded primly, turned, and began walking away as briskly as her stiff and weary body would permit. She heard Gideon asking Arion to back up a few steps. She didn't look over her shoulder as they made a tight turn and drove back the way they'd come.

Well, Hanneke thought. My foray into the role of Underground Railroad conductor is over. Was she overthinking to feel offended anew because he'd thanked her for agreeing to travel with him, but not for actually helping? Well, there was nothing for it now, she counseled herself, except try to

128

dismiss his condescension.

Twilight was descending by the time Hanneke emerged from the woods and approached her own farm clearing. She'd been laboring on this land for almost a year and was proud of what she'd accomplished. Today, though, something felt different. A quiver of apprehension prickled her skin, and she scrutinized the farmyard for several minutes. She didn't see anything amiss.

As she trudged up the drive, she did what she had chided herself for doing at least a hundred times—she glanced up at the *fachwerk* dwelling's chimney. It was, of course, barren of smoke. Stifling a sigh, she headed for the barn. Greeting her sheep, confirming that all was well, would lift her spirits.

William had, as expected, tended the animals well. Hanneke checked all the outbuildings with a sickle in hand—more to bolster her own courage than anything else—to satisfy herself that a vindictive slaver had not hidden himself away.

Finding no sign of an intruder, she went inside the house. The dim structure was colder inside than out, but she soon had fires going. Still feeling restless, she leaned against the dry sink and considered her options for an evening meal. By Hanneke's standards, the food she'd eaten on her trip with Gideon had been hearty but bland. Now, she had a sudden longing for a good German meal—the smoked eel and herring her mother had served during her childhood near the Baltic Sea, or perhaps the spicy tang of a good marjoram-spiced bratwurst served with mustard.

Hanneke frowned. What under heaven was this? She never indulged in nostalgia, preferring instead to face the future with her head held high. With a firm mental shake, she fetched some potatoes and smoked ham from the root cellar.

That evening, she huddled near the parlor stove with her knitting. Tonight, however, she discovered that she felt too edgy to find comfort even in her beloved handwork and had to set it aside. *Mein Gott!* she thought, exasperated. This simply would not do.

She picked up the small wooden bird a runaway had once left in her barn. Fingering it when she needed to think had become a habit. There in the chilly, candlelit room, she allowed her mind to drift…and at once found herself thinking about Celia.

Since leaving The Milton House, Hanneke had tried not to think about the girl, actually. The personal bond they'd developed during their brief, but powerful time together was real…and yet, the hard truth was that she'd likely never learn if Celia survived her journey north. What was she experiencing right this minute? Was she still huddled in the Goodriches' cellar? Or was she shivering her way onward with a new shepherd because someone had deemed her sturdy enough for travel? Was her mother still alive, or had she given up hope after Celia stole away? Hanneke knew that the not-knowing would gnaw at her soul.

Well. She would simply have to learn to live with it.

And I will, Hanneke vowed staunchly. Somewhere between her home and Milton, she'd lost something but gained something as well. Yes, her existence at Safe Haven Farm was often lonely…but *true* loneliness was running from slavers, as Celia had done. Or being alone in an unknown place with the weight of responsibility for someone's life pressing on her shoulders like a millstone, as she had done.

In truth, Hanneke felt shame for all she'd taken for granted before her sojourn to Milton. Her home might be icy, but at least it had windows. The parlor stove might be tiny, but it did throw heat. She owned this house and forty acres. She had so much more than Celia probably dared dream of.

I was privileged to meet her as I did, Hanneke mused. Experiencing what she had learned from reading *Uncle Tom's Cabin,* a couple of memoirs, and newspaper accounts of slavery now seemed dry and distant. Gideon might feel dispassionate about the people he helped, but she would never understand how.

Gideon. Bunching her mouth, she put the wooden bird aside and picked up her knitting again. Perhaps God wanted Gideon to save me from pride, Hanneke thought wryly, for if he hadn't spoken as harshly as he had, she would indeed have felt proud of what she had accomplished. However, despite Nancy Goodrich's praise, his accusations had undermined Hanneke's confidence.

You failed. You faltered.

Hanneke leaned closer to the candle to see a hidden stitch. She wished she knew more about Gideon. He'd been silent when she'd told him that his life mattered too. He had an uncanny ability to present himself as emotionless in general, and to stay thoughtful and steady in emergencies. Despite recent attempts on his life, he seemed to think he was impervious to death.

Or…perhaps the man simply did not care if he lived or died. Perhaps he was so completely devoted to his cause that he'd accepted the possibility of being killed.

If that were the case, Hanneke reflected, she shouldn't find it surprising. After all, Asa Hawkins, a wealthy, hate-filled man, had accepted the risk and been willing to die for his anti-slavery beliefs. Should she be surprised that Gideon would act as he had? For that matter, Hanneke noted sardonically, *she* was well aware of the dangers, yet she had chosen to embark on this trip anyway.

She would always regret, however, that her brief acquaintance with Gideon had not been more amicable.

Well, it certainly wasn't the first time she'd crossed paths with a difficult man. Hanneke snorted as she unwound another length of yarn from its ball. Her relationship with Deputy John Barlow had begun with him calling her a liar and ordering her to leave town. Unlike Gideon, John was often annoyed and impatient. He had a quick temper, and she never had to guess what he was thinking or feeling. Her efforts to do what she believed was right, especially during the early months of their acquaintance, had often irritated him. And yet, Hanneke thought, our relationship improved dramatically over time.

Remembering that pleased her. It also reminded her that reporting to John what she'd learned about Asa Hawkins from Celia was a high priority. She had also promised to study Asa Hawkins' ledger in hopes of prying some insight from its pages.

Perhaps I'm not *completely* useless, she told Gideon silently, and got ready for bed.

Chapter Fourteen

The next morning, Hanneke was up before dawn. After pulling on a sturdy work dress, she paused. Was it safe to go out to the stable? Might a slaver be lurking in the shadows? As far as she knew, Hiram Aubuchon was still in the area. And one of the slavers who'd attacked Gideon near Milton was still…somewhere. She wished she'd thought to ask Gideon, who had said he knew one of the men, for a description. It would be helpful to have, in case he showed up at Safe Haven Farm. Although Gideon had said that was unlikely, Hanneke couldn't set aside her trepidation. Perhaps she should postpone chores until the sun had fully risen.

Nein, she decided, annoyed by her own hesitation. She might have to carry this fear with her, but she wouldn't let it cripple her. She had every intention of going about her business as usual.

She strode to the stable and turned her sheep out to their fenced field. She was mucking out the stable when a familiar voice called a greeting. "*Guten Morgen*, Frau Bauer!"

She looked up, pleased to see her friend William Bluewing at the door. "William! It's good to see you." She pitched a shovelful of dirty straw into a pile, which would later be worked into the fields. "I can't thank you enough for tending to the animals while I was away. Especially since my journey lasted a bit longer than expected."

William grabbed a second shovel. He was dressed in work clothes today, a linen shirt, and leather trousers, and looked just as handsome as he did when attired as the teacher he aspired to be. "I was happy to help," he assured her, and shot her a crooked smile. "Put in a good word for me with Jacobine's mother, and I'll do your chores for a month. Jacobine and I have yet to convince her to consent to an early wedding."

"Ah, young love," Hanneke said with a smile of her own. "Jacobine will turn sixteen soon, and Karoline has promised that you two can marry then. What's the rush?"

William sobered. "I do feel a sense of urgency," he allowed. "The truth is, none of us knows how much time we have. Jacobine and I want to spend every moment we can as husband and wife."

Hanneke's teasing smile faded as well. A chill shuddered over her skin. His statement about time was true for everyone…but local Indian people had particular reason to worry. The government wanted to exterminate the Ho-Chunk, or at least exile them somewhere beyond the Mississippi River. The people who'd made their way back to Wisconsin, and the families like William's who'd never left, had suffered terribly. Things were relatively quiet at the moment. Nonetheless, Hanneke was aware that hatred of and fear about all native people simmered in the hearts of many whites—government officials and private citizens alike. She wasn't so naïve as to believe that some Yankee and European immigrants' hostility, or government policy, could never again lead to more violence and anguish.

Thinking about what that could mean for William and Jacobine made Hanneke feel sick with dread. She knew that Karoline, Jacobine's mother, felt exactly the same way.

As if sensing that Hanneke's mood had darkened, William said staunchly, "Well, our time will come."

Hanneke nodded. "I believe it's meant to be, William." That was true. She'd never seen a young couple so devoted to each other.

William seemed ready to steer the conversation in a new direction. "Say, that mare John loaned you is a beauty."

"She is." Hanneke glanced toward the far end of the stable, where Cinder contentedly munched her own grain. "I'll miss her when he takes her back, but it's been a blessing to have had her this long."

They finished chores by spreading fresh straw on the floor. Hanneke leaned her pitchfork against a stanchion wall. "Well. I want to check the ewes' hooves, but it's best they have a little more time outside to settle down." She trimmed hooves once a month or so, carefully cutting back the extra accumulation of horn that could hobble a sheep. "Let's go back to the house. I'll brew some coffee and we'll figure a fair payment for your help."

She often bartered produce or warm woolens in exchange for the Bluewings' help with farm work, and they had no trouble reaching an agreement: three pairs of socks knit in gray two-ply yarn. Hanneke always had sturdy socks and stockings on hand.

William tucked the socks away. "One more thing. The combination of cool nights and warmer days we've had recently has started the maple sap run. Didn't you mention an interest in learning how to tap the trees?"

Hanneke remained quite curious to see how it was done. "I did indeed."

William looked pleased. "My uncle and his sons have come to help. We'll be cutting wood and placing the spiles today, and we'll start processing the sap tomorrow. We can always use an extra pair of willing hands. May I take you to our sugar camp tomorrow morning? It's a quarter mile away from the spot where we usually camp, and you'd have trouble finding it alone."

"Of course. Perhaps…eight o'clock?"

With an affirmative nod, he rose to take his leave. "Jacobine and Frau Ketzler will be there. And my mother will be glad to see you."

The young man had just stepped outside when the sound of hoofbeats coming up the drive drifted through the wavy window glass. John Barlow appeared, riding his black Morgan. At the gate, he swung to the ground and strode forward with a hand extended. "William! I'm glad to see you."

It did Hanneke good to watch the two men greet each other with warmth and mutual respect. Not all government officials hate Indians, she reminded herself. Or Negroes. Or immigrants. She feared that John's position in the sheriff's department was a lonely one, but she was profoundly grateful that her neighbor, the deputy assigned to handle most area crimes, was, at heart, a decent man.

After William left, she turned to Barlow. "You're here early! Is there something I can do for you?"

John prodded a fence post with the toe of one boot before saying gruffly,

"I mostly just wanted to make sure you got home safely."

Hanneke was touched. Her conversation with John about traveling had been oblique, but he'd had a general idea of what was happening, and he hadn't liked it. It had never occurred to her that he might stop by—perhaps more than once—to check on her well-being.

"*Danke*," she said lightly. "Do you have a few minutes to spare? I have some news to share about the night Asa Hawkins died."

When they were settled with coffee and anise buns at her table, Hanneke offered a somewhat cloaked version of Celia's account of Asa Hawkins' demise. "To summarize, according to Celia—his hidden passenger—Hawkins left the wagon to speak to someone. When he returned a few moments later, he was furious. Sometime later, he apparently got dizzy or lost consciousness and drifted off the lane. He was thrown from the wagon and tumbled down the incline into the gully. Celia made sure he was dead before fleeing."

John twisted his mouth sideways with frustration. "Is the girl willing to testify to what happened?"

Hanneke tipped her head, not bothering to hide her exasperation. "Of course not. And as you well know, that wouldn't help anyway. But we do now know more details about the night he died. It's extremely unlikely that Hiram Aubuchon was responsible for Hawkins' death. Celia was clear that Hawkins voluntarily stopped the wagon and went to speak with someone. I can't imagine Asa Hawkins conversing with Hiram Aubuchon by chance or by design." She sighed. "I would have taken great satisfaction in proving that the wretched man was a murderer, but it just doesn't fit."

"In other words, we're no closer to knowing who struck the fatal blow that killed Asa Hawkins." Barlow rubbed his face with his hands. "I've assembled a list of Hawkins' friends and associates, and I've questioned about half of them without turning up anything useful. I also spent two days looking for a lost child while you were gone." Anticipating her question, he flapped a reassuring hand. "I found him. He's safe."

Gott sei dank, Hanneke thought.

"Too much time is passing." The deputy got up and began prowling the small room, then stopped and glared at her. "And what, pray tell, do you find amusing?"

"Nothing." Realizing that a faint smile had curved her mouth, Hanneke quickly schooled it away. The truth was, she'd been thinking that of the two difficult men she'd worked with recently, John's irritability was a pleasant change from Gideon's silence.

He snorted.

"Why are you so agitated?" Hanneke asked gently. "We still have ideas to pursue."

He shook his head. "Jerome Hawkins has been storming into our office every day, demanding to know why we haven't arrested his brother's killer."

"That does sound most unpleasant."

"The sheriff's in a foul mood. He wants this case solved quickly."

The fact of which he no doubt reminds John frequently, Hanneke thought with a small sigh. Frequently and forcefully.

"He also wants me to find the person who stole goods from the clock-maker's shop two days ago and track down a heifer missing from a farm out towards Lebanon."

Hanneke sighed. "I truly regret you are being pulled in so many different directions." She had nothing to offer him but sympathy.

And perhaps it helped, for Barlow stopped pacing and reached for his hat. "Well, I best get to it. Thanks for the coffee."

"I haven't had a chance to look at Hawkins' ledger yet, but I will soon." Hanneke rose to see him out. "Is there still no word from the gray mare's owner?"

"No." John clapped the hat on his black hair. "We usually sit on stolen property for four weeks. If no one claims the horse after that period, she'll be sold at auction."

"Of course." Hanneke hated to think of Cinder being sold. She couldn't afford to buy the beautiful mare herself, though. I must simply enjoy whatever time I have with her, Hanneke vowed, and tried to be content.

With that in mind, she decided to run some errands of her own after breakfast. When her morning skillet was scrubbed and tipped upside down to dry, she bundled into her cloak and saddled Cinder. After being gone on Gideon's errand, she was eager to check on some of her neighbors.

At the König cabin, Hanneke was relieved to find the new baby girl doing well, and the new mother weary but dry-eyed. I'll keep my eye on them, Hanneke thought, but progress is being made.

After leaving the little family, she made a point of riding to the junction where she'd ripped down the broadside offering a $300 reward for Celia's capture. To her dismay, a duplicate broadside had been nailed to the same huge oak tree.

Hanneke felt a flush of searing anger. She *knew* Celia now. She was a friend, of sorts, and harsh white men were still trying to make money by hunting her down and feeding her to the vultures.

The situation was intolerable.

Well, Celia is a two-day drive away, she consoled herself. Or perhaps even farther along by now. She *was* here, Hanneke told the slavers silently, and you failed to find her.

When she'd calmed herself, she continued on her rounds. She checked on a young boy whose broken leg she'd set and splinted, and an elderly couple who craved company, before stopping for a quick chat with Gerda Muehlhauser.

"I've been hoping you'd visit!" Gerda offered an eager smile. "Please, sit."

Hanneke peeled off her outer layers and settled at the older woman's table. "I was away for a few days." She hoped that this kind soul who had kept Fridolin's secrets when he needed a friend would not ask questions that would make it awkward for Hanneke to protect her own.

Fortunately, Gerda had other things on her mind. "May I offer you some *Lebkuchen?*" She opened a tightly lidded crock on a shelf in the kitchen corner, removed several cookies, and arranged them on a plate. Only when satisfied did she place the plate on the table. Hanneke didn't miss the hint of pride in Gerda's thin face. And she understood why. Gerda almost never offered guests refreshments because Oscar, her husband, was generally a poor provider.

"These are delicious," Hanneke assured her. "What a treat."

Gerda tipped her head sideways. "Are you unwell, my dear?"

The question was startling. "Why—I'm fine." Hanneke felt her brow furrow. "Why do you ask?"

"Because I sense that something is troubling you." Gerda's wrinkled face, framed by a blue and white striped headscarf, was concerned.

"I'm *fine*," Hanneke reiterated. But a short time later, after she'd left the Muehlhauser place and stopped to visit her friend, Clara Steckelberg, she was surprised to receive a similar question.

She'd found Clara behind the house, making firewood on the old stump she and Charles used as a chopping block. Clara took one look at her, slammed the axe blade into a log, and crossed her arms. "What's bothering you?"

"Nothing!" Hanneke protested. Gracious! Although she loved Gerda and Clara and appreciated their concern, their insights made her uncomfortable. As much as she wanted to discuss her recent experience, she simply could not. "I've visited several people this morning. I discovered that everyone is either doing well or improving, and that lifted my spirits."

Clara snorted, but she was a good enough friend to let the matter go.

* * *

After tidying up from a late-morning meal at home, Hanneke fetched the ledger Asa Hawkins had used to record goods bought and sold in his freight-hauling business. Then she settled near a sunny window. She was well aware that she was unlikely to find something helpful, but there was no harm in looking.

The leather book was nicely bound. Hawkins' notations filled perhaps three-quarters of the ledger. The transactions were noted in a heavy-handed scrawl with neat columns showing the date each transfer was made, what was hauled, what the cargo weighed, and what Hawkins delivered or received. Since the railroad had reached Watertown the previous autumn, his schedule sometimes included a stop at the depot to drop off loads of products and produce from interior Wisconsin, or to pick up goods—anything from kegs of nails to barrels of seaweed-packed oysters to bolts of printed cotton. Fascinating, Hanneke thought as she considered the geography involved.

The only frustrating aspect of deciphering the ledger was that Hawkins had abbreviated locations. It didn't take long to discover that "WT" meant Watertown and MKE meant Milwaukee, but OT, LC, and WTO were more difficult to discern. Hanneke didn't know Wisconsin's landscape well and could not decipher many of the abbreviations.

Well, she thought staunchly when she reached the final page, that was merely an introductory look. All she'd done was read through each entry. What she needed to do next was to comb through the now-familiar pages, looking for anomalies or patterns or whatever else might provide a kernel of insight.

"But not right now," Hanneke told the dust motes dancing in front of the window. The work was tedious. She needed a break before going back to the beginning.

Once she'd set the record book aside, however, she found herself feeling restless. It fretted her to know that some mix of her fear and worries had been apparent to Gerda and Clara that morning. For almost a year, she'd kept her own sheltered spot in the barn hidden. Keeping the secret had not been a challenge. Her expedition with Gideon had left her feeling more vulnerable. That was not good.

She had plenty of chores to occupy her time, but instead, she decided to ride north. Charlotte Stofeldt had urged her to visit, and she might as well make good use of Cinder while she could.

When she trotted up the Stofeldt drive an hour later, Hanneke met Charlotte driving down in a small cart holding her well-bundled children. Charlotte waved cheerfully and pulled her horse to a stop as Hanneke and Cinder approached. "Hanneke, good afternoon!"

"I see I've caught you at a bad moment," Hanneke said ruefully.

"No, not at all!" Charlotte shook her head in denial. "I was just on my way to visit the Pohl sisters. Why don't you simply follow me to their home?"

The Pohl family—Berta, Erna, and their brother Felix—lived in a tidy frame house painted white with blue shutters, in the tiny crossroads hamlet of Clyman's Corners, just a mile or so from Charlotte's housebarn. A dark-haired man with a bushy beard was driving a wagon from the barn as they arrived. The wagon was painted a cheerful blue, with "Felix Pohl, Fine Carpentry" in black letters inside a yellow ovular frame on the side. He doffed his warm knit cap respectfully but did not stop to chat.

"Hanneke!" Berta exclaimed when she saw she had more company than expected. "How nice to see you."

Hanneke and Charlotte stabled their horses in the barn before heading to the house, where Berta stood beckoning in the doorway. "Come in, come in."

"Did I see you pass our brother Felix as you arrived?" Erna ushered the others into a well-furnished parlor. "He's heading out to deliver a chest of drawers. You probably noticed the sign by the road. He's a carpenter and cabinetmaker."

"He does fine work," Berta said with a hint of pride. "Since he's out, however, we can have a nice ladies' chat."

The room was over-furnished, in Hanneke's opinion, with curtains at every window, figurines and colored glass dishes on every shelf, and heavy chairs and settees finished with dark green horsehair upholstery. Perhaps Felix Pohl used the space as a showroom, for the bureau and chairs and a glass-fronted hutch were beautifully crafted. Or perhaps, Hanneke thought sardonically, I'm so used to my austere house that I don't know good taste when I see it.

She and Charlotte sat down with knitting projects. Erna was embroidering a picture of George Washington in colorful silk threads, and Berta was working on a net embroidery table runner. Charlotte had given little Beatta a piece of linen so she could practice her own stitchery, and baby Henni was soon settled with a rattle in a basket near a barrel stove with pretty nickel plating. The four women talked of the best kinds of apples for pie, and which local creamery produced the richest cheese, and—in time—abolition.

Hanneke found herself oddly restless. After the pure camaraderie she'd enjoyed at the letter-writing party, she had believed that sitting with these people, others who believed that slavery was a stain on the nation, would settle her. Instead, she felt as if a veil had dropped between her and the others.

The sisters served hot chamomile tea and gingerbread before the impromptu work party came to a close. Erna loaned Hanneke a copy of *Narrative of the Life of Frederick Douglass, an American Slave.* Berta wrote out a receipt for corn muffins that Hanneke had complimented.

Soon, Hanneke had left the others at their respective homes and begun the ride to Safe Haven Farm. Twilight was lowering its cape over the landscape, sending long shadows over the road in wooded areas. Pleased as she was with the memoir in her saddlebag, her mind slid back to brooding all too quickly. Why had she had such a reaction to good company that afternoon?

Because I am not, she reminded herself, the same person I was before going on the journey with Celia and Gideon. How under Heaven did people who'd been helping the Underground Railroad for years—people like Nancy and Joseph Goodrich—go about their daily lives with such apparent ease?

Hanneke was almost home when Cinder abruptly began favoring her front right leg. "What is it, girl?" Hanneke asked. They had stopped near a massive bur oak tree standing sentinel over the snow-matted prairie stretching into the distance beyond. She'd passed another rider earlier, but no one was in sight now.

After dismounting, Hanneke patted the horse's withers affectionately. "I need to check your hoof and shoe, all right?" She took a moment to murmur encouragement to the mare before running her hand down the troubled leg. Her father had always reassured his horses that way before checking a hoof.

Hanneke leaned gently against her mount and lifted the animal's hoof. Just as she'd suspected, the mare had picked up a stone. Bizarrely, it occurred to her that it would be handy to see Gideon appear around the bend, with Arion pulling his wagon and the heavy farrier tools it contained.

"Or perhaps not," she muttered, quickly and disdainfully dismissing that thought. She carried a hoof pick in one saddlebag. She was perfectly capable of clearing the debris from Cinder's foot, *Vielen Dank.*

Hanneke easily removed the stone. But as she was straightening up again, something flashed in her peripheral vision with a whistling sound. Before she grasped what was happening, it struck the oak with a loud wooden *thwack.*

Cinder shrieked and reared on her hind legs. Hanneke felt a harsh jolt of pain in her left shoulder and stumbled to her knees. I've been kicked, she thought, but that seemed inconsequential. Cold gooseflesh dimpled her skin as she stared open-mouthed at the oak. Part of the wicked blade was embedded in the tree trunk. Its wooden handle quivered in the fading light.

Someone had thrown a hatchet at her.

One of Cinder's distress cries, high and trembling, punctuated Hanneke's shock. Ears back, the mare was prancing with anxiety. I must get her away from here, Hanneke thought. And myself as well.

She leapt to her feet and snatched the reins. The road was still empty. The hatchet had been flung from a small shrubby thicket on the far side of the lane. If the person was still there, he was well hidden. She considered grabbing the sharp-bladed tool, to defend herself or at least to show evidence of the attack, but she didn't dare take an extra moment. Managing to grab a stirrup in one hand, she flung herself into the saddle and kicked the mare to a loping run. Hanneke leaned low over the pommel. Her heart was pounding so fast she could feel blood throbbing through her veins. The skin between her shoulder blades prickled with a dreadful anticipation.

Someone had just tried to kill her.

Chapter Fifteen

Hanneke reached Safe Haven Farm without further attack. She forced herself to take the time needed in the stable to properly care for Cinder. She didn't realize what comfort she'd taken from the sweet mare until forced to cross the open yard alone. She thought with longing of Charlotte Stofeldt's housebarn as she hurried to her back door.

Her hands shook as she let herself in and locked the door again behind her. Her boot heels clicked on the floorboards as she circled the house. Even though she knew all too well that securing her home in that manner was not enough to discourage a determined intruder, she felt a compulsive need to make sure that all windows and doors were locked.

Wincing, she rubbed her shoulder gingerly. Well. She now knew how it felt to be kicked by a horse. She'd prefer not to experience that a second time.

Then she circled again, cupping her elbows in her hands, trying to calm herself. In truth, the cold house felt lonelier than ever. On her mad dash home on Cinder, she had briefly considered riding straight to the Barlows' home in search of shelter, but she'd feared that her assailant might be following her. The last thing she wanted to do was draw such a *Teufel* anywhere near Ulricke. She yearned to tell John what had happened, but what could she say without revealing more than she should? She hadn't seen the hatchet-thrower, she wasn't physically injured, and she had not lingered long enough to gather any evidence of what had happened.

I *chose* to accompany Gideon in the first place, she thought. I accepted the risks. It would not be fair to John if she reported the incident without providing details about the attack near Milton…which she could not do.

As her heart rate eased to a more reasonable pace, Hanneke kindled a fire in the parlor stove. She fetched her Rolling Wheels shawl and tucked it beneath her cape before pulling her chair as close to the stove as possible. Her shakes turned into shudders that trembled through her limbs, and for a few moments, she could do no more than sit. All she could see was the hatchet blade, glinting in the gloom as it whirled just inches from her head. All she could hear was the faint whistling noise it made as it spun and the solid *thunk* of sharp iron digging into hardwood.

Hanneke pressed her fingertips against her temples. Who could have *done* such a thing? Who would even have such a skill? Anyone could have fired a gun, but hurling the hatchet with such precision required a special ability. She imagined that some Ho-Chunk or Potawatomie men might possess that skill, but the notion made no sense. The only Indian people she knew were the Bluewings, and the image of her trusted friend William hurling a hatchet at her was ludicrous.

Gideon, then? Hanneke rubbed her upper arms with her palms. He had mentioned that he "fought best with a knife." Perhaps knives weren't the only bladed weapons he had mastered. He was obviously no stranger to violence, and she had not lived up to his expectations on the journey. But…she was no threat to him, so why would he want to harm her? Even if he did, he'd had plenty of opportunities on their way back from Milton.

Perhaps one of the slavers prowling about had thrown the hatchet. After all, anti-abolition sentiment had already taken a horrid toll since she'd arrived less than a year ago. Loomis, the abolitionist she'd become aware of the previous spring, had been killed. Asa Hawkins was dead. Gideon had been injured while trying to help Celia in the first place, and two slavers had stalked them almost to Milton and attacked. One of the slavers had died on that quiet lane. She and Celia and Gideon easily could have as well. And now, someone had stalked her on a lonesome country road.

Gideon had known the identity of one of the slavers near Milton. Hanneke closed her eyes, thinking back. Levi Cox, that was it. Someone—either Cox or an informant—had known where to find Celia and her protectors, and probably known that Frau Hanneke Bauer was along.

Hanneke frowned, tapping the arm of her chair with one finger. Even in a slaver's mind, was her minor role as escort on Gideon's wagon seat truly enough for her assailant to want her dead? Had the man thrown the hatchet to scare her away from the Underground Railroad as part of a broader effort to eliminate help for passing runaways altogether?

She snorted bitterly. "What you apparently don't know," she told her attacker, "is that my trip with Gideon was my first and, evidently, my last."

In the kitchen area, she fetched some leftover potato soup seasoned with onions, caraway seeds, and dried parsley, and heated it in a small pan on the stove. Spooning the simple meal restored some of her energy and cleared away more of her shock and confusion. She reached for her nearby knitting bag. Her hands felt steady enough now to work the needles.

After establishing a cadence on the simple sock she'd chosen to work on, her thoughts quickly swiveled back to the attack. The most likely theory, she thought, is that Levi Cox had thrown the hatchet at her. She pinched her lips together. But why had he tried to kill her? Why had he assailed her in such a brutal and frightening way?

The answer struck Hanneke with such force that her fingers stilled. He hadn't wanted to kill me, she realized. He wanted to intimidate and frighten me.

He had succeeded. But now that she'd had a chance to actually think about what had happened, anger was starting to overwhelm the raw terror that had chased her home. That was a good thing.

Much of her fury was aimed at Levi Cox—or whoever had thrown the hatchet—but an equal part devolved onto Gideon's shoulders. He's made a difficult situation worse, Hanneke thought. The man seemed to think he could entice her to help on a journey that turned deadly, then ignore the aftermath. I asked Gideon if a threat remained, Hanneke reminded herself. And what had he said? "It's unlikely that he'll trouble you further, but…you would be wise to remain vigilant."

I don't even know what Cox looks like! Hanneke fumed. How am I to "remain vigilant" without knowing what or who to watch for?

Hanneke understood the need to keep secret anything pertaining to lambs being shepherded north, but surely Gideon could share with her helpful information—information that might save her life—if he wished. His silences and evasiveness had galled her during their journey to Milton and back. Now that she'd watched a hatchet whirl past her head, not knowing all the facts was unacceptable.

Nein, she thought. This was absolutely intolerable. The last of her patience was gone. She was not going to sit quivering in her home, wondering if or when a slaver might threaten her again. It was time to confront Gideon.

Hanneke always felt better when she thought an issue through, made her own decisions, and took action. Before going to bed, she felt calm enough to return to Asa Hawkins' ledger. She did so slowly in order to become more familiar with Hawkins' system. Managing a successful freight business was complicated but, she grudgingly admitted, the man had clearly been well-organized and meticulous. Beyond that, no insights emerged, and the meaning of many abbreviations remained elusive.

You failed.

Hanneke slapped the ledger closed. *"Mist!"* she muttered in frustration. Promising herself that tomorrow would be a better day, she went to bed.

* * *

Hanneke had a restless night, startling awake at the slightest sound. She rose to tend her animals before dawn had crawled over the landscape. If someone was lying in wait to attack her, she wouldn't offer him daylight to do it. She needed a moment to summon the courage to open the back door. "I will not be bullied," she reminded herself, and opened the door.

By the time she got back to the house, her body ached with the strain of clenched muscles. Still, she would not cower inside. Her animals—all of them—meant everything, and deserved the best care she could give them.

She was eager to track down Gideon but knew it would not happen that day. The Bluewings expected her help at their sugar camp. Besides, she wanted to learn about tapping maple trees, and to spend the day with people who had become dear to her.

When William came to guide her, she put one hand on his arm to stay him for a moment. "William," she said quietly, "I need to tell you that someone threw a hatchet at me yesterday. It came *very* close to hitting me. I was alone, coming home from a friend's house."

William's eyes widened for a half-second, but otherwise, he didn't respond. This granite-like composure was one of the things Hanneke loved about William. In addition to being absolutely dependable, he was steady and proactive in a crisis.

"I didn't see who did it," she continued, "and I'm not exactly sure why I was targeted like that. I think the person was trying to frighten me, not kill me. I'm unable to explain any more. However, if you're going to walk me to the sugar camp, you deserve to know. Perhaps it would be best that I simply stay home." William's mother and sisters, and his fiancé Jacobine and her mother Karoline, were at the camp.

William was silent for a long moment as he considered. Then he shook his head. "The clearing is mostly open, with little underbrush. My uncle is there, and three of my male cousins. No one will get close to us without them knowing." He offered his arm. "Shall we go?"

He understands, Hanneke thought as they set out. He understood that this was something she needed to do to reclaim her equilibrium. And although she had no proof, something about his expression made her believe that he understood—at least generally speaking—what she'd involved herself in.

No wonder Jacobine had fallen so deeply in love with William Bluewing.

The air was still chilly, but only patches of snow remained, glittering in shady spots. The earth smelled muddy. Shards of sunlight filtered through the dense canopy to dapple the matted brown layer of oak, maple, and basswood leaves on the forest floor.

Fifteen minutes or so after leaving her own clearing, they reached the Bluewings' new home. New camp, she reminded herself, for they'd moved their former home to a new spot in a glade of sugar maples. Her Ho-Chunk friends lived in a dome-shaped shelter constructed of sheets of birchbark affixed over pairs of tall saplings that had been pounded into the ground, bent over, and lashed together near the top. Hanneke had been astonished when she realized that it was not unusual for the structure to be assembled and reassembled, but obviously, their system was efficient and readily manageable.

Earlier that winter Hanneke had visited with William's mother, Annie, several times. They'd sat on the thick woven mats covering the earthen floor while Hanneke worked on knitting or coiled straw basketry. Annie worked on black ash baskets of her own, or helped her young daughters learn how to stitch applique. The experience of sitting inside a wigwam had felt strange at first, but not for long. A warm fire burned beneath a ceiling hole, and the small space was certainly no smokier than her own *schwartze Küche.* Sitting with Annie in the cozy wigwam made Hanneke feel warm inside and out.

Now Jacobine scurried forward to meet them. "Frau Bauer, welcome!" she called happily. "Welcome to the sugar camp."

"Danke, Liebchen." Hanneke schooled away a faint smile to see Jacobine, who had always been a shy girl, display self-confidence and a perhaps-premature sense of gracious hostess. Hanneke did hope that Karoline would relent soon and allow Jacobine to marry William.

As they approached the camp, the first thing Hanneke noticed was one of Annie's larger baskets sitting near the entrance to the wigwam. "That's particularly gorgeous," she murmured to William, gesturing. The basket was square, perhaps a foot tall, woven in a herringbone pattern of perfectly even strips removed from black ash saplings. A decorative row of symmetrical points, crafted of the same strips, adorned the top rim. "I've seen others' work, but never anything as beautiful as your mother's baskets—especially when she gets fancy like that."

William smiled, then sobered. "My mother keeps the skill alive. The forced removals almost destroyed the practice. Even people who evaded the soldiers, like my family, were constantly on the run. Basket makers need enough geographic stability to cut and debark a tree, and carefully pound out the splints. It's almost impossible to make something so complicated and time-consuming when you're always on the move."

"Oh, William. I'm so sorry." Hanneke touched his arm. "How did Annie ever manage?"

"It was important to my mother, and she is the most stubborn person I've ever met." He gave Hanneke a wry glance. "She still insists on going out into the swamps and choosing the tree she wants to work with herself, even though I know what to look for." Then he cocked his head. "Come and meet the others."

The clearing smelled of wood smoke and was dominated by several towering piles of cut wood. Two large iron kettles hung over a fire near the reassembled wigwam. A roof had been constructed to protect the maple sap in the kettles from rain or falling sticks. William's uncle had come to supervise, and several male cousins in their late teens or early twenties were helping. All of the men greeted Hanneke with friendly smiles. "*Haho!*" she said each time. The greeting was one of the few Ho-Chunk words she knew. "I've come to be useful."

"We do appreciate your help," William assured her. "It takes about forty gallons of sap to make one gallon of syrup."

Hanneke's eyebrows rose. "Gracious."

"We'll take most of whatever syrup we attain and boil it until it crystallizes into sugar. That's easier to store and carry than the liquid. Do you have a preference, Frau Bauer?" He shot her a sidelong look. "By American law, it all belongs to you."

She waved a dismissive hand. "I will gratefully accept a share of maple sugar, but that's all." She knew that the Bluewings could sell or trade whatever excess they produced, and she had no intention of reducing their modest profit.

"Come see the trees the men have tapped," Jacobine urged. "One of our jobs is to collect the jars and baskets as they get full."

They walked toward a bark basket placed beneath a dripping spile that had been struck into a massive maple tree trunk. The tree's sprawling limbs were bare, but Hanneke appreciated the hint of protective canopy overhead, nonetheless.

William spoke quietly. "Before you begin work, please take a moment to thank the trees. We sprinkle tobacco in gratitude as well."

It was a new idea for Hanneke. She knew William would not tolerate doing any permanent damage to the sugar maples...but pounding spiles and taking gallons of the released sap must surely wound the trees. Actually, the request sounded like a respectful idea. "I will," she promised.

Jacobine's mother, Karoline, was already helping Annie Bluewing and her two daughters collect the buckets and baskets that caught the clear sap dripping from the spiles. Moving with care on the uneven ground, the women carried it to the "starter" kettle, which was constantly filled with the clear, water-like sap. As that cooked down and gradually became tawny, one of the men transferred the hot liquid to another kettle to cook down further.

Hanneke spent most of her day stirring the kettles with a wooden paddle to keep the sap from scorching. "When we have thick syrup," Annie told her, "I'll cook that into sugar." Getting the perfect consistency for granular sugar was apparently tricky, so Hanneke didn't mind Annie's refusal to delegate that particular task. By the end of the afternoon, Hanneke's upper body muscles ached—especially the badly bruised shoulder where she'd been kicked by Cinder.

What she hadn't known to anticipate, however, was how sociable the day would be. William's uncle, a stocky man with a pockmarked face, liked to tease his sons and nephew. The campsite's quiet was frequently punctuated with shouted jokes, bursts of laughter, and the whoops that accompanied the occasional impromptu wrestling match.

What a joy to see William so completely at ease, Hanneke thought. He and Jacobine managed to exchange frequent murmurs and knowing glances as they worked. He helped his young sisters pour squiggles of maple syrup on a small snowbank. The shapes turned into candy, and the girls' eyes glowed with pleasure.

Best of all was working with her friends. Annie's placid but watchful demeanor was always somehow reassuring. Hanneke had also missed having the Ketzlers for company at home, and it was good to catch up with Karoline and Jacobine. "I'm glad you could come," Jacobine told them both earnestly towards the end of the day. Her large blue eyes sparkled with the pleasure of having her mother, her future mother-in-law, and her surrogate mother all in one place. "It's nice to do things as a family." She gestured, indicating all of the people in the clearing.

Karoline shot her a *Don't push me* look. "It's nice to be getting acquainted with the Bluewing family," she said pointedly.

"It's good to be here for many reasons," Hanneke said placatingly. She was also glad that Karoline had come. Her friend looked well. The simple green work dress visible beneath her shawls was a good choice for her coloring, and looked new. Setting up her tin shop in Watertown must have been good for business. After what Karoline had endured on her farm, that was good to see.

In late afternoon Annie prepared stew thick with beans, corn, and venison, served with frybread. The women ate by themselves inside the warm shelter where woven bullrush mats covered the earthen floor. Hanneke relished the hearty meal, flickering fire, and the company of women.

Annie told stories about her ancestors making maple syrup. "My grandmother spoke of letting sap freeze in whatever containers she could find. That forced the water to separate and rise, and she simply removed the ice every few hours until nothing remained but thick syrup."

Karoline's brows had risen. "That must have taken even longer than boiling does."

"Oh, much longer," Annie agreed. Crinkles fanned from the corners of her eyelids, which some might mistake for a secret smile. Hanneke, however, briefly saw shadows in the older woman's eyes. She remembered what William had said earlier about people hiding from soldiers or angry white settlers. People on the run couldn't carry iron kettles with them.

She glanced at Jacobine, who was listening intently, her face tipped toward the older woman, the sprinkling of freckles barely visible in the low light. Annie had already approved the match between Jacobine and William. Hanneke had as well, but at moments like this, doubt puddled in her soul. Karoline was right to be concerned. Did Jacobine truly understand what she might be facing as William's wife? The thought of her sweet Jacobine running from soldiers made Hanneke want to weep.

Halt, she scolded herself, and resolutely shoved the mental images away. Brooding about events that might never come would do more harm than good. She was grateful when Karoline got to her feet, taking the conversation in a different direction. "Jacobine and I must start home. I want to reach Watertown before full dark."

Annie insisted that her daughters would tend to the dishes, so Hanneke followed the Ketzlers back outside. The men, who'd also eaten, had spread a blanket on the ground and were seated in a circle. Hanneke leaned closer to see what they were doing—and paused with astonishment.

William had already scrambled to his feet in preparation for walking the women home. Hanneke gestured him closer. "William," she murmured, "what are your cousins and uncle doing?"

After glancing over his shoulder, William turned back with a perplexed expression. "They're just playing a game. It's similar to dice. Why do you ask? Is something wrong?"

Hanneke waved his concern away. "I was simply curious," she lied, but summoned a smile. William had chosen not to broach a complicated conversation about what had kept Hanneke busy lately. She would show him the same courtesy and do her best not to burden him with unnecessary details. "Thank you for inviting me to visit your sugar camp. I learned a great deal." More, actually, than she'd expected.

Chapter Sixteen

Hanneke was up and out early on Monday morning, trotting toward Watertown on Cinder's back. She was still anxious about going out—fearful, in truth—but she knew that if she backed down even once, she would lose whatever sense of self-worth she had left. Staying home would hand her attacker a victory on a silver platter. There had been no more assaults or threats. She *would* go about her business.

Apprehensive as she was, she had plenty to occupy her mind. In addition to fretting about Gideon's pique, and Celia's health, she still wanted to help identify Asa Hawkins' killer.

Usually, mental challenges like that kept her occupied, but today, she felt melancholy. She'd started reading Frederick Douglass' book, and descriptions of the brutality of his childhood had sickened her. The day before, in the churchyard after Sunday service, the main topic of conversation seemed to be the coming of spring—when to plant, when the last snowstorm might come, when the first pasque flowers would emerge. For Hanneke, the talk was a reminder that this spring would mark her one-year anniversary of coming to Wisconsin. It was not a celebratory thought, for her arrival had been wretched. *Fridolin, I wish you hadn't died,* she thought. One year of widowhood was not a milestone to savor.

The best thing she knew to do was keep busy. She had several errands to run in town. She decided to confront the most unpleasant one first: visiting Asa Hawkins' freight yard, near the Rock River.

When she got there, seeing the familiar business sign made her clench her teeth:

Asa Hawkins, Auctioneer
   Dealer in Merchandise of All Kinds
   Freight Hauling, Livestock Sales, Etc.

Today the yard looked deserted. Hanneke walked through gingerly, for melting snow had left behind mud and puddles. The animal pens were empty. For all she knew, the padlocked wooden buildings where crates and barrels had once been piled high were empty as well. The property would likely be sold.

Hawkins had once locked her up here, and now, even walking through the freight yard was distasteful. Hanneke knew that Deputy John Barlow had already searched the yard and found nothing helpful. However, Hanneke thought, sometimes a fresh pair of eyes found details previously missed.

Hawkins' office was in a main building near the drive. To Hanneke's surprise, the front door was not locked. "Hello?" she called cautiously as she crept inside. The last person Hanneke wanted to confront was Asa's brother Jerome, an avowed nativist and—according to John Barlow—an active member of the Know-Nothing party. Thankfully, although he'd no doubt come to see to urgent matters, there was no sign of him today.

Hanneke had never visited an auctioneer's office before, but the small main room seemed to hold no surprises. Near the door stood a well-polished wooden piece, six feet tall, that was half umbrella stand and half coat rack, with a small shelf near the top for hats. Hawkins' cherrywood desk still gleamed with polish. Two comfortable chairs sat in front of the desk for colleagues' use while conducting business. Although Hawkins' most recent ledger was, of course, not there, Hanneke found other business tools lined up neatly: a pen, wipe, and inkwell; a gleaming scale, a clock, an oil lamp, a box of cigars. Hanneke imagined Hawkins offering one to seal a deal with a favored customer, the two men contentedly blowing smoke rings as they chuckled about how much money there was to be made on this sale or that.

Today, though, the space seemed hollow and lifeless. Hanneke's search led to no discoveries of hidey-holes, no secret compartments. She twisted her mouth with frustration. Had she really expected to find something that

John Barlow had missed?

Ja. She had.

It would help, she thought, if she knew who the real Asa Hawkins truly had been. The big man had been arrogant and unkind. As a Know-Nothing, he didn't shy from torchlight parades intended to intimidate and threaten honest people just trying to make a life for themselves and their families. He had despised the foreign-born, Indian people, and Negroes.

More than anything else, though, he loathed slavery. He'd risked his life to help runaways, and in the end, he had probably died for the cause. She hadn't liked Asa Hawkins, but he hadn't deserved to die alone in a gully.

She considered her surroundings again. Asa Hawkins had been tidy, she thought grudgingly, and organized. The Spartan furnishings here included a few personal touches, such as the books standing on a shelf beside two older business ledgers. *I would not have guessed that Hawkins read novels!* Hanneke mused. She pulled down his copies of *Moby-Dick* and *David Copperfield.* Hanneke had not read either of the famous books, and for half a second, she considered slipping them into her basket. John Barlow hadn't taken them, and it appeared that Jerome was interested only in closing whatever business deals had been left unfulfilled by his brother's death.

Then she realized how uncomfortable she would be reading volumes once owned by Asa Hawkins. After quickly replacing them on the shelf, she turned instead to the ledgers. She should only be considering items that might have relevance to the crime. Very well, she told herself. *Think.* She would never make sense of Asa Hawkins, but she had a mind of her own. What had she missed? With one hand on the desk, she closed her eyes…and thought of something she should have considered from the beginning.

Hanneke grabbed the two older ledgers and plopped into one of the guest chairs. Using fingers stiff with cold, she flipped through the pages until she found what she was looking for.

"Da ist es!" Hanneke breathed, reading the entry again. Then she tucked both ledgers into her basket. After one last look, she left the freight yard.

Her next task was to track down Gideon. He'd left her with no contact information. Going back to the carding mill where they'd met would be pointless, since he didn't work there on a regular basis. She wasn't even sure that "Gideon" was actually his name.

He'd told her that he was an itinerant farrier, so presumably, he did not have his own shop. That made sense for a man who wanted to come and go on his own terms.

Well. Most smiths shoed horses and oxen on the side, so how many specialized farriers could there be in Watertown? He had to have *some* way to attract potential customers. And she thought she just might know what it was.

When Hanneke had first arrived in Wisconsin, she'd stayed in Watertown with Angela at the Red Cockerel until she found her footing. While trying to understand how her husband Fridolin had died, Hanneke had learned that the best and most inexpensive way to find people providing goods and services was to check the broadsides and notes that were tacked to the doors of every blacksmith shop she'd ever seen. Several blacksmiths had established shops in Watertown, and she knew where to find all of them.

She started in the familiar north-central part of the city, which was the heart of Watertown's German settlement. Gideon didn't speak the language—at least, Hanneke thought darkly, not that I know of—but someone could have helped him write a notice in *Platt Deutsch*, the dialect common in northern regions where she and many of her neighbors were from.

She had no success at the German shop. Well, that was hardly surprising. Most immigrants preferred to conduct business of any kind with fellow countrymen, and so many German-speaking people were settling in the area that doing so wasn't difficult to accomplish.

Hanneke visited two more blacksmith shops before finding what she wanted at a narrow red-frame building in the Second Ward. As she approached, she heard the clank of hammer on anvil and smelled the acrid smoke drifting from the building. In a nod to the weather, one of the big swinging doors was closed, and the other only ajar. Hanneke slipped through the crack.

The smith, a surprisingly skinny man, looked up when she entered. So did the half-dozen men lounging in a back corner not too far from the fire. For the fourth time, Hanneke smiled politely and pretended the proprietor wasn't gaping at her in astonishment. "Pardon me, gentlemen," she said in English. "I only came to look…." She gestured, then began to study the placards and notices covering the doors. One caught her attention almost at once:

Gideon Sparrow, Master Farrier
   Specializing in General Equine Health
   No Animal Too Large or Difficult
   All Work Done in the Comfort
   Of Your Own Stable
   To Obtain Service, Leave Word
   at The Barking Dog

Hanneke read the notice twice. So, she thought, "Gideon" really is his name—or at least the name he uses publicly. She took a morsel of gratification in that. The promise Gideon had made in his advertisement, "No Animal Too Large or Difficult," bordered on overconfidence, but she knew him well enough to know he probably felt no fear in approaching even the most unpleasant draft-breed stallion.

She turned again to the skinny blacksmith, who had not gone back to work. The other men were silent as well, apparently unsure of what to do or say with a female inside their domain. "Can anyone tell me how to reach The Barking Dog?" She assumed it was a tavern, with the name chosen to discourage thieves.

A man with a drooping mustache who was holding a fan of cards used his free hand to point north. "Two…." The word came out scratchy, and he cleared his throat. "Two blocks up, on the left side."

"Thank you kindly." Hanneke's broad smile included all of the men. Then, she left them in peace.

She had no trouble finding The Barking Dog. There, she spoke with the tavernkeeper and delivered a message for Gideon Sparrow: *My mare is lame and in need of attention at your earliest convenience. Hanneke Bauer.*

Once that was accomplished, Hanneke made her way back to the German neighborhood and the comfort unique to time spent at the Red Cockerel Tavern with Angela. She approached from the rear, so she could settle Cinder in Angela's stable, and then let herself in the back door.

Hanneke's friend welcomed her warmly, as always, but she was preparing the noon meal and didn't have time for a good talk. Hanneke visited with her beloved goddaughter Liesl, and chatted briefly with Gerlind, the older woman who minded the baby and sometimes helped in the kitchen as well. Then Hanneke pitched in with the lunch crowd, helping serve a hearty pike and walleye stew fragrant with onions and dried parsley. Hanneke suspected that Adolf, Angela's assistant, had caught the fish in the Rock River that morning. It was an economical meal at a time when root cellar stores were running low.

The pace didn't slow until they ran out of stew, well after noon. Adolf, Angela's helper, took a quiet moment to lean against the bar. *"Danke* for helping, Hanneke."

"My pleasure," she assured him. When she'd lived here, she had also worked in the tavern, so the routine was familiar. Besides, Angela and Adolf were family. The pace was hard on them. She enjoyed occasionally helping out. It made her feel useful.

Angela was about Hanneke's age. Life had honed her to an immensely practical and reliable woman. She had high cheekbones and wore her light brown hair in a thick coil behind her neck. What Hanneke found most striking were Angela's eyes, ever vigilant. She was a quiet woman who could quell a taproom brawl with one stern command. She labored ceaselessly to run the tavern and raise her daughter. Despite her status as a husbandless mother, she had many friends and admiring customers who would do anything for her.

Adolf soon left the tavern to purchase beer for the evening crowd. Angela and Hanneke settled in to wash stacked dishes. "So," Angela began without preamble. "What's troubling you?"

Hanneke scraped morsels of food into the slop bucket, giving herself a moment to think. Somewhere deep inside she had known that if Gerda Muehlhauser and Clara Steckelberg had seen that she was burdened, Angela would as well. She also knew that, unlike those friends, Angela would not be put off.

Finally, she handed the plate to her friend, who had already filled a basin with soapy water. "As you know, I have dipped my toes into certain waters. Illegal waters." Soon after Hanneke's arrival, Angela had helped her keep a young black child safe from slavers at the tavern. They hadn't discussed the incident since, and to the best of her knowledge, Angela did not know that Hanneke's barn was a stop on the Underground Railroad. Although she trusted Angela with her life, Hanneke had no intention of providing any specifics of her trip to Milton.

Angela merely nodded as she plunked the plate into the rinse water.

"Someone asked for my assistance with a certain task," Hanneke continued, choosing her words with care. "I did my best, and things turned out all right, but he called me a failure."

Angela crossed her arms and leaned against the dry sink before facing Hanneke. "I can't imagine you failing at anything you put your mind to."

"I do believe his standards were unreachable," Hanneke conceded. "And I've tried to focus on the good I did accomplish. Nonetheless, I haven't been able to stop brooding about what he said."

"Well." Angela briskly returned to her task. "I can't imagine anyone being so unkind. Perhaps this man was only frustrated at that moment."

"I don't think so." Hanneke set one full bucket aside and reached for an empty one. "I haven't heard from him again." She clamped her mouth shut and focused on the task at hand. It felt good to unburden herself to such a close companion in even this oblique style, but she had a dread of whining about the situation. "I still very much want to help the effort, but I don't think I'll be asked again." She shrugged, as if it didn't matter. "I've never been called a failure before."

Angela wrung out a dishrag, draped it over a string, and picked up a clean one. "Why are you letting one comment from someone you hardly know affect your self-esteem to such an extent?"

The question was unexpected. The point Angela had raised was also too complicated and new to adequately answer right now. "I just want to be truly helpful," Hanneke said instead, hating the plaintive note that had crept into her voice. She cleared her throat and tried again. "You help many people here at the tavern, and now you're also a mother. I know it's all been horribly difficult for you, but…."

Angela placed one understanding palm on Hanneke's arm.

It helped enormously for Hanneke to be reminded that she had one dear friend who truly understood what life was like for a single woman trying to find her own purpose. "This is something incredibly important," Hanneke murmured, "and I want to help."

"As I understand things," Angela said carefully, "most of the effort doesn't take place in this area. I believe there is a much greater need in the eastern states and along Wisconsin's Lake Michigan coast. It would be a mistake to think that your willingness and strength of character will be ignored forever. Perhaps there's simply been no need of your services."

"Perhaps." Hanneke wanted to believe that was true, but she still carried doubts…and the niggling fear that she was, in fact, not strong enough to do the work she desired to do.

As much as she wanted to stay at the tavern and help with the evening crowd, Hanneke needed to get back to the farm before dark. Besides, if Gideon had the decency to respond to her note, he would presumably appear at Safe Haven Farm.

"I wish I could linger," she confessed when the kitchen was tidy, "but I have animals waiting."

Angela wiped her hands on her apron and gave Hanneke a hug. "You are an extraordinary woman," Angela said quietly. "Don't let anyone tell you otherwise."

Hanneke inhaled deeply. "*Danke.*"

As she left, she picked up the two covered slop buckets and set them on the back stoop. She knew Angela routinely traded kitchen scraps for eggs from a local farmer—probably pickled at this time of year, but certainly better than none at all. Then she crossed the alley to fetch Cinder.

She'd done no more than step inside the stable when she saw Gideon sitting on a keg in the nearest stall, whittling a piece of what looked like basswood with a small knife. Hanneke managed to swallow her startled exclamation, but whatever peace she'd gained while talking to Angela disappeared in an instant. Stay calm, she willed herself. With Gideon, losing her temper or showing emotion would not help anything.

"Frau Bauer." He did not look pleased to see her. He took a swipe with his knife, honing the basswood toward a point. "Why on earth did you risk sending a note for me at The Barking Dog?"

Hanneke's composure vanished. Honestly, was a polite greeting too much to expect? "Good afternoon to you as well." She pulled the door closed behind her and fetched a stool that Adolf used out here in warmer weather. Since Gideon hadn't had the courtesy to rise when she entered, she didn't want to loom over him.

He snorted. "What is the problem?"

"The problem," Hanneke snapped, "is that someone threw a hatchet at me the other night. It came inches from killing me. And I think you know who did it."

As he absorbed those words, Gideon's face slowly tightened, muscle by muscle. He went very still, but she could feel the anger emanating from him like heat in the cold stable. "Tell me."

She did. "I didn't see him, or discern anything else helpful, but it seems extremely unlikely that a woman threw the hatchet. I don't know what might happen next—" she heard her voice tighten "—and I don't even know who to watch out for! I understand the need for general secrecy, but the fact that you've kept whatever you know from me—"

"I've been trying to protect you." The words escaped through gritted teeth.

"Well, you most certainly have not done so!" Hanneke jumped to her feet, cupped her elbows in her palms, and began prowling the small stable. "I *insist* that you tell me whatever you know or suspect about my attacker. *Mein Gott*, I deserve that much!" Although she kept her voice low, well aware that someone might be passing in the alley, her last sentence was hissed more than spoken. Just talking about the incident on that lonely twilight road brought those moments back in shocking detail—the whistling sound of the whirling blade, the solid *thunk* of it hitting the tree, the terror pounding in her chest when she realized what was actually happening, and how vulnerable she was.

Gideon didn't respond for several moments. Hanneke was gathering words and sentiments for another expression of ire when he finally began to speak. "I once mentioned a man named Levi Cox to you."

Hanneke stopped pacing. "You did."

"I've…." Gideon paused. "I won't say I've *known* him for years, but I do know who he is. He used to work solo as a bounty hunter. Sometime in the past year, he's gone to work for Hiram Aubuchon."

Cox must be one of the men Deputy Barlow had met when Aubuchon arrived in Watertown with two employees. Hanneke felt her eyes narrow. "He was one of the men who attacked us near Milton."

"Yes." Gideon studied his whittling, then started again with his knife. "I didn't get a good look at him, but I know his style. We've tangled before. More than once."

Hanneke sat down again and leaned close. "Someone told those men where to find us that night. It seems safe to assume that this Cox knows exactly who I am."

"That appears to be so. Yes."

"But why did he come after me? Was it simply because I accompanied you that one time?"

Gideon shaved another curl from the basswood. "I suspect he did it to goad me."

"To *goad* you?" Hanneke repeated, not sure she understood. "I assumed they were after our lamb that night. Was this a personal vendetta?"

"No. He is only in Wisconsin to do Hiram Aubuchon's bidding, and he expects to be well paid for it." Gideon took a savage swipe with his knife. "But I have bested him before in this business. I suspect he felt especially motivated."

"Is the lamb safe?" Hanneke asked anxiously. "Have you heard anything?"

"Of course not. I don't expect to."

Hanneke looked away, watching dust motes dance in the weak sun streaming through a crack between two wallboards. "I suppose not."

Gideon's hands stilled, and he looked up. "I deeply regret that you experienced such a moment when you were traveling alone, Frau Bauer."

That was more than she had expected from him, but she was not appeased. "What does Cox look like?"

"Long dark hair, past his shoulders. I've never seen him without a black felt hat. About my height. Wiry build. A scar on his left cheek." Gideon drew an imaginary line with one finger to illustrate, looking faintly pleased with himself. "I gave it to him."

Ignoring that, Hanneke drew a picture in her mind. At least she had *something* to go on now. "How likely is another attack on my person? What can I do to protect myself?"

"Do you own a firearm?"

"I do not."

Gideon's mouth tightened. "Then you must be especially watchful."

Watchful? She needed to be *watchful*? Hanneke folded her arms and abruptly turned away to keep from shrieking at him.

After a pause Gideon said quietly, "When you agreed to help me, you did know there were risks involved."

That was absolutely the wrong thing to say. "I accepted the risks inherent with our journey," Hanneke snapped. "There was no mention of the possibility that someone would throw a hatchet at me once that journey was over."

Seconds ticked by. The faint but lively shouts of boys at play drifted into the silence. Clopping hoofbeats sounded down the alley from the main street. Hanneke tried to think of something reasonable to say and simply could not.

Eventually, Gideon rose to his feet. "You did the right thing by getting word to me and telling me what happened. I'll do what I can."

Hanneke had no idea what that meant. I'm on my own, she thought. Well, she was used to that.

Then, as Gideon was walking to the door, she heard herself say, "Will you ever ask me for help again?"

He paused without turning around. "Not if I can help it," he muttered, and left her alone.

Chapter Seventeen

I n the moments after Gideon had disappeared from Angela's stable, Hanneke thought of many things she wished she had said. Gideon's final conclusion—that he wouldn't ask for her help again if he could avoid it—had been quite clear. Her fingers fisted in her cape. He had rejected her all over again.

Why are you letting one comment from someone you hardly know affect your self-esteem to such an extent?

Because I wanted to do more work with Gideon! Hanneke answered Angela silently. She wanted to be a trusted partner in this illegal and sacred business of helping people escape bondage and suffering. Obviously, though, she'd burned her bridges with him.

Perhaps that wasn't a totally bad thing, she thought. She didn't feel capable of trusting Gideon again anyway. He was a brave man, good at his job of ferrying runaway souls where they needed to be. He was also insensitive and, in her view, dangerous.

Well. Her barn would remain a refuge for any traveler in need of shelter. And maybe one day, another competent shepherd would approach and ask for her help. In the meantime, she was grateful to have occasional challenges from Deputy Barlow to give her something important to do, breaking up the monotony of chopping firewood and shoveling dirty straw from her animal pens.

So I shall focus on that, Hanneke told herself, and tried to set aside her anger and bruised feelings. Now was as good a time as any. Stiffening her spine, she strode from the stable and turned toward the sheriff's office.

Deputy Barlow wasn't in but was expected back soon. Hanneke left a message and went back to the Red Cockerel.

Twenty minutes later, Deputy Barlow found her in the taproom, studying the older account books. He greeted Hanneke with a frown and slid into an empty chair. "What have you got there?"

"The earliest two business ledgers that belonged to Asa Hawkins."

John's frown deepened. "Where did you get those?"

"His office, of course."

"What were you doing there?" He raised a hand, caught Adolf's eye, and pointed one finger skyward to ask for a beer. "You can't just—"

"Of course, I can," Hanneke said impatiently. John must be especially frustrated today. "You'd already been there, and Jerome Hawkins has obviously already been there, and neither one of you were interested in these. You already gave me the most recent book, and I'm here now to show these to you. You're welcome to take them with you, if you wish."

"I don't wish. Besides, I don't think it's likely that Hawkins would have actually recorded details of his illegal dealings."

"I don't agree," Hanneke insisted. "Everything about these ledgers, and his office, paints the picture of a man who was extremely well organized. I believe he took pride in efficiently running his own business. It's possible he felt compelled to keep records of his work on the Underground Railroad, no matter how cryptic or obscure. Perhaps he needed to make *some* mark of what he was doing." She imagined Hawkins taking a secret pleasure in hiding his records, as it were, in plain sight. "What I'm trying to tell you is that Hawkins did make extra notes in his ledger, in a way. Would you like to stop grousing and hear what I discovered?"

John waved a hand in grudging acquiescence. Hanneke looked over her shoulders to make sure no one could hear her. It was early for the evening crowd, and only a few other people were in the room, nursing drinks alone or with companions.

Leaning closer, she explained what she'd spotted at the freight yard earlier that day. "It occurred to me that we do know for sure of one Negro person Hawkins aided. Last spring, soon after I arrived in Watertown, Hawkins somehow ended up taking in a lost colored child. Remember?"

"Of course, I remember. I risked my career and livelihood to help you both."

"Yes, and I'm still grateful." She flipped through one of the ledgers. "Here's his notation for that day: 'Carried a load of furniture from CC to Watertown. Three chests of drawers, one table and two chairs, two storage trunks.'" Hanneke looked up. "Each item includes a notation for dimensions, weight, and wood type. He was thorough. But here's the important part. The entry ends with this: 'Also carried one tiny parcel.'" She looked at Barlow triumphantly. "I believe that 'tiny parcel' was the baby who'd been separated from its mother while the woman ran from slavers."

John Barlow scratched his jaw. "You may be right," he conceded, more thoughtful now. "But how does this—" He stopped as Adolf approached with a foaming tankard. When the young man had disappeared back toward the bar, John continued, "help us identify the killer?"

"Well, it doesn't," Hanneke admitted. "However, it does give us some insight into Hawkins' system. These books here include five notations of 'parcels,' always marked 'big' or 'small.' If someone idly glanced at such an entry, there was nothing to attract attention, nothing to suggest he was breaking the law. The most recent ledger is at my house, but I can tell you that it also contains two notes about 'parcels.'"

John raised a quizzical eyebrow. "How can you be sure, if you only figured this out today?"

"I'm sure. I've read the ledger you gave me at least a dozen times."

John sipped the amber liquid in his stein, looking at her over the foam. "Why did you do that?"

"Because that's what it took to start to understand what Hawkins wrote." Hanneke felt herself growing impatient again. Wasn't that exactly why he asked for her help? She could pursue lines of inquiry that he had neither time nor patience for.

John nodded slowly. "Well done," he allowed.

Hanneke felt a flush of satisfaction.

Pulling the ledger closer, John took another look at the entry. "'CC,'" he murmured. "I wonder if that's Clyman's Corners."

"Oh!" Hanneke said softly. The Pohl family lived in Clyman's Corners. "I didn't see it, but that certainly could be. Hawkins made note of frequent business there. A carpenter and cabinetmaker named Felix Pohl has a shop there, and he would likely need help getting his big pieces to market. I just hadn't made the connection to 'CC.' The ledgers are riddled with such initials, and I could only guess at a few of them."

"How do you know this Felix Pohl?"

"In truth, I don't. However, I have become friendly with his sisters, Berta and Erna. They're both abolitionists."

John nodded thoughtfully. "From what I know, Clyman's Corners is small, but local residents are largely anti-slavery." His mouth twisted in that familiar way. "I assume Hawkins did not make any entry for the day he died?"

"That is correct," Hanneke agreed sadly. It would have been helpful to know who Hawkins visited shortly before his death, but he never got the chance.

She and John simply needed to keep thinking and looking.

* * *

Days passed, and winter turned toward spring. John came to take Cinder back, and that sad day left a void that even Hanneke's beloved sheep couldn't fill. She did her best to keep busy. She planted seeds in a sunny window and hauled barrow-loads of manure to the big garden. She helped ladies at her church host a fund-raising dinner. She delivered a pair of twin boys in Lebanon, and did her best to check on Gerda Muehlhauser, and the König family, and others in need. In truth, though, nothing filled her soul like the work she had done with Gideon and Celia.

Fridolin, I'm floundering, she told her husband one evening as she sat on the back step and stared at the stars appearing in the sky. He didn't answer, but it always helped to unburden herself to him in this way.

A quiet movement behind her farm clearing, at the forest's edge, caught

Hanneke's eye. She jumped to her feet, heart racing like a thoroughbred on Independence Day. Levi Cox? Hiram Aubuchon? Another of Aubuchon's employees? She stood by the back door, poised to jump inside and lock the door.

Then she recognized Claudette Bluewing, William's youngest sister, making straight for her. Hanneke pressed a hand over her chest, missing the days when she was not afraid of every visitor to Safe Haven Farm. She hurried out to meet the child. "Claudette?" she called as the girl reached the yard. "Is everything well?" Any Bluewing was welcome at her home, but neither of the two girls had ever come to the house alone before.

Claudette didn't answer right away. She was a thin girl of perhaps five, wearing moccasins and a faded cotton skirt and blouse. Her black hair was tied back behind her head, and her eyes were dark and inscrutable. She waited until she had reached Hanneke's side and lowered the blanket she'd held over her head before speaking. "William wants you to come."

Frowning with worry, Hanneke leaned closer. "Is someone sick? Or hurt?"

"Sick," Claudette confirmed soberly. "Very sick."

Alarm blossomed in Hanneke's ribcage. "Of course, I'll come back with you," she assured her young visitor. "We can go as soon as I grab my bag of medicines."

Twilight was fading fast as the two of them headed back into the forest. Hanneke hesitated in the gloom, but Claudette seemed confident of the route to the sugar camp. Before too long, the glow of a campfire flickered through the underbrush. The towering trees cast giant shadows.

After the cheerful sugaring work party she'd attended here, the clearing seemed eerily still and quiet. In addition to the fire blazing outside, she could tell a smaller fire was burning inside the wigwam. She was glad for both of them.

William must have been listening, for he emerged from the wigwam as Hanneke and Claudette reached the clearing. "Frau Bauer." His voice was as steady as ever, but Hanneke could tell that he was glad to see her. "Thank you for coming."

She kept her voice low. "What's happened?"

"A man I don't know stumbled into the clearing here about an hour ago and collapsed. I got him inside, but he's burning up with fever."

"Where is your mother?" Annie Bluewing was quite capable of tending most illnesses.

"She's away visiting my aunt. Claudette and I are the only ones here right now." He put a hand on Hanneke's arm as she started for the wigwam. "You should know—he asked for you."

She whirled. "For me? By name?"

William spread his hands. "Most of what he's said has been incoherent. But when I got to him, he begged me to 'Fetch Frau Bauer.' Quite clearly."

Now Hanneke had a suspicion about the ill man who'd stumbled into the Bluewings' camp. But why, under heaven, she thought, would he ask for me?

She stooped to enter the wigwam. She usually loved being inside the Bluewings' home, for it smelled fresh, like the forest itself. Tonight, though, she was greeted with a sour smell of sweat and illness.

Gideon lay on blankets that had been arranged on one of the family's beautiful bullrush mats. Hanneke could hear him muttering, and in the firelight, it was clear that he was insensible. Claudette, who'd already slipped inside, was kneeling beside Gideon and patting his face with a cloth. Hanneke knelt on the other side and placed the back of one hand on his forehead. The heat in his skin felt scorching. This was worse, Hanneke thought grimly, than even Celia's fever and illness had been.

William had followed her inside. "Is there anything you can do for him?"

"I'm certainly going to try." Hanneke fretted her lower lip with her teeth. "This man is dangerously ill, though."

"You know him?"

"His name is Gideon."

William accepted her terse response. "What do you need?"

"Clean cloths. Any kind of broth if you have it. Water." She reached for her bag. "And I have some herbs—if you could make a tea…?"

"Of course."

Hanneke did what she could for Gideon: echinacea and elderberry juice for strength, and the tea of elderflower, white willow bark, and ginger to fight the fever. She had to hold his head and dribble the liquids between his lips. Sometimes, he moaned. Sometimes, delirium pulled nonsensical words and phrases from him. Sometimes, he called for people she didn't know—Tabitha, most often, but also Sarah and Amy.

The evening felt dreamlike. This man had vexed her mightily, but Hanneke certainly took no pleasure in his misery. How he would hate this situation! Gideon guarded his person closely. If he knew he was helpless, and at times delirious, he'd be horrified.

She didn't know how long they'd all been sitting vigil when she noticed that Claudette was struggling to stay awake. "Is there a quiet place where you can fix beds for yourself and Claudette?" Hanneke whispered to William. "I'm going to stay with him." She nodded toward Gideon.

William offered to stay, but she waved that idea away. "I'm accustomed to sitting with the sick," she reminded him gently. That was true enough, but there was another motivation. Gideon hadn't said anything he shouldn't, but if he did, it would be best if no one else was there to hear it. "I could use your help with one more thing, though. Can you spare a shirt? This man's is filthy and soaked through, and we need to get him out of it."

Soon, William had his young sister settled near the fire outside, beneath the birchbark ceiling affixed on poles. Then he rejoined Hanneke and offered her a knee-length linen shirt—the kind men often labored or slept in. "That will do nicely," she murmured.

William went to the far side of the pallet. Between them, they managed to pull off Gideon's sturdy shirt.

Hanneke froze in horror. *Mein Gott.*

Unwilling to believe her eyes, she held a candle close. Gideon's back was a mess of scars. Long, thin stripes latticed his skin from collarbone to waist. Somewhere, at some time, Gideon had been viciously whipped. Perhaps more than once.

For a long moment, Hanneke could only stare, open-mouthed. She was afraid she might vomit. Her mind struggled to accept what she was seeing— and what it meant.

When she finally lifted her gaze to William's, she saw, even in the low light, a similar revulsion glittering in his black eyes. "Maybe…maybe he used to be a seaman?" William whispered hoarsely. "With a harsh captain?"

Hanneke looked away. She didn't believe that. She thought about Gideon, and how he approached work on the Underground Railroad with the intensity of a religious calling. She thought about all she'd witnessed. Recent events had made it clear that Gideon would do anything—*anything*—to help a runaway escape north.

"Tabitha?" Gideon mumbled. "I'm cold."

Hanneke's first instinct was to return Gideon's original shirt and pretend that she and William had not just seen something Gideon would surely not want them to see. But…*nein*. She was a healer. She'd been right to remove Gideon's sweat-soaked shirt.

"Let's get this clean shirt on him," she murmured. When Gideon was settled back on the blankets, she looked gravely at her young friend. "And William…."

"I'll never speak of this. To anyone."

Hanneke believed him. She compulsively reached out. He squeezed her fingers in reassurance.

She blinked back tears, grateful for the darkness. If Karoline doesn't give this young man permission to marry Jacobine very soon, she thought, I shall help them elope myself.

It was a long night. After William went outside to get some rest, Hanneke put down a blanket of her own and settled herself near Gideon. Sometimes, he flailed so wildly that she feared he would hurt himself. Sometimes, he spoke of things she didn't understand. Hanneke listened to the wind rustle against the birchbark, thought about Celia, and occasionally added another log to the interior fire. She slept in snatches and continued to give Gideon sips of water and tea and venison broth. Twice, she went outside to relieve herself among the trees and was glad for William's presence in the grove.

Gideon was quiet in the hour or so before dawn, and Hanneke closed her eyes to rest. She startled from a doze when she heard him croak her name. "Frau Bauer."

Immediately alert, she scrambled to her knees. *"Ja.* I'm here." She studied his face, where perspiration was forming rivulets as drops ran down his cheeks. His fever had not broken.

His eyes, though…they were aware. He was staring at her when he managed, "You must go."

She pressed her lips together against her instinctive declaration that her ministrations might just be keeping him alive, and that she wasn't going anywhere. "Just rest," she murmured.

"You—have to—go!" he managed hoarsely. "What day is it?" When she told him, he closed his eyes for a moment, as if in despair. With an obvious effort, he opened them again and held her gaze. "There is a boy…waiting in the brickyard. Fetch him and keep him safe."

Hanneke felt her heart sink. She briefly wondered if God was laughing at her. She had prayed to be given another opportunity, but not like this. Alone? In charge? *Nein.* "It would be better if William went. The Ho-Chunk man who took you in."

"His skin…is not white."

She knew what Gideon meant. An Indian man creeping about one of the industries along the Rock River would be much more likely to attract attention than a white person.

"There's no one else," Gideon rasped. His eyes were glittering. "Don't bring the boy here."

"So where—" Hanneke began, but Gideon had again lost consciousness.

She sat back on her heels, feeling numb. *There's no one else.*

Of course, I will go, she thought, but the lack of instructions was daunting. Assuming she could even find the boy, and get him out of the brickyard, where was she supposed to take him?

Well. She didn't know, but she did know that crouching here and dithering wasn't doing anyone any good.

Hanneke went outside and softly called to William. He leapt to his feet at once, and she suspected he'd spent more time that night listening for any sign of trouble than actually sleeping.

Quickly, without providing any backstory, she told him about the conversation she'd just had with Gideon. There was no one she trusted more than Jacobine's fiancé, and she believed he was no stranger to this business. She was proud of the steadiness in her voice, and proud also that she managed *not* to beg William to accompany her. "I'm leaving at once," she finished. "You can look after him until…until I return?"

"Yes, but…." William looked troubled. "I don't like this."

Hanneke felt a raindrop hit her nose. "I don't either."

"At least wait until darkness falls."

She tipped her head. "William. It's barely dawn. I can't wait until twilight. I fear this boy Gideon mentioned has already been waiting too long, wondering if he's been forgotten."

The patter of rain against the earth and bare tree limbs grew stronger. "You know…." William held her gaze. "I hope you know that you can bring the boy here."

"I do understand that. But Gideon doesn't think he'd be safe here."

William took that in, jaw tightening. Then he said, "Wait," and ducked into the wigwam. Returning a moment later, he held out his fist. "Take this."

Hanneke accepted his offering and almost smiled when she realized that he'd given her one of the carefully incised disks his relatives had used in their gambling game—the one so similar to the piece she'd spotted among Celia's things. "Do these circles have some special meaning about abolition?"

"Honestly, I don't know that they do," William admitted. "Two years ago, a Negro man in tattered clothing presented himself in our clearing. I wasn't there, but my mother saw the desperation in his eyes. When he produced a similar game piece, she knew he needed help, and that another Ho-Chunk family had sent him to us. How did you know?"

"When I saw the men playing with these the other day, I suspected as much." Hanneke thought about the disk she'd inadvertently spotted in Celia's travel bag. "Someone else I…I knew briefly was carrying one. Did you make these?"

William shook his head. "No. They're common game pieces. Many Ho-Chunk people are nomadic these days, and it's difficult at best to find our lodges. But it seems that someone gives these pieces to…to travelers in need of help. Seeing one would certainly give any Indian pause." He nodded toward the game piece in her hand. "It can't hurt to carry it."

"*Nein*, it can't." Hanneke tucked it away. "Thank you. Now, I really must go."

"I still don't like this."

"I'll manage," Hanneke told William. "Take care." With that, she lifted her chin, pulled up her hood, and walked from the glade.

Chapter Eighteen

By good fortune, Hanneke was offered a ride to town before she'd walked a mile from Safe Haven Farm. She passed the journey in the back of a farm wagon with a jumble of children huddled together for warmth. Once they'd reached Watertown, she asked to be let off near the industrial district that ran along the Rock River. She didn't know where the brickyard was, or even if there was more than one, but she didn't ask. She didn't want anyone to have a memory of her inquiring about it.

A light but steady rain still beat down as she began looking for it herself, striding through the district in what she hoped was a confident, purposeful manner, as if she had business at one of the mills. As a widow, at least this much was familiar—taking care to present herself as someone competent and assured, ready to convince whoever needed convincing that yes, she was here to conduct business and no, her husband would not be stopping by to take care of the details and payment.

Watertown was only twenty years old but growing quickly. Even on this gray and drizzly day, there was an air of busy-ness here—shabby laborers and shouting dray wagon drivers and business owners wearing fine top hats trotting past. The Rock River made a deep oxbow turn within the city, so waterpower was plentiful for the flour mills, sawmills, oil mills, and other enterprises.

Hanneke knew little about brickmaking, but she didn't think such an enterprise would be too active in winter. That makes a brickyard a good spot to hide, she thought. To the best of her knowledge, the process required no water wheel. It did require good clay, however, and she was guessing that one of the best places to gather it was along the river. Even if the yard owners were preparing for their prime season, snow had been on the ground so recently they could—she hoped—only be beginning to ramp up the operation.

She walked for over an hour before the sign for a brickyard appeared. It was what she wanted, but the discovery still wound up her apprehension. Were slavers about? Was this the right brickyard? If it was, where might the boy be hiding? She took a deep breath, trying to calm the panic swirling inside. Be deliberate, she counseled herself. *Think.*

A graceful elm tree grew near the brickyard. There, Hanneke sheltered and thought. She had stopped briefly at her own home after leaving the sugar camp that morning and pulled on an old work dress made of brown wool for just such a moment. Her cloak was dark as well. She took refuge beneath its vase-shaped branches so she could study the yard.

As she'd hoped, it was largely quiet. At this distance, it was difficult to tell if anyone was working in the main structure—a nondescript frame building—or not. No smoke puffed from the dome-shaped building where, Hanneke assumed, dried bricks were fired. The earth was bare, and the rain was reducing the last patches of snow to slush and mud. She could imagine long rows of bricks drying in the sunshine, but there were none now. Empty racks waited forlornly for new-formed bricks. The brickyard owners probably sold out stock in autumn, she thought, given the rate at which new buildings were being constructed. Just a couple of low piles of actual bricks remained, stacked in the lot's corner near to where she stood. The only other thing on this side of the yard was a small outhouse roughly constructed with makeshift planks and tar paper.

On the far side of the lot, though, a few people were working at a table beneath a wooden roof. Over the next few minutes, a handful of people came and went, delivering loads of clay. The men trundled wheelbarrows heaped with slick earth the color of yellowy cream. Hanneke realized with dismay that the few women and children involved carried heavy lumps of raw clay without aid, usually on the tops of their heads.

Abruptly, the heavens opened. Angular torrents of water slashed the ground, creating spreading puddles in all directions. In mere moments, the rain had soaked through Hanneke's boiled-wool cloak. She felt a chill settle deep in her bones.

The storm, however, was providing her best chance to look for the boy. She took one last, penetrating look around. The few outdoor workers had disappeared. No one was in sight, even on the road. Across the river, a few black umbrellas bobbed as pedestrians hurried on their way, and a freight wagon splashed along the lane. Hanneke could just make out the driver, hat pulled low, hunched over his knees.

No one was paying attention to the dripping brickyard.

After pulling her wet hood as far forward as possible, Hanneke walked from the elm toward the outhouse. Blood thumped in her ears. The drumming rain seemed deafening. Her ears strained to hear an outraged yell. The skin between her shoulder blades prickled with dreadful anticipation. No one accosted her, though.

She picked her way around a low heap of bricks that had been tossed against the northern wall of the outhouse. All of the bricks were cracked, misshapen, or broken, which was no doubt why they hadn't been sold. Ignoring them, Hanneke approached the outhouse with caution. "Hello?" she called softly. "I've come to help."

Silence from the outhouse was her only response.

Hanneke crept closer. "Don't be afraid. I'm here to help." She winced, realizing belatedly that her words were probably exactly what a slaver might say at such a moment, but Gideon hadn't advised her about how to approach a frightened runaway. Was there a secret word or phrase? She didn't know.

She still got no response, but when she opened the door, there he was: a skinny boy with black skin huddled on the floor. His hair was close-clipped, suggesting ease of travel more than anything else. He had a narrow face with sunken cheeks, and enormous dark eyes. His skin had an ashy look. She knew better than to ask his age, but guessed him to be no more than eight years old. He was shuddering with cold or fear—perhaps both—and cowered when she came into sight. Tear tracks stained his cheeks.

Hanneke wanted to cry in sympathy. Instead, she quickly slid inside and shut the door. The small space smelled of old lime, but the fresh scent of rain flowed with the wind through large cracks and rips in the tar paper.

"Well," she whispered, "at least we're out of the storm." She settled down on the floor across from him. "Please don't be afraid. I'm truly here to help you. Would you like some food? You must be hungry." At home, she had wrapped several slices of good German bread in pieces of oilcloth and stuffed them, with two wrinkled carrots and a wedge of cheese, into her basket. Now, she held out one of the packets.

Eyeing her with distrust, he snatched the parcel and began devouring bread like he hadn't eaten in days. Only when he'd gobbled two pieces did he speak. "The man said another man would meet me here."

"Which man told you that?"

The boy shrugged. "Graybeard down the river."

Hanneke reminded herself that questions about shepherds were inappropriate. "When was the second man supposed to meet you here?"

"Yesterday." The child's lower lip trembled. "I don't know if he forgot, or if he got in trouble, or if he thought someone was watching."

Hanneke swallowed hard. "Are you aware of anyone watching? Is anyone trying to find you?"

"I believe so, mistress." His gaze darted to her, then away. "Folks in Illinois told me so."

Someone was tracking this child. Hanneke felt a sinking sensation in the pit of her stomach. Was it Hiram Aubuchon or Levi Cox? Or some other depraved bounty hunter who'd been hired to chase this boy down? Hanneke sent a prayer skyward: *Oh, Fridolin, please guide me. I didn't expect to find myself in a situation like this, and I don't know if I can keep this child safe.*

She felt more than heard Fridolin's response. *You **can**. Keep your wits about you, Hanneke. I have every faith in your ability.*

He rarely responded when she talked with him, and this message from her husband heartened her immensely. *You're right*, she told him. *I can do this. I **will** keep this boy safe.*

Hanneke crawled to the northern wall, where there was a low six-inch hole in the flapping tar paper. After snaking her hand through the gap, she blindly reached about before choosing a rough-edged chunk of brick and drawing it inside. It was no match for a gun, or a determined man with a knife…but she felt better for having it.

The boy was watching. "What's that for?"

"Nothing, I hope." Hanneke looked back at the boy. "Would you like to sit right here by me? It would be warmer."

For a moment, he looked tempted, but he shook his head. "No, Mistress. I'm fine right here."

Too soon, Hanneke counseled herself, trying to think of something else to say or do to convince this poor child that she really was a friend. "Is there a name I can call you?"

He thought for a moment before saying, "My master says my name is Apollo."

"Apollo?" Hanneke was appalled by the arrogance. If she remembered correctly, Apollo was the Greek god of sun, poetry, and music. This boy's poor clothing suggested he spent his days digging potatoes or some such, not reading verse or playing the flute.

The boy must have sensed something of her feelings. "My mama called me Daniel," he whispered. "From the Bible."

"Ah." Hanneke knew her Bible. The biblical Daniel grew up a slave but had eventually reached a much more important position in life. Daniel's mother was a clever woman. "May I call you Daniel?"

The boy gave her a dubious look, perhaps not used to white people taking an interest in such personal details. But he nodded.

Hanneke pinched her lips. What should they do? Now that she'd found Daniel, it was all up to her.

Celia's low, rough voice spoke in her memory: *Run at night, hide by day.*

Hiding here is the best choice I can make right now, Hanneke thought. Then Daniel and I will run. She could see no other option. Even if she got Daniel out of the brickyard, what then? She'd been lucky to pass through this industrial area earlier without attracting attention. A woman and a Negro child would probably not be so lucky.

She leaned closer to Daniel. "I don't believe we should try leaving this spot until nightfall. For the moment, we're at least hidden, and I don't think anyone will wander this way." He offered no argument.

The time passed slowly. When sitting on the floor proved unbearable, Hanneke perched on the space between the latrine's two holes. She worried that any moment, the door might bang open, and she and Daniel would suddenly confront a slaver. At the same time, crouching for many hours in a ramshackle outhouse seemed strange and somewhat ridiculous. All she had to do was glance at Daniel, though, to be reminded what this truly was about. She wanted to tell him that she cared about him. She wanted to tell him that she was sorry for whatever brutalities he had experienced in the past. She wanted to ask why he was braving this dangerous flight alone. Instead, she ripped the wedge of cheese in half and handed him one of the pieces. He accepted it gratefully, but then subsided into stillness again. Apparently, Hanneke thought sardonically, *he is better used to such waiting than I.*

Slowly, *slowly*, the light creeping through cracks began to wane. Hanneke found a knothole more or less at eye level, and periodically checked the little slice of the outside world. Did Watertown's police officers patrol this area? Probably. She and Daniel needed to move on, but she had to pick her time carefully.

When dusk descended, Hanneke inhaled a long breath. Neither staying nor going seemed like a good idea. She still didn't know where they would go. Gideon would know where to find a safe house. Gideon was not here. He'd told her that the Bluewing wigwam wasn't safe, and she knew her own home wasn't either—not when Hiram Aubuchon had already shown up once, not when someone was, she feared, watching her place. The only plan was to somehow pass through the city and head north, losing themselves in the more open countryside.

"It's time," she whispered. As Daniel started to rise, she spotted a small smudge of light in the distance. A streetlamp, maybe? *Nein.* The light was moving. A lantern.

"No, stay still!" she hissed, one eye pressed to the hole. "Someone's out there. Maybe they'll turn off, but right now, they're coming this way."

Daniel silently dropped back down to the floor. His face was expressionless, but his eyes were alert, darting from the door to a loose sideboard near where he sat. His body was still, but Hanneke could tell the boy was prepared to take explosive action if need be.

Actually, his air of suppressed tension reminded her of Gideon.

But she didn't have time to think about Gideon now. She crouched, keeping one eye close to the knothole that provided a limited view of the makeshift alley that ran between the brickyard and the gristmill it neighbored. She could make out two men now, sharing the lantern. They were still coming closer, but stopped often so one of the men could beat occasional shrubbery with a long stick. They're looking for us, Hanneke thought. Her stomach cramped. Why had she decided to stay in the old outhouse? You trapped yourself, she thought. You should have been long gone.

When the duo drew parallel to the main brickyard building, one man broke left and disappeared around the front of the low frame office structure. The second man kept walking, swinging his big stick even if there was nothing apparent to investigate. He stopped, scanning the empty yard, then kept walking.

"One of them's coming this way," Hanneke whispered to Daniel. "I'm so dreadfully sorry."

He waved away her apology as if baffled. "We ain't done yet."

His words shamed her. If this young man could find resolve, she could too. "No. You're absolutely right. We're not done yet."

She took stock of her meager resources. An abandoned outhouse didn't provide many weapons. Any, really. But she still had a few tools at her disposal. One of them was surprise. This slaver will have to go through me, she thought, to reach Daniel. She imagined herself being handcuffed, dragged away in one direction while Daniel was dragged in another. The image produced smoke inside of her.

She would not make it easy on the man.

With every step that drew the man closer, a spring beneath her ribs pulled tighter. She didn't think the man approaching the outhouse was Hiram Aubuchon, but it might be Levi Cox. It was impossible to see the man's features behind the globe of lamplight. He was wearing a hat, though, and had long hair that dangled past his shoulders.

Hanneke's heart was thumping so hard that she expected the man might hear it as he drew ever closer. He was making straight for the outhouse now—there was nowhere else to look. She left her post by the eyehole and crouched by the door. Waiting. *Waiting.* She imagined the slaver drawing close now, step by step. Her lungs seemed incapable of drawing breath, as if she and Daniel had already used all the air in this tiny place.

Then she could hear the fall of the man's booted feet on the hardpacked earth. She and Daniel exchanged a silent, wide-eyed look.

"Boy? You in there?" the man hollered. "Come on out, or I'll make you sorry you didn't."

It took all of Hanneke's self-control to wait until she saw the wooden door handle move before launching. Then she gathered herself like a hunting cat and hurled herself into the door and out into the night. In a dizzy instant, she heard the man grunt, and she noticed the scar on his left cheek. He didn't fall, as she had hoped, but he did stagger backwards.

"Good evening, Mr. Cox," she heard herself say. Then she swung her right arm in a big sweep. The broken brick she clutched in her fingers met his skull with a sickening thud. He went down like a dropped piece of laundry.

She reached back into the outhouse, but Daniel had already plunged outside. His little fists were clenched. Something about that made tears burn Hanneke's eyes.

They instinctively clutched each other's hands. "Run!" someone implored. Hanneke wasn't sure if the word came from Daniel or her or both of them at once. She heard Cox groaning. Some part of her was glad that she hadn't killed him outright. Another part of her wished she had.

Then she and Daniel ran into the night.

Where, where, where. The word thrummed in Hanneke's head. Her instinct was to turn away from town towards the Rock River. The bank here had been cleared, though—there was no place to hide. Cox might be down, but his companion would surely be upon them very quickly. A shout from somewhere behind them confirmed her fear.

Daniel was putting pressure on her hand. She followed his persistent tug toward the building next door, a three-story brick gristmill perched on the riverbank. To her surprise, the building was not quiet. A steady mechanical hum shuddered from the mill. All of the local farmers who had spent the winter shelling their cobs bit by bit must be clearing out their barns to prepare for the spring, and bringing wagonloads of corn to the mill.

Hanneke and Daniel ran past the side wall, along the front, and turned the corner. Daniel stopped abruptly, crouched, and wrenched a small pane of glass free from the wall just above the earth. Before Hanneke could say a word, he slithered through and disappeared.

Hearing another shout, she dropped her basket inside and followed.

Chapter Nineteen

The idea of eeling into the mill's basement room terrified Hanneke. She did it anyway. The interior was dark and noisy, and she had no idea where she was landing. The windowsill scraped painfully against her chest and stomach. She heard fabric ripping. Daniel's small, firm hand gripped her forearm before they crashed together onto the floor.

She pushed herself slowly to a sitting position, trying to assess. Daniel was already clambering up onto a heavy beam near the window. Reaching through the empty frame, he grasped the piece of glass he'd removed and carefully pulled it back into place.

They were in the mill's gear room. Except for the high windows, most of the room was underground. A lone lamp placed high in one corner cast the room in shadows. Hanneke didn't see anyone working, but the room was full of wheels and cogs that powered the actual mill upstairs. Leather belts disappeared through holes in the ceiling on their way to other parts of the machinery. The sound of running water was also noisy. A man-made channel against the building diverted water from the Rock River, providing force to the turning wheels.

Hanneke was breathless and achy, but none of her bones seemed to be broken. She wouldn't have chosen to secrete themselves inside anywhere, but what was done was done. She looked at Daniel as he crouched back beside her. "Did you fix the window in advance?"

"I done got here early. Took a look around. This be the best place to hide that I saw." He lifted one shoulder. "Can't be too careful on such a journey."

"No," Hanneke said weakly, raising her voice to be heard over the continuous rattle and splash. "I'm glad you did." Forcing herself to her feet, she took a hard and careful look around. She made her way cautiously through the crowded room, careful not to get caught on some piece of machinery. The room's floor was packed clay, and its walls were stacked stone. Heavy wooden beams supported not only the ceiling, but many moving iron parts.

She'd never been inside a gear room before. Several weeks earlier, she had brought her own shelled corn to a similar gristmill owned by a Pomeranian couple, but never left the main floor where the massive millstones did the actual grinding. Now, she took a moment to consider their options. "We can't stay here for too long."

Daniel shrugged. "Where we gonna go from here?"

It was a reasonable question. She glanced at this child. Clearly, it had not occurred to him that she didn't know exactly where she was taking him. In truth, she didn't care a fig about what Gideon thought of her anymore, but she must not fail Daniel. So, don't panic, she thought. Think calmly.

Hanneke was trying to do just that when a sudden commotion drifted down the open staircase. Voices…and one of them sounded familiar. She swallowed hard against a flood of something metallic and bitter on her tongue. The familiar voice belonged to Hiram Aubuchon.

Boots began thumping down the wooden stairs. "…telling you," a new male voice was saying, "there's nobody down here! I haven't left the main floor in hours. I would have seen anybody trying to slip by me."

Hanneke grabbed Daniel's hand and yanked him hard toward the back wall. *Be quick,* she told him with her eyes. The boy leapt to follow without wasting time replying or even nodding.

"They left my man down at the brickyard next door." That was Aubuchon again, and his voice had lost all pretense of civility. A pool of splintered light suggested he was carrying a lantern. "But he did see them come this way. They must be here somewhere."

The men were almost down the stairs now. The machinery provided places to hide, but Hanneke knew Aubuchon well enough to know that— particularly so driven to find them, and especially in this foul mood—he would check every cranny. She grabbed her basket with a pang of remorse, but there was no time to waste on regrets. She threw it from the open access door she'd seen earlier in the back wall. The doorway was intended to allow men inside the mill to service the big water wheel outside. The basket and all of her supplies dropped into the channel directly below. The basket might be found in the morning, but she didn't want Aubuchon to find it in the gear room.

She squared her shoulders. With her pulse pounding in her ears, she climbed out and motioned fiercely for Daniel to follow. She kept going, a now-desultory rain plopping upon her.

Only a narrow ledge of decorative brick led across the back wall, inches from the rotating wheel. The mill's overall design brought water up from the river and shot it over the top of the paddles, causing it to power the massive wheels. The wheel splattered Hanneke with cold water. For a moment, she felt incapable of moving her limbs.

Somehow, she kept from falling into the swift and powerful waters flowing below and behind her. She clung like a limpet, her face against the wall. Reaching out blindly, she connected with Daniel's arm. He was already climbing out to join her on the skinny protuberance, nimble as a spider.

Hanneke forced herself to slide each foot along the decorative ledge, distancing herself from the hatchway and giving Daniel a bit more room. Now what? The gritty brick wall dug into her cheek. Her legs trembled. She willed them to stay still. Darkness had fallen, and she didn't think anyone passing on the river would see the two of them cleaving to their perch. She and Daniel couldn't go back inside until she was sure Aubuchon had moved on, but she couldn't hear anything but splashing water. She was wet and cold and shuddering so hard she feared she would shake herself from the ledge.

There was nothing to do but wait.

* * *

Hanneke didn't know how long they'd been clinging to the brick wall above the river when she became aware of a gentle tug on her skirt. Daniel. She didn't dare turn to look at him.

"Mistress, they be gone," he muttered. "We can go in now."

I'm not sure I can, Hanneke wanted to say. She gritted her teeth instead. Trying to pivot on the ledge seemed a fool's task, so she slowly, *slowly* slid one foot sideways a few inches. When stable, she dragged her second foot after it. After an interminable time of sliding and clinging, she felt the hatch's open space in front of her foot. Daniel, who was already inside, helped her through the opening.

Once within four walls again, Hanneke's knees gave out, and she crouched, flexing and unflexing stiff and clumsy fingers. Daniel crouched too, arms hugged across his shoulders, waiting silently.

The sight of him wet and cold affirmed what she already knew. "We can't stay here," she told him. "Even if the slaver is gone, the miller could come back at any time." The gear room felt like a haven, after being outside, but Hanneke felt a compulsive urge to be *out*.

Climbing back out the side window was harder than diving through had been. With Daniel's assistance, though, Hanneke managed with only one more tear in her skirt. At some point, the rain had stopped. She lifted her head to the heavens, instinctively looking for stars, gulping in the nighttime air, savoring the earth's firm feel beneath the soles of her shoes. "Daniel, could you hear anything while we were out on the ledge?"

"Just bits and pieces." His hitched thin shoulders, trying to hide his shivering. "One of them men be powerful mad, that's all I know. He was yelling by the time they left."

"Did you happen to hear what he was yelling about?"

"Not particular," Daniel said, "but I'm pretty sure he was looking for me. Wants to drag me back to Arkansas, and you to jail for helpin' me." He looked up at her with unblinking eyes. "What we do now?"

"Now," Hanneke told him, "we run."

She led the way as if she knew what she was doing. The skinny boy followed without pause. Their eyes had adjusted to the darkness, so travel was manageable. She kept to the riverbank at first, skirting Watertown proper, with the idea that, if nothing else, they could plunge into the Rock River, grab some bit of flotsam for buoyancy, and let the current carry them beyond Aubuchon's grasp.

Twice, she and Daniel crouched behind some flimsy shelter—a wall of scratchy winterberry, a decrepit chicken coop—when the sound of angry male voices came too close. They're searching for us, Hanneke thought, holding her breath each time until the danger had passed. Levi Cox had seen them race from the brickyard, and he'd been coherent enough to send Aubuchon after them.

Hanneke cut north after they'd finally cleared the industrial district. She and Daniel moved with stealth and she worried that she should have taken the extra time to circumnavigate Watertown proper. There seemed to be too much traffic in the streets. It only feels like the middle of the night, she reminded herself.

Dray wagons, farm wagons, carts, and buggies passed on the street. The young man who served as lamplighter made his rounds, carrying his ladder from post to post so he could light the jets. Foot traffic to *Bieirwirthschafts*—German taverns—and other gathering spots kept them dodging into alleyways and around corners. Once, peeking around a corner, she saw a tall policeman, identified by a shard of lamplight glinting on the tin star pinned on his chest.

Soon, they were in farm country, with plenty of open prairies and dense forests between the clearings. Hanneke knew they weren't any safer in this terrain, but she felt more comfortable here. She was grateful to leave behind streetlamps and noisy taverns and patrolling policemen carrying heavy batons. She didn't want to answer any questions about why she and Daniel were scuttling about together. She didn't want to—once again— bring trouble to Angela's door. Aubuchon was probably keeping an eye on the tavern, anyway. All she could do was keep running, checking over her shoulder every few steps to make sure Daniel was still on her heels.

They made their way along farm lanes and rutted roads, diving into the understory whenever they heard voices or a passing vehicle. But where to go?

Since Gideon had lost consciousness before finishing his instructions, all Hanneke knew to do was head north. The half-moon and towering trees cast shadows of deep blue and gray. The woodland seemed hushed, as if waiting for something to happen. The damp cold made her bones ache.

There were only patches of snow on the ground in shady spots now, and they instinctively avoided those. The earth had refrozen, but mud formed during the recent rain left her fearful of leaving the occasional footprint. Daniel knew to hop from stone to stone when possible, and to walk on compressed piles of leaf litter. Would it be enough to throw off the tracker? She didn't know.

Hanneke stole quick glances skywards, taking comfort in knowing that Fridolin was watching her from somewhere up there. *And*, Celia might, right this moment, be searching for the North Star as well. Presumably, Celia was somewhere east and north of Milton. It was an uplifting thought.

After Hanneke got her bearings, she made sure to detour around her own farm and the Bluewings' sugar camp. Daniel was clearly flagging. She was so exhausted that she was afraid she'd do something truly foolish and give them both away.

We need a spot to rest, Hanneke thought. They weren't too far from the Steckelberg place, so she decided to slip into Clara and Charles' corncrib for a rest break.

It was harder than she'd anticipated, however, to creep along the side of their farm lot like a burglar. It was also hard to see the soft lamplight glowing in the kitchen and know that Clara had no doubt cooked a delicious supper.

The corncrib was a small rectangular building, built on posts that lifted the structure a couple of feet above the earth. Tin pie pans had been affixed upside down to the posts. Both measures were designed to repel rodents. During construction, spaces had deliberately been left between logs to let breezes flow through and keep the corn dry. It was a dubious hiding place, but Daniel didn't complain when she told him they were taking a rest.

Clara had left the corncrib door unlocked, probably because the small building was almost empty. Hanneke felt only a few stray hard kernels beneath her boot soles as she crept inside. A bubble of laughter rose inside her chest. The Steckelbergs had probably been among those who'd recently finished husking and shelling their corn and had taken it to a gristmill for grinding.

The cornmeal was stored elsewhere, but a pile of empty burlap sacks had been tossed in one corner. Hanneke dropped and patted the sacks beside her. "It's better than nothing," she promised Daniel. "But I am sorry that I don't have any food left. It all went out the window with my basket." The zwieback and dried apples she'd wrapped in a towel for the journey hadn't seemed particularly appealing at the time, but envisioning them now made her stomach growl.

"I've gone longer than this without food," Daniel said bravely, but he looked so miserable that Hanneke thought her heart might crack in two.

"Peel off that damp shirt," she told him. "I don't have a needle and thread, but I can fashion something dry for you." She chose a newish-looking bag—silently promising Clara to replace it—and managed to rip holes for Daniel's head and arms in the seams. In the end, the upside-down bag made a voluminous shirt of sorts, the bottom falling to the boy's knees. "At least it isn't wet," she observed, and he nodded. The makeshift shirt didn't seem to bother him.

It suddenly occurred to her that she'd tucked the game piece that William had given her into a pocket instead of her basket. It wasn't much to give this child, but it was better than nothing.

She withdrew it. "I want to give you something." Hanneke handed over the small wooden disk.

Daniel studied it in his palm. "These marks mean something?"

"I don't know," Hanneke confessed. "A Ho-Chunk friend gave it to me. If you ever need help and meet a Ho-Chunk person, this marker will identify you as a friend. And *I* believe it will help protect you on your journey."

She could see that Daniel accepted her words. He rubbed the piece between thumb and finger before securing it in his own pocket. Hanneke wasn't sure where her words about protection on the journey came from, but she didn't regret what she'd said. If they gave Daniel a bit of solace or comfort, all the better.

Hanneke held out one arm. "Would you like to sit by me so we can warm each other up? You can sit on my lap if you'd like."

This time, Daniel didn't hesitate to crawl closer. He's just a child, Hanneke thought, wrapping her arm around him. She felt every rib. He was mature and experienced and capable. But he was just a child.

Her heart ached.

She tipped her head and rested her cheek on the top of his head. His close-cropped hair felt rough against her skin. I'm sorry, she told him silently. I am so, so sorry.

Neither one spoke for a long while. Finally, Hanneke's curiosity overcame all else. "Daniel," she murmured, "might you be willing to tell me why you're running by yourself? Where are your parents?"

He didn't stir. "My daddy be sold off years ago," he told her in a low voice. "I don't even remember him."

"I suspect he remembers enough for both of you." It was the only thing Hanneke could manage.

His shivers had stopped, and he was very still. "My mama was with me when we left. 'We're going on a most perilous journey,' she whispered. 'But in the end, you and me is gonna be free.'"

After a pause, Hanneke asked with trepidation, "What happened to your mama?"

"She done got sick and died. Back in Illinois." His tone was expressionless. "But she made me promise to keep going. Said I was the only one left with a chance." A fierce look came into his eyes. "I *am* gonna find freedom."

Hanneke's eyes burned. A salty lump thickened her throat. "I'm sure your mama is watching your journey. Maybe she's traveling with you yet, even though you can't see her." Hanneke made a small noise, clearing her throat. "The only thing I know for sure is that she's very, very proud of you right now."

Daniel seemed to be thinking that over, but abruptly, he jerked upright in her arms.

Hanneke heard it too: hoofbeats, drumming fast up the lane. They pulled close before stopping. Then came a bellow: "I want the boy!"

It was Hiram Aubuchon.

A cold hand fisted Hanneke's heart. *Mein Gott.* She'd brought them into a corncrib and let this slaver corner them. There was only one door, and Aubuchon could see it from where he stood. The spaces between logs were too narrow for even Daniel to squeeze through. They were trapped—

Halt, a voice in Hanneke's mind commanded. She didn't have time to count mistakes. Aubuchon didn't have his hands on them yet.

"I'm not leaving without the boy!" Aubuchon roared. "Bring him out! *Now!*"

After a minute or two passed, Hanneke heard the house door open and boots step onto the porch. "What's this all about?" Charles sounded as angry as the tracker. "You're not welcome here. We already told you that!"

"I don't care if I'm welcome or not!" Aubuchon retorted. "The law is on my side. I'm hunting a slave boy called Apollo. He ran away from his rightful owner. The owner wants him back."

"We can't give you what we don't have." That was Clara. She must have stepped outside with Charles. "As my husband said, you are not welcome in our house." There came the distinctive sound of a shotgun being cocked.

"Federal law says—"

"But as a good American citizen," Clara continued, speaking clearly, "I will tell you that I saw a light across the road, maybe half an hour ago, where there's no reason for a light to be."

No one outside spoke for a long moment. Daniel trembled in her arms. Hanneke's lungs stopped working. Peeking through a wall gap, she could actually see Aubuchon—no more than a shadow in the night, but she recognized his silhouette, his hat. He was close enough to spit on.

After long deliberation, Aubuchon growled, "I'll go check it out. But if you're lying...." He let the threat hang in the air.

"Slavery is a vile sin against human nature," Charles called sternly, "and against God. You will answer to your Maker!"

Aubuchon muttered what was probably a curse and moved out of Hanneke's sight. A moment later, hoofbeats sounded on the drive again.

There was no time to exhale, much less rejoice. "We must go *now!*"

Hanneke hissed. Clara had sent Aubuchon on a fool's errand, and he wouldn't linger long.

Tempted as she was to explode from the corn crib, she forced herself to crack the door and slide outside with stealth. Daniel was right behind her, clinging to her skirt. Hanneke didn't dare glance toward the house. She prayed Clara didn't see them so she wouldn't have to lie. Had she somehow known that Hanneke was hiding with a runaway in the corncrib? Or had she simply done what she could to confuse and delay Aubuchon? Either way, Clara had given them a chance, and might pay a heavy price for it. Hanneke's eyes burned with gratitude. *Gott segne* Clara, Hanneke thought fervently. God bless Clara.

Keeping to the deepest shadows cast by buildings, Hanneke scurried down one side of the open courtyard formed of farm structures—corncrib, smokehouse, ox barn. She and Daniel held hands as they stumbled along the rutted stubble of the Steckelbergs' hay field. Hanneke's back quivered, every muscle tight, her ears tuned for angry shouts.

"All right, Daniel," she whispered hoarsely when they'd reached the wooded land backing the field. "Let's head north." Without another word, they began to run.

They raced through the forest as if chased by hounds, tripping over roots buried in leaf duff, banging toes on hidden stones, getting scratched on unseen branches. The world dwindled to this blue-black-gray landscape they ran through. I've done this before, she reminded herself. I can do it again.

They ran blindly, skirting farms, until Hanneke no longer recognized her surroundings. She paused to catch her breath, bent over, hands on her knees. They had, she thought, lost Aubuchon.

Or had they? She'd hoped for that when they'd left the gristmill. Instead, he'd chased them to her neighborhood, still on the prowl. Much as she wanted to believe she and Daniel were now safe, in her heart, she knew they were not.

After a few minutes Daniel asked, "You be all right, Mistress?" Evidently much more used to running, his skinny chest was not heaving.

Hanneke forced herself to straighten and speak the truth. "I fear we left a trail that would prove easy to follow." A tracker like Aubuchon could probably follow their trail blindfolded. Especially in the daylight. They had, she judged, hours to pass before the rising sun presented a new problem for them to navigate. Nonetheless, she needed to stop letting panic and fear dictate their journey, and let common sense take charge. The sky was clearing, and Hanneke blessed the stars twinkling overhead. *We're not alone on this journey*, she thought, and felt a tiny bit better.

Daniel was still waiting. For better or worse, he had put his fate in Hanneke's hands.

"It's time to make more effort to cover our tracks," she told him somberly. She hated her own idea, but there appeared to be no help for it. "Let's look for a creek or other waterway."

It took a while to find what she wanted. It was Daniel, bless his heart, who announced the existence of a nearby marsh. "I can smell it," he told her earnestly, and she accepted his word.

They eased through a final fringe of alder, bog birch, dogwood, and willows. Then a pond opened before them, reminding Hanneke of the lake she'd encountered while searching for The Milton House. This one was smaller, though, and weedier.

Perfect.

"In we go," Hanneke murmured, as cheerfully as she could manage. She thought Daniel might protest, but he merely nodded. Taking a deep breath, Hanneke waded in.

The cold water bit at her feet and ankles like fire. She compressed her lips against the whimper trying to escape and took another step. She sank deeper this time, up to her knees in the mucky mix of mud and water. The air smelled fetid, of rotting things. Daniel kept pace with her.

Many plants grew in stands near the pond's edge—bulrushes and cattails mostly, their silhouettes black and clear in the starlight. There were also clumps of pickerelweed, and a scattering of sedges she didn't recognize. That was all right. The bulrushes and cattails were larger, and even in their winter-dead and shriveled states, would provide what was needed.

Daniel's hushed words came clear in the stillness: "Here's a good spot." He'd found a particularly dense group of plants.

Hanneke followed his voice around a thick stand of cattails, lifting her feet carefully and taking time to set each down before moving farther. The icy cold was already gripping her legs like a vice. If she actually fell in this water, she would surely freeze to death.

"Take my hand," Daniel offered, as if wading in a foot of half-frozen mud was something he did every day. Hanneke clutched his calloused hand, and he gently pulled her into the center of a clump of cattails.

"This *is* a good spot," Hanneke told him. She doubted that anyone on shore would be able to see them.

Now, once again, there was nothing to do but wait.

Chapter Twenty

Hiram Aubuchon appeared shortly after dawn.

The morning's first bird chirps had been drifting through the maple trees on shore. Although many of Hanneke's summer avian friends had fled and not yet returned, finches and chickadees provided a reassuring sense of normalcy.

That sense quickly vanished when the birds went silent. Then Aubuchon stepped from the woods. A few red-winged blackbirds flew up from the sedges.

Hanneke would have sworn that she didn't have it in her to react. Her feet and lower legs were blocks of ice. Her body felt wooden. She wasn't sure she'd still be erect if she and Daniel weren't propping up each other. Her brain felt frozen as well, unable to parse information.

Nonetheless, as soon as she heard footfalls in the woods, she prickled alert. "Someone's coming," she told Daniel, the words barely audible. He nodded. She was grateful for his acknowledgement. Somewhere in the lonesome hours, when the stars had begun to fade, she'd started worrying that Daniel would not survive the night. That her choices had been all wrong. That he would pay the ultimate price for her mistakes. That this time, she'd be forced to admit that she had indeed failed.

A second man—not Levi Cox—was with Aubuchon. How many men are on the slaver's payroll? she thought bitterly. Glimpses revealed that this man was small in stature, dressed as a laborer in worn boots, heavy trousers, and a wool coat with the collar turned up.

Aubuchon traced the shoreline in both directions as far as conditions would permit, beating the tall grasses savagely with a long stick. It seemed to Hanneke that as much as searching, he was venting anger. She winced to imagine what he would do to her and Daniel with that stick if he discovered them.

The slave catcher came within several feet of their hiding spot in the reeds. She tried to think about what to do if Aubuchon realized that she and Daniel were almost within arm's reach. *We can't flee deeper into the water,* she thought grimly. *That would surely kill them both—although if given a choice, perhaps Daniel would choose death before going back south as a slave.*

Nein. The best thing they could do was stay hidden in the cattails and hope.

Hanneke could now hear Aubuchon's breath coming in heavy pants and glimpse the black wool of his coat. If he did spot them, would Aubuchon drag them to shore and tie them up? Would he leave his assistant guarding Hanneke and Daniel while he went to fetch an officer of the law? *Lieber Gott,* what if John Barlow were the one sent to get them? She *hated* the possibility that he'd be put in such a position.

She felt Daniel's shoulder twitch beneath her fingers, and realized she was squeezing too hard. He didn't move, though. She didn't either.

After an absolute eternity, the two men finished thrashing the shrubbery and marshland grasses where water and land met. "They're not here," Aubuchon called, clearly frustrated. "Let's go."

When the smaller man turned obediently to follow, Hanneke got her first quick look at his face. She had to bite her lip—hard—to keep from squawking in indignation.

The man helping Hiram Aubuchon search for them was Oscar Muehlhauser, husband of her dear friend Gerda. Oscar Muehlhauser had not hired himself out for odd jobs on someone's farm. Oscar was clearly in Aubuchon's employ.

Did Gerda know what her husband was doing? That was too much for Hanneke to contemplate just then. As she peeked through the foliage, Oscar trudged from the open shoreline and disappeared after Aubuchon, into the forest.

"Wait," Daniel whispered.

They did, until the morning birds returned to their song. Finally, Daniel glanced up at her. She jerked her chin up and down. Staying hidden would no longer help them.

Leaving their dubious refuge, however, was even harder than she'd expected. Her limbs felt as stiff and heavy as oaken planks. She and Daniel held on to each other as they staggered from the clump of cattails. Despite his help, Hanneke lurched in the mud and fell to her knees just inches from dry land. Finally, *finally*, she felt the earth solidify beneath her boots.

She and Daniel collapsed together and indulged in a few moments of rest, right there on the shore. They were wet, though. The air was chilly, and their clothes clung clammily to their skins. Normally, Hanneke would use a towel to gently coax warmth into feet as cold as theirs, but she had to do the best she could with her hands.

"We have to keep moving," Hanneke told him. She believed she'd developed several blisters the day before, and she grieved for her basket and the warm socks she'd thrown away at the mill.

"Where we goin' next?" Daniel's teeth were chattering, and his eyes were dull. His earnest question made it clear that he'd put all of his hope into her trembling hands.

Hanneke didn't know this part of Southern Wisconsin well, and she had no idea if Gideon had visited any safe houses nearby, but she had tried to keep her general bearings by watching the stars. We can't be more than five miles from Clyman's Corners, she thought. John Barlow had said that there were many anti-slavery citizens living in that area. Even better, she had friends there who were definitely committed to ending human bondage. The thought of curling up in Charlotte's tidy barn, safe in a dry stack of hay with perhaps a piece of hearty bread spread with salted duck grease, brought tears to her eyes.

But it was too soon to think of relief. Hanneke stumbled to her feet. "We're going north. We both need food, and to dry out, and to rest."

Hide by day, Celia had said. *Run at night.*

Thank you, my friend, Hanneke thought. She turned to Daniel. "I have an idea of where to look for those things. First, though, we're going to find a spot to hide until the sun sets."

Daniel didn't argue. All I have to do is keep this boy safe, Hanneke reminded herself, and they set out.

* * *

Crouching with one palm against a fence rail for balance, Hanneke eyed the laundry flapping on three clotheslines outside the log farmhouse. Was she truly contemplating thievery?

Ja. She was.

Hanneke had left Daniel about a mile from the marsh. She'd found a decent hiding place where a great fallen log in the midst of a shrubby alder thicket formed a tiny cave of sorts. The boy didn't offer a word of complaint, but he was shuddering with cold and could barely speak when spoken to. They'd passed this farm earlier, and Hanneke had come back in hopes of finding something to eat.

In that, she had failed. She wasn't brave enough to break into the home, although that was probably exactly what Gideon would have done. However, the good wife here had chosen to peg out her laundry, despite the cold. Hanneke was mesmerized by a particular pair of boy's trousers that would likely fit Daniel. And three pieced quilts hung on the line closest to the fence, their geometric shards of color astonishing in the gray and white landscape.

Hanneke had never stolen anything in her life. Just the thought made her feel as if she was crossing an invisible line, and that it would have implications for her soul.

But Daniel is suffering, she argued with herself. He is a malnourished child. The cold could kill him. Stop dithering!

Without giving herself time for further thought, Hanneke grasped the top fence rail with both hands and began to climb, kicking away her skirt when it got in the way. Her legs trembled with fatigue, and hunger was making her light-headed, but once she was moving, she didn't stop. Linen sheets dangling from the farthest clothesline created a partial barrier for anyone glancing out through a window, and she prayed it would be enough. "Forgive me," she whispered to the occupants. "I'm trying to save a child. I *will* provide recompense. I promise."

She first snatched the trousers, which were made of thick wool and only showed one patch. Half a dozen work shirts hung nearby, and she took one of those as well. Then she grabbed the most faded quilt—a star pattern done in brown and yellow calicoes—and threw everything over the fence. She heaved herself over and fell upon landing but was on her feet immediately. Clutching the laundry against her chest, she ran in the direction from which she had come.

The pants and quilt were chilled, but dry. Her reward came when Daniel shed his wet trousers and makeshift corn sack shirt. When he wriggled into his new clothes, each was a little too big for him, but he obviously didn't care. "Thanks," he mumbled. Then he curled up in the quilt and went to sleep.

Hanneke claimed a corner of the quilt and settled down as well. She thought about the next leg of the journey, which would commence when the sun set. She thought about Oscar Muehlhauser working for Hiram Aubuchon, and how much good the money earned had done Gerda—whether she knew where it came from or not. Hanneke wondered where Oscar and Aubuchon were, right this moment.

She wondered if Gideon had recovered or died in the Bluewings' wigwam. Then, like Daniel, Hanneke closed her eyes and slept.

* * *

Hanneke slumbered fitfully, dreaming of opening her eyes to find Hiram Aubuchon staring down at her and Daniel. She jerked awake for good when a talkative gray squirrel skittered over their sheltering log. It took a moment to understand where she was, and with whom. The sun was setting, and here in the woods, the world was already turning azure and cobalt, ash and iron. The woods were so quiet that the gurgling and rumbling sounds from her stomach seemed especially loud. She felt groggy and had developed a headache.

There was nothing for it but to find assistance. "Time to get moving," she murmured, gently shaking Daniel's shoulder. "We're going to a community where I think people will want to help us."

They stumbled into the night, heading for Clyman's Corners. Hanneke took roads to make walking easier. This was farm country, and largely quiet, so they only had to dive for cover a few times.

Hanneke aimed for the Stofeldts' place. Berta and Erna Pohl had been welcoming as well, and had spoken vehemently against the evils of slavery, but Hanneke knew Charlotte best. More importantly, Charlotte's place was closest.

When the housebarn appeared from the darkness at the top of their drive, Hanneke's knees went custardy with relief. The massive building gave the impression of safety and stability. All we need is a bite of food and a decent place to rest, Hanneke thought. Then, she could figure out what to do. Maybe Charlotte could even advise her on where to take Daniel next.

The living space was largely dark, but when Hanneke crept around the side of the housebarn, pulling Daniel with her, she did spot a soft glow at the main room window. "Go hide, but not too far," she whispered. The boy silently disappeared.

Hanneke tiptoed closer, dodged several barren planters waiting for spring, and almost tripped over a child-sized sled that had been left against the wall near the door. Trudging up the steps felt like a monumental task. A rising wind whistled around the eaves and made the bare tree branches bob and dance. She hopefully glanced heavenwards but sailing clouds had covered most of the sky. Her knock sounded blasphemously loud in the silence.

No one came for so long that Hanneke feared there would be no response. Then, a curtain, at the near window, moved before dropping back into place. The door opened a crack, and Charlotte's pale face appeared. She carried a glass-paned lantern, and still wore a plaid work dress.

Her eyes grew wide. "Hanneke?" she gasped. "Whatever are you doing here? Come in, come in." She held the lantern high, her face puckered with concern. She'd already uncoiled her hair for the night, and the loose strands hung almost to her waist. "Why…are you all right, my dear?"

"*Nein.*" Hanneke allowed herself to be pulled inside. Beyond Charlotte, shadows cloaked the main room. She heard faint, rhythmic breathing from the depths.

"Beatta and Henni are asleep," Charlotte whispered. "Now, whatever happened? What do you need?"

"I need help. Something to eat and a dry corner of your barn."

A confused frown formed on Charlotte's face. "A dry corner of my barn…?"

"I'm traveling north with a companion." Hanneke chose her words carefully and gave her abolitionist friend an intense look.

Understanding crept into Charlotte's eyes. Her jaw hardened. "*Nein.*"

Charlotte must have misunderstood, Hanneke thought. "*Ja.* I wouldn't have stopped if we weren't exhausted and half-frozen and very hungry."

"You can't stay here."

Hanneke's brain didn't accept what she was hearing. "Just for a day or so. We don't need to come inside your home."

"*Nein.*" Charlotte took a step backwards, deeper into the shadows. "Helping you would be against the law!"

Hanneke blinked at her friend. Charlotte may not be an active shepherd on the Underground Railroad, but she loathed slavery. She was a staunch abolitionist who rallied her friends and neighbors to work for the cause. Hanneke had believed they were friends. "Please, Charlotte. I'm *begging* you." Hanneke heard her voice tremble and simply couldn't help it. "It's a child I have with me. He's suffering."

"*Nein!*" Charlotte put the lantern down and crossed her arms. "I am an honorable, law-abiding woman. I once broke German law. Although I truly believe I had no choice, I live with that knowledge every day." The muscles in her jaw tightened. "My family and I have a good life here. I simply will not risk everything by breaking American law. I won't turn you in, but you *must* go somewhere else."

Hanneke wanted to argue. To help Charlotte realize how desperately she needed assistance in this moment. That a life was at stake—maybe two. That

Daniel was a helpless child who'd known nothing but brutality and grief in his short life, but was resolved to do what it took to find freedom or die trying.

Hanneke clamped her lips tight to hold in the beseeching words rising from her tongue. Clearly, Charlotte had made up her mind. "Please leave my property at once," she muttered.

Then she stepped deliberately around Hanneke and opened the door again. Hanneke left slowly and with head held high, unwilling to scuttle away. A gust of wind hit her as she walked onto the top step. She felt ready to cry. If Daniel hadn't been waiting for her, she would have.

She swayed on her feet for a moment, composed herself again. *Surely* Charlotte would at least allow her and her charge to get a sip of water. She turned and dared try. "If we could just use the pump—"

"I asked you to go!" Charlotte hissed, stepping outside and closing the door behind her. "What on earth were you thinking, Hanneke? My *children* are inside." She put a firm hand on Hanneke's upper arm, as if to escort her.

Hanneke wrenched her arm away. Somehow, in the fluster, her foot partially missed the next step. She fell to one knee on the ground, hard. Pain shot through her leg like a dagger. Worst of all, her left cheek slammed into one of Charlotte's big blue flowerpots. Pain exploded in her face. For a few seconds, she feared she would pass out.

"Hanneke!" Charlotte cried. She raised the lantern again, shining more light on the steps.

Hanneke couldn't answer right away. Tentatively, she tried bending her leg. Nothing appeared to be broken, *Gott sei dank*. Her mind overflowed with the surprise of falling, the sharp pain, the worry for Daniel, and her inability to find a decent solution for his needs.

Then, another thought managed to briefly push those things aside. Later, she would marvel that at that terribly low moment, a disparate but cogent thought suddenly crystallized with complete clarity in her mind. But in that second, Hanneke saw what she hadn't been looking for. Hadn't even been thinking about.

Her fuzzy brain tried to make sense of the possibility. *Es kann nicht sein,* she thought. It can't be possible.

Can it?

She staggered to her feet. Charlotte had frozen with her mouth in a perfect O of distress.

Before she could summon her common sense, Hanneke hoarsely demanded, "Charlotte, what did you do?"

The other woman seemed incapable of responding.

Turning her back on Charlotte, Hanneke limped away.

* * *

Daniel's voice was low. "The woman won't help?"

"No, she won't." Hanneke squeezed his shoulder. "We'll try a different place."

She'd had no trouble finding him in the woods, close to the road near the Stofeldt housebarn. She hadn't walked a quarter mile when she heard a whip-poor-will call twice. Although it wasn't an unusual night sound, the birds who'd nested near Safe Haven Farm had not yet returned for the summer. Following the sound, it wasn't long before she heard the call again, and then almost inaudible calls: "Mistress! Mistress! Here I am."

Hanneke put a hand on his shoulder, already trying to decide their next move. Erna's and Berta's house wasn't too far away…but Hanneke was now suspicious that the Pohl sisters would give her the same response that Charlotte had. Besides, their brother was an unknown. The chance seemed too great to take. She'd met no one else.

Glancing up, this time she spotted the North Star, seemingly darting in and out of racing clouds in the night sky. *I suppose,* she thought, *we can just keep walking north.* She didn't like that idea, but it was better than no idea at all. How far away was the Canadian border? She didn't know. Hanneke thought she'd read somewhere that one of the Great Lakes stood between Wisconsin and Canada, which complicated the situation, but she'd confront that obstacle when they got there. Or…perhaps she should head east to Milwaukee and try to find a sympathetic steamer captain who would let Daniel hide on his boat while he traveled north.

Daniel's fingers dug into her arm. He pointed with his other hand. A spot of light had appeared among the skeletal black branches. Someone was driving a wagon along the road, coming from the east. A lantern hung near the seat, casting a soft glow of light but keeping the driver in shadows. Hanneke could just make out the silhouette of a top hat. Presumably a man, then. It was nighttime, but early enough that it wasn't shocking to see someone finishing their errands for the day.

He seemed to be driving very slowly. Too slowly, actually. Hanneke's tired muscles went rigid. Her tongue turned to parchment. Why was the man creeping along? Was the driver searching the underbrush beside the road? What was he looking for? *Who* was he looking for? Was he coming for them?

Daniel turned silently and gazed up at her. His eyes looked huge. He seemed to be waiting for Hanneke to tell him what to do.

Hanneke tried to think. If they moved now, deeper into the woods, the man would likely spot them. If they did *not* move from their spot, the same might be true. Fear nibbled mouse-like at her belly. Her breath quickened. She felt a chill in the marrow of her bones that had nothing to do with the temperature.

She did not know what to do.

The driver was drawing nearer. He would pass very close by their thicket. Daniel's head was bowed. Hanneke held her breath.

Then she heard her name, little more than a whisper. "Frau Bauer? Frau Bauer?"

Hanneke couldn't think of any good reason someone would be calling her name here on the outskirts of Clyman's Corners. She feared a trap.

"Frau Bauer?" Low and soft, the words came clear.

Hanneke clenched her teeth. It appeared that this wagon driver was alone. Her right hand moved slightly, slowly, among the leaf duff where she crouched. She had brained Levi Cox with a broken brick. She'd fight this man if she had to, but a weapon—a stone, perhaps—would help a great deal. She clenched her teeth when her fingers found nothing helpful. It was too late for a wider search.

The wagon pulled alongside. "Frau Bauer?"

It did not sound like Hiram Aubuchon's voice, but she didn't recognize it either. Hanneke saw four equine legs plod past the shrub that cloaked them. Through the leaves, the wagon seat came into sight. She still couldn't see the driver, only one dark boot.

"Frau Bauer?"

Daniel started to quake. Hanneke's heart tried to climb up her throat, and she tasted something bitter. Was she about to fail…again?

Chapter Twenty-One

The single lantern hanging from the stranger's wagon cast only a pool of pale-yellow light as the vehicle passed. Before it disappeared, Hanneke got a glimpse of the last three dark letters visible on the side. "...t-r-y," had been painted in a yellow oval on the side of a pale blue wagon. She had the sense that she'd seen it before, but it took her a moment to place it.

Then she remembered. What she'd glimpsed was part of "Felix Pohl, Fine Carpentry."

Hanneke shot to her feet. Daniel tried to grab her hand, but she strode forward to meet the man. "Herr Pohl, *da ich bin,*" she croaked. It is me. She knew she was taking an enormous risk, but every instinct told her that if she and Daniel didn't get help—soon—the consequences could be dire. Felix Pohl seemed her best chance of getting assistance.

The wagon stopped at once, and she sensed him climbing to the ground. "Frau Bauer?"

"*Ja.*"

"Oh, *Gott sei dank.* I've been searching and *searching* for you." The bushy-bearded man made as if to reach for her arm.

Hanneke stepped sideways, out of his grasp. "Why have you been searching for me?"

"I've come to take the boy to safety!" The man rapidly looked over both shoulders at the dark road. "I trust he's still with you? Fetch him, quickly! He can hide in my wagon."

The words were welcome. Still, Hanneke couldn't let go of her wariness.

"Who sent you?"

"Gideon."

Hanneke's mouth opened. The last she'd known, Gideon was lying unconscious in a Ho-Chunk camp on her property. "How—" she began but stopped herself. Explanations would have to come later.

In short order, Daniel had joined them at the wagon. "This man is going to take us to the next safe place," Hanneke whispered. He nodded.

Several pieces of heavy furniture had already been loaded into the wagon. One was a heavy German-style *Schrank*, lying on its back. The tall wardrobe had double doors and gleaming hardware. Felix climbed into the wagon bed, opened one of the Schrank's doors, and jerked his chin in Daniel's direction.

The boy didn't need encouragement. He scrambled to the wagon bed, scurried between pieces of furniture, and slid into the *Schrank's* open space. The quilt Hanneke had given him—stolen for him, really—was still wrapped around his shoulders. She was glad he had that small comfort in his wooden box.

Felix Pohl looked at her. "Frau Bauer, I can't just leave you standing here. Climb up to the seat. If anyone asks, you're simply keeping me company on my delivery run."

And thus it ever is, Hanneke thought sardonically, but she also didn't feel like walking home alone in the dark. It took every ounce of energy she had left to heave herself up to the seat. Part of her wished she could climb into a huge *Schrank* with a quilt herself and go to sleep.

As soon as Hanneke and Daniel were in their places, Felix Pohl picked up the lines again. After performing a tight turn in the lane, they drove on. He did not tell Hanneke where they were going. She did not ask.

They passed through Clyman's Corners. The hamlet was dark and quiet, but Hanneke recognized it from her earlier visit. She was startled when Felix Pohl made an unexpected turn, and it took her a moment to realize that he was detouring to avoid driving past his own house, where Erna or Berta might be glancing out the window. Perhaps he was trying to protect them. Perhaps they did not know about Felix's secret efforts.

In a moment, they turned again. North this time, which was reassuring.

They left the tiny village behind and drove on into terrain not too dissimilar to what she knew—a few farms, open prairies and solitary bur oaks, marshland, stands of leafless hardwoods. Hanneke gripped the wagon bench tight with one hand so she wouldn't fall asleep.

Perhaps an hour later, Herr Pohl eased the horse and wagon into and down a long farm drive. A fortunate family lives here, Hanneke thought. Everything was neat—no banging shutters, no agricultural clutter in the yard. The Greek Revival-style farmhouse was painted white with green shutters. There were two outhouses, half a dozen outbuildings, and a high and sturdy fence around the dormant vegetable garden.

Felix Pohl parked near the stable. "Stay here," he muttered, as a shadowed figure slipped from the door. He was waiting for us, Hanneke thought. She'd stopped trying to figure out how this was all coming to be.

After a brief whispered conversation and firm handshake, the two men parted again. The shadowed figure disappeared back into the stable. Herr Pohl walked to the wagon, reached inside, and managed to open the *Schrank*. Hanneke couldn't hear what he murmured, but he helped Daniel climb from the wardrobe before lifting the boy to the ground beside him. Then, with a hand on Daniel's shoulder, Herr Pohl guided him into the dark barn.

Hanneke had turned on the seat to watch, and an alarm bell rang in her brain. "Wait!" Her voice was raspy.

There was already no one to hear. Before she could gather her wits, Felix Pohl returned to the wagon and climbed to the seat. *"Aufstehen!"* he called in a low tone, flicking the leather lines. In response, the horse moved forward, and the wagon began to rumble slowly back up the drive toward the main lane.

"Where is the boy?" Hanneke hissed frantically. "Please, wait! *Halt!*"

"The boy is being taken care of," Herr Pohl muttered, without slowing the wagon. "He'll be transported to his next stop."

Hanneke wanted to protest further. She wanted to insist that she and Daniel both needed a few minutes to absorb this astonishing turn of events. She wanted to yell that she hadn't even had a chance to say goodbye.

She was, however, learning a bit about this business. After swallowing her own sputters of dismay, the best she could do was say, "He needs food."

"He'll get it."

"And someone needs to check his toes for signs of frostbite."

"It will be taken care of."

Hanneke's heart felt like a smoldering lump of coal. Grateful as she was for receiving help, and for getting Daniel back on the Underground Railroad, everything had happened too fast. She'd come to care for him, but she hadn't been given a chance to share a few last words and wish him well.

When he finally spoke, Herr Pohl's voice was no louder than a dried corn husk whispering in the wind. "It has to be this way. Safest for everyone, you know."

Hanneke sighed heavily, blinking away hot tears. "*Ja.* I know."

Then, for some reason, an image of the Ho-Chunk game piece she'd given to Daniel popped into her mind. He does have something from me, Hanneke thought. And from William Bluewing as well. That knowledge did not compensate for Daniel's hasty transfer, but it helped a little.

They didn't speak again until they were halfway back to Clyman's Corners. "Where do you live?" Herr Pohl asked. "I'll drive you home."

Hanneke started to tell him, then stopped. "Please take me to the home of Deputy John Barlow, who lives near me. I have to talk to him."

Herr Pohl cast her a glance. Even in the gloom, his apprehension was apparent. "That's a very bad idea."

"What?" His response startled Hanneke from her slump. It took her a moment to realize that he'd mistaken her intent. "*Nein, nein.* I won't tell him about any of—of this." She waved a vague hand. "Believe it or not, I need to speak to the deputy about something else entirely."

* * *

Hanneke hunched deeper inside her cloak on the drive to Deputy John Barlow's farm. By the time they finally reached the lane that led to the Barlow drive, she had to clear her throat before murmuring, "Just leave me here. We're very close."

Felix Pohl did as she asked. He didn't speak, but he did take Hanneke's hand for a moment. She pressed his fingers, trying to convey her gratitude. Then she clambered from the seat and walked down the dark, silent lane.

She was afraid she might find the house closed up for the night. To her immense relief, light from an oil lamp still glowed in a sitting room window. It must not be as late as she had feared.

She knocked softly when she reached the Barlow door. After a moment, John opened it with the lamp in one hand. His eyes went wide with obvious shock. *"Guter Gott!* Hanneke, what on earth happened to you?"

Hanneke was so thankful to see Deputy John Barlow that she couldn't find words. Her muscles softened with relief. The left side of her face still pulsed with pain, though, and swelling was making it increasingly difficult to see out of that eye. She expected that bruises were beginning to appear. Probably horrific ones. I must look like a street brawler, she thought, but there was nothing for it.

John seemed to move beyond his astonishment, for he opened the door wide. "Please, come in. Ulricke has already gone to bed, but we can talk in the parlor. Shall I go for Dr. Rausch?"

She accepted the invitation to come inside but told him there was no need to fetch the doctor. "I just need some food and rest."

He walked out of the room. He still wore his boots, but he walked silently across the hardwood floors. He probably doesn't want to disturb Ulricke, Hanneke thought, with her usual selfish and shameful pang of envy. Fridolin likely would have done the same thing for her.

John returned with a cup of water and two slices of heavy rye bread, speckled with dark seeds and spread liberally with honey. Hanneke took one bite and almost groaned with pleasure.

He watched her eat before saying, "We thought you might be dead, you know."

"What? Why?"

"Because your basket was found floating in the millrace. The miller called for a lawman, and it happened to be me." John Barlow leaned forward, forearms on his legs. "I recognized it. The poor man was beside himself. He claimed that 'whatever lady' had lost it must certainly be dead because no one could survive such a fall." One corner of his mouth quirked slightly. "I didn't assume that was true, actually. Nevertheless, I'm very glad to see you. Battered as you are. I'm afraid that some of the local citizens have decided that the unknown lady, after being jilted in love, so despaired of her future that she took her own life."

"Gracious," Hanneke said weakly. The idea of her basket being found, and becoming a point of such speculation, hadn't crossed her mind.

"Now. Tell me what happened to you." He seemed to have a second thought, and held up a palm. "Or do I not want to know?"

"You do not want to know."

He frowned at her. "*Hanneke—*"

"It's my problem." She held up her own palm, not in the mood for a scolding. "But please, listen to me. I think I might know who killed Asa Hawkins."

Barlow was silent for a long moment. Then he folded his arms and leaned back in his chair. "Go on."

"You remember Charlotte Stofeldt, *ja?* We've become friendly since you first sent me there. I was at her housebarn this evening, and I tripped and fell on the front steps when leaving. It wasn't pretty," she gestured toward her face, "but it did bring me in contact with one of the large ceramic flowerpots Charlotte keeps near the front door."

The deputy raised both eyebrows, clearly unimpressed. "I'm very sorry that happened, but—"

"It looked black at night, but I remember seeing it in daylight. It's actually dark blue. As close as I recall, it was a very similar shade to that chip of glazed porcelain that Dr. Rausch found in Hawkins' hair."

Barlow did her the respect of thinking that statement over, but then shook his head. "That seems extremely unlikely."

Hanneke scooched her chair closer to the fire. She'd thought about this all the way home with Felix Pohl, and she still wasn't exactly sure what to tell John. He needed to know enough to believe her, but not enough to put his standing as a deputy sheriff in jeopardy.

Finally, she drew in a slow breath and released it again. "You already know that Asa Hawkins was occasionally using his freight business to help runaways. I think it's possible that on the day he died, he was looking for a safe spot where his cargo could hide. That would have been the person I mentioned, who was with Hawkins when he died."

"I remember what you told me before." John nodded.

"Things hadn't gone as planned that day, so perhaps he was desperate. Hiram Aubuchon and his men were already causing trouble in the area." She hesitated. "I believe that one of them is Levi Cox."

John's face tightened, but all he said was, "When Aubuchon came to Watertown, he brought Cox and another man with him. That third man seems to have disappeared."

That's because Gideon killed him on the road near Milton, Hanneke thought. She fought to keep her face still and inexpressive.

John gazed at her with narrowed eyes, rubbing his chin, before motioning for her to continue.

"You said yourself that the whole area around Clyman's Corners is heavily anti-slavery. Charlotte Stofeldt is an avowed abolitionist." Hanneke rubbed her palms on her thighs, still trying to get warm. "If Asa Hawkins found himself in that general area and needed a place to hide his cargo—the woman I told you about—it's not unreasonable to imagine him talking to Charlotte." I drew the same conclusion, she added silently. I thought she would be willing to provide assistance.

He shook his head. "Of all people, why would Hawkins pick out Charlotte Stofeldt to ask for help?"

"We'll never understand for sure," Hanneke conceded, "but he might have known that Charlotte had strong opinions that seemed to support what he was doing. She's written to politicians and composed editorials for the local and state newspapers. Hawkins would surely know who she was." Hanneke re-pinned her shawl, wishing she had knitting to occupy her hands. When things calmed down, she would ask John if he'd kept her recovered basket, and if her favorite knitting needles were still inside. "I have reason to know that although Charlotte is a vocal abolitionist, she *only* wants to change the law. Having done what she did in the Old Country, she is...." Hanneke paused as she searched for an appropriate word. "Charlotte is vehemently opposed to breaking the current law and helping any runaway. Terrified, actually."

John stood up and began prowling the quiet room. "Even if that's all true, are you really suggesting that she struck Hawkins hard enough to kill him, just because he asked for aid?"

Hanneke was still painting a possible picture. "Not on purpose, I don't think. However, based on my own experience...I think it's plausible that she was the person Hawkins argued with that night. Celia said Hawkins was furious, remember?" Hanneke bit her lower lip for a moment, imagining the scene. "Hawkins was always brusque at best. Appallingly rude at worst. It's entirely possible that Charlotte turned Hawkins away, perhaps even giving him a little push for emphasis. Hawkins easily could have tripped in the same place I did and knocked his head on the planter."

"And he didn't die right away," John mused. He was still pacing back and forth.

"I don't know anything for sure. I do think, however, that when the sun is up tomorrow, you should take the porcelain chip Dr. Rausch gave you up to the Stofeldt place. Look to see if a matching chip is missing from the blue pot on the left. Talk with Charlotte and see what she says."

"Frau Stofeldt will know that you were the one to give me this tip," John observed. "She has a great deal to lose. Aren't you worried that she might retaliate?"

"I'll take care," Hanneke promised. She'd given the matter a lot of thought herself. Honestly, though, she didn't think Charlotte would actually come after her. *That* could quickly get her into exactly the kind of legal trouble that she feared.

John frowned at her. "Based on what you're saying, and what you're implying, it's a delicate situation."

"I'm very sorry." He'd helped her before, but Hanneke truly didn't want him to end up in a compromising position.

"I'll have to think about how I want to handle this." John Barlow's mouth was twisted sideways in vexation. "Including the right words to use with Jerome Hawkins."

Hanneke expected him to say more—a lot more—but he did not. Instead, he said, "I think it would be a good idea if you spent the night here. Ulricke can provide company in the morning."

It was an incredibly gracious suggestion. Hanneke was both tempted and touched by the gruff man's kindness. Without much thought, though, she declined. She wanted to talk with Gideon, but she didn't know where he was. That left her only one option.

"I'll be all right," she assured John. "All I want to do right now is go home.

Chapter Twenty-Two

The next day was gray. Dark, low-hanging clouds frowned at Safe Haven Farm all morning. Hanneke avoided heavy labor and was grateful for her long-sleeved green-and-brown work dress. It was loose and comfortable, easy to put on. She was ready for company by the time John Barlow rode into her yard on his black Morgan about noon. She had been expecting him.

The night before, John had actually asked Hanneke if she wanted to accompany him to the Stofeldt place. She'd said no. "Probably for the best," he'd said. "What you need now is time to recover."

"*Ja.*" Although that was true, Hanneke didn't tell him that she didn't have the heart to face Charlotte Stofeldt right now. Intellectually, Hanneke understood Charlotte's fears. She had the right to make her own decisions, and she should not be judged harshly for obeying the law. But on a deeper level...Hanneke couldn't help feeling that Charlotte had betrayed her when she was most desperate for a bit—just a bit—of compassion.

Heaven help me, Hanneke thought. This business had turned her into someone she didn't recognize.

After their conversation the night before, John Barlow had driven her home to Safe Haven Farm. He checked on her stock but reported that they'd recently been fed and watered and provided with clean pens. "William," Hanneke murmured, almost speechless with gratitude.

The deputy also insisted on checking Hanneke's window and door locks. She did not object. Hiram Aubuchon had more reason than ever to despise her. And if Levi Cox had survived the head blow she'd dealt him in the brickyard, he had personal reason to come after her.

Since she'd been sleeping in thickets lately, her cold and empty house didn't seem so bad. After a quick meal of applesauce, more bread, and coffee, she had gone to bed and dropped into a heavy sleep.

Now, she met John at the back door and invited him inside. "I've got coffee on," she said.

"What you have is an impressive black eye," John observed. "Hanneke, I do try not to mind your business, but you simply can *not* do—whatever you did—again."

And you simply can *not* tell me what I may or may not do, Hanneke thought, but she withheld the acerbic reply. Instead, she brought the steaming coffee pot, toast spread lightly with lard, and her last bowl of preserved currants to the table. Utensils, plates, and cups were already in place. "I'm waiting to hear what Charlotte had to tell you."

John sighed and scrubbed his face with his palms before sliding into his usual chair. "Well, you were right."

Hanneke paused for a moment, taking that in. "That news brings me no happiness." She had wondered, perhaps even suspected…but hearing it from John Barlow made it real. "So. Charlotte Stofeldt killed Asa Hawkins?"

"Indirectly." John reached for a piece of toast and set it on his plate. "Evidently, Hawkins appeared unexpectedly to—to ask a favor she did not wish to grant." He gave Hanneke a sardonic look, and she was quite sure that Deputy John Barlow knew exactly what the argument between Hawkins and Charlotte had been about. "She swears his head injury was an accident. That Hawkins tripped and fell when he was leaving, just as you did. He hit his head on that big flowerpot. Frau Stofeldt said she thought he was well enough when he left her farm."

Hanneke thought that over. They needed real evidence instead of memories. "Did you find a damaged spot that matches the chip that Dr. Rausch found in Hawkins' hair?"

"I did."

Hanneke sat down and poured herself a cup of coffee. "That scenario matches what Celia told me," she mused over the rim of her mug. "Are you going to charge Charlotte?"

"I'm still thinking about that," John admitted. "She should have come forward and shared what she knew. Instead, she withheld that information, which created extra work and worry for us. But if her tale is to be believed—and I think I do believe it—there was no intent to harm Hawkins."

I don't know, Hanneke thought. She remembered the feel of Charlotte trying to hold her arm on the steps. It was not beyond imagination to think that Charlotte might have grabbed or even pushed at Hawkins.

There was, however, no way to prove that. No way to ever truly know. And Hawkins had been a big man. Intimidating. It was not surprising that Charlotte had reacted poorly to Hawkins showing up one night on her front step while her husband was away—especially when what he wanted violated her convictions. Charlotte Stofeldt had a lot to lose if caught breaking the Fugitive Slave Act.

John looked at Hanneke glumly. "You've pushed me into a dilemma, you know."

"I know." Hanneke was glad she didn't have to decide if and how Charlotte Stofeldt would be punished.

* * *

"Frau Bauer! *Frau Bauer!*"

Hanneke looked up from the chickens she was gingerly feeding and saw Jacobine Ketzler running across the yard. The young woman was waving excitedly with one hand and clutching up her skirts with the other. William, moving at a more normal pace, appeared a moment later.

Jacobine skidded to a stop when she got close. "Frau *Bauer!*" she gasped in a more alarmed tone. "Are you all right? Did someone hit you?"

"*Nein,*" Hanneke said quickly, wondering just how awful she looked. "I took a bad fall. It looks worse than it actually is, I assure you." Jacobine looked ready to launch more questions, so Hanneke asked one of her own. "What has you so excited today?" William had caught up, and they exchanged a meaningful glance over the girl's shoulder. He offered a tiny, reassuring nod: *All is well.*

Jacobine's smile returned. "We came to invite you to our wedding!"

Hanneke clutched Jacobine's shoulders. "Your *wedding*?" That was the best news Hanneke had heard in a long time.

Jacobine was practically bouncing on her toes. *"Ja!* We finally convinced *Mutti* that it doesn't make sense to wait. We're going to get married as soon as we can figure out a plan."

"Congratulations to you both," Hanneke declared, beaming at both young people.

Jacobine was dressed in a simple, and worn, gray work dress. Her lightly freckled face emanated happiness and resolve. She'd never looked more beautiful.

William spoke up. "Thank you, Frau Bauer. Your support means a lot."

"I don't think we'll be able to marry in our own church," Jacobine added, and lost a bit of her glow.

Hanneke fought down her own sadness. "I believe you'll find a way," she told Jacobine consolingly.

Jacobine, however, didn't seem to need consoling. She'd clearly already prepared herself for community objections. "We will," she affirmed. "And, of course, we want you to come."

"Oh, *Liebchen!*" With a clatter, Hanneke dropped the pan of seeds and corn she'd been sprinkling on the ground for her mixed flock so she could embrace Jacobine. The birds got extra noisy, flustered by the largesse. "I'm very happy for you both."

She glanced at William. He managed to grin and also to look sober at the same time. "I will do everything in my power to take good care of Jacobine for the rest of her life," he promised.

Hanneke couldn't ask for more. "And I'm quite sure Jacobine will do the same for you." Both of the young people were gaining a fine spouse. Their skill sets were very different, but that would make them a good team.

"Mama said she'd make me a new dress," Jacobine confided. "That will be lovely, but I told her that it must be something practical."

Hanneke held her at arm's length. "May I knit some lace for your special day? I think you need a lace collar and some cuffs, all easily removed." And a lace shawl, she was thinking. Of course, she would gift Jacobine a lace shawl.

"That would be lovely!" A distant look came into Jacobine's eyes as she imagined the possibilities. "*Danke*, Frau Bauer."

"Do you remember where I keep my collection of samples in the workroom? Why don't you go on inside and start choosing some favorites? We'll be right along."

When the young woman had disappeared, Hanneke turned to William and said in a low voice, "I'm extremely grateful that you tended my animals while I was away."

"Are you truly all right? I've been terribly worried."

"I'll be fine," Hanneke assured him, then leaned closer. "Does Jacobine know what I was doing?"

William shook his head. "Of course not." He was dressed in Yankee clothes today and looked like a sober young businessman. "I hate keeping secrets, but...."

"I know exactly how you feel," Hanneke murmured. "It's awful, but it is for the best. For Jacobine's safety as well as ours." It was good advice, but she felt uncomfortable giving it. *It's for the best.* Isn't that what everyone had—to her annoyance—told her?

Wanting to change the subject, she stooped to pick up her pan, shooing away excited Rhode Island Reds, German Leghorns, and Plymouth Rocks. "How has your guest fared since I was there?"

"Not fully recovered but doing much better. His fever has broken, and he's up and around. Perhaps you could check on him. We're staying at the sugar camp until my mother comes home, but Claudette and I will be visiting with Frau Ketzler and staying for dinner."

"I'll go this afternoon," Hanneke promised, trying to sound nonchalant. The truth was, she wanted to see for herself that Gideon Sparrow had improved.

* * *

When Hanneke entered the Bluewings' sugar camp clearing that afternoon, Gideon was approaching from the opposite direction, carrying a pail of water. He stopped moving when he saw her. Something she didn't recognize crossed his face. He put down the pail by the wigwam and slowly came to greet her.

"So," Hanneke said. "You're doing better."

"Much." Gideon was studying the bruises on her face. Muscles worked in his jaw.

His scrutiny made her uncomfortable. "I'm not seriously hurt. The bruises will go away."

He jerked his head toward the outside fire, under the shelter. "Let's sit."

The afternoon was just a promise of spring, and it felt good to settle on a log near the fire. The camp was peaceful. A few more songbirds chirped from the trees, and an occasional squirrel or chipmunk skittered across the open ground. A light breeze nipped at Hanneke's cloak, and the air smelled of woodsmoke and dank earth.

Gideon sat next to her. "Tell me what happened."

As concisely as possible, Hanneke did.

Gideon threw a log on the fire, sending a cascade of sparks arcing from the burning logs. Then he sat in silence for several long moments, as if considering what she'd told him. Hanneke stared at the flames, unwilling to say any more. If he told her again that she'd failed, she decided, she would get to her feet and go home. After she gave him a jagged piece of her mind.

Finally, he said, "I should never have asked you to go find the boy."

"I managed," Hanneke said curtly. "Besides, there was no one else."

Gideon picked up a hunk of wood from a saddlebag that had been left near his seat. He also pulled out his carving knife. She could see he was making a little man astride a horse, perhaps to give Claudette. He nodded his head. "It was a difficult situation. Still. I wish I had not—"

"I *managed*," Hanneke repeated.

Gideon took a heavy swipe with his knife. Then he stared at the ground for several moments. Finally, he said, "You did extremely well in a tough situation."

That observation was so astonishing that Hanneke almost fell from her log. It was more than tough, part of her wanted to say. *Daniel and I were cold and tired and hungry, and Aubuchon and Cox were after us, and I was terrified every single minute.*

At the same time, though, she realized that Gideon's rare praise had eased a certain weight from her shoulders. His earlier criticism had frayed the core of her confidence. Now, evidently, she had managed to redeem herself in his eyes.

Angela's voice spoke in her memory: *Why are you letting one comment from someone you hardly know affect your self-esteem to such an extent?*

Once again, Hanneke shoved the question aside. She felt emotional. Covering her confusion, she pulled out her knitting and busied her hands. "It was very challenging," she allowed, keeping her gaze on the stitches. She was proud that her voice remained steady. "I didn't know where to take the boy." She darted a quick sideways glance at Gideon. "But you somehow got word to the shepherd in Clyman's Corners...?"

Gideon nodded. "After gaining my sensibilities—" He tightened his jaw for a moment, apparently angry that he'd lost his sensibilities in the first place— "I talked with William Bluewing about our predicament. We guessed you might go to Clyman's Corners because of its reputation for anti-slavery sentiments. William went to pass the word to our shepherd, who said he'd go looking for you." Gideon shook his head, briefly distracted. "William is an extraordinary young man."

"He is," Hanneke agreed. "Thank God that you and he *did* pass the word. I don't know how much longer we would have lasted on our own." She sighed heavily. "But things happened so quickly at the end that I didn't even get to say goodbye to the boy."

"That's what happens sometimes." Gideon shaved a curl from his wooden man's hat. "If you want to continue in this business, you have to accept that it's...." He hesitated, as if searching for the right term. "It's hard."

'Hard,' Hanneke thought. A small, straightforward word with enormous and layered meaning. In her limited experience, helping runaways could be physically demanding, exhausting, and dangerous. But honestly, the emotional toll of taking charge of another human being, only to have them disappear into the unknown, was worse.

"I didn't know," she heard herself saying. "I didn't know how difficult it would be to take responsibility for someone's very life, to come to care for them, then have them abruptly disappear. It's brutal. I'll never know if Celia makes it to Canada. Or Daniel." She shrugged, chagrined for speaking so candidly.

Gideon used one thumb to rub a rough spot on his handiwork. "You once asked how I could bear passing runaways along without wondering how they fared." His voice was very low, as if unsure he should continue. "You should know that every single day, I think about each soul I've ever helped. But I determined a long time ago that I would do whatever it took to pass them farther up the line. I'd go insane if I got to know every person I met. And, my way is safer."

"Yes, I see," Hanneke said slowly. And she did, even if she wasn't willing to make the same vow. She realized that—even though she was only working on a basic sock—she'd made a mistake in her knitting and needed to pick out several stitches. She suddenly felt a little wobbly. Her head still ached. It was all so annoying! It was too soon for me to come here, she thought. And yet…Gideon had said, "If you want to continue in this business…." Did she honestly have a choice? Was *he* giving her a choice?

"Is something wrong?"

She drew in a deep breath, struggling for equilibrium. "I'm just…well, your cordial words surprised me."

"Have I really been that difficult?"

Her eyebrows rose. "Yes. You have."

Silence stretched between them. A twig fell from one of the towering trees. A blue jay announced his presence. What an extraordinary moment, Hanneke thought. She'd come to Wisconsin to start a family and settle into the role of *Hausfrau*. Yet here she was, sitting in a Ho-Chunk camp, discussing the Underground Railroad with a man who was himself a fugitive.

Gideon started carving again. Finally, he said, "Well, I apologize. The truth is, I don't spend much time with other people. I'm not good at it."

CHAPTER TWENTY-TWO

"At The Milton House, you called me a failure."

"I did?" Gideon looked taken aback. "I'm used to focusing on nothing but my work. I become especially withdrawn while on a trip of that nature. I must have spouted off in a stressful moment."

The defense felt simplistic. My sense of worth was attacked, Hanneke thought, and he doesn't even remember the moment?

And yet…she'd never before met anyone so dedicated to a purpose. Even now, after his oh-so-cutting comments, she had to admit that she admired him for that. A lot. *And,* as grueling and frightening as her time with Daniel had been, and as hurtful as watching him disappear had been, knowing that she'd made a difference—saved a life—buoyed her in a way she'd never known before, even as a healer.

The truth entered her soul like a physical thing, rich and profound. I do believe, she thought, that I've found my true calling.

Gideon was watching her.

Hanneke cleared her throat. "So, just to be clear…will you ask for my assistance again?"

He crafted the slope of the wooden man's shoulder before saying, "I'd prefer that you retire from this business."

"But you admitted that I did 'extremely well' on this latest adventure. Why should I retire?"

He turned on her. "Because I don't want you to get hurt! Listen, most of the time, this work isn't noble. It's dirty and dangerous and sometimes unspeakably ugly. Someone like you shouldn't be caught up in it."

His vehemence left her floundering. "Do you mean…you think I'm too sensitive?"

"You *are* too sensitive."

I guess he's not leaving the question of my participation up to me after all, Hanneke thought. She was having trouble keeping up.

In any case, Gideon was wrong. Deputy John Barlow had once scorned her abilities as well, but he'd come to see that her "sensitivities" could be assets.

She opened her mouth, then shut it again. Her headache was gnawing at the back of her skull, and the temperature was dropping as the afternoon eased toward night. Now was not the time.

Gideon seemed to come to the same conclusion. "You should go back home and take care of yourself."

"No," Hanneke said deliberately. "I believe we have something else to talk about." She'd seen the horrid scars on his back. Whatever happened in the future, she didn't see any point in pretending otherwise. They needed to be acknowledged.

"Oh, Lord." Gideon put his carving down and rested his elbows on his knees. "You saw."

Hanneke wet her lips. "I did."

"So you know."

"I do," she said slowly, "and I do not." She struggled against the questions agitating to be asked. This was his story to tell, if he would. She wasn't even sure if she wanted to hear it. She felt as if she were standing on the edge of a gaping abyss, and if Gideon did tell her—truly tried to tell her—she might fall into a blackness too dark to bear.

He was silent for so long that she thought he'd made his choice. She startled when he did speak, his voice low and husky. "I am a fugitive slave."

Hanneke swallowed hard. She'd known, of course. Still, it seemed impossible. Gideon's hair was a silky wheat color. His skin was no darker than her own. "No one would ever know," she murmured. Even as she spoke, though, she remembered what one of the Pohl sisters had said about a woman in Wisconsin who'd passed as white for years—only to be tracked down by slavers and dragged south in bondage. The same thing, it seemed, could happen to Gideon. At any time. Any moment.

"I am the result of generations of southern white men raping enslaved African women."

Hanneke searched and failed to find an appropriate response. Eventually, she said, "The words 'I'm sorry' are grotesquely inadequate, but...I truly am. For every bit of what you've been through. I've read a little about the brutal treatment slaves endure, but after seeing your scars...."

"You *didn't* see my scars." For the first time, Gideon's composure wavered.

"No one can see my scars."

The sudden anguish in his voice tore at Hanneke's heart. Beneath his customary rigid composure, Gideon was carrying some pain so deep, so enormous, that she sensed it was consuming him from within. Although her first instincts had counseled respect for his privacy, she now suspected that the kindest thing she could do was gently encourage him to share.

She felt as if she were sliding along the thinnest of ice. "Do your scars have something to do with Tabitha?"

He jerked at the name. "What do you know about Tabitha?"

"Nothing at all. Only that when you were badly fevered, you called her name." Hanneke hesitated. "And sometimes Sarah and Amy as well."

Gideon turned his head, avoiding her gaze. "I do not discuss my past."

"Well, perhaps just this once, you should," Hanneke dared. "I think you need to unburden yourself. Then we'll never speak of it again unless you want to."

He hunched his shoulders. His chin dropped toward his chest as if his past was a crushing weight. Finally, he gritted out the words. "Tabitha was my wife."

'Was' my wife. Hanneke's chest turned leaden. She'd assumed as much but hadn't known if Tabitha was dead or still enslaved. It took all of her courage to get the next question out. "What happened to her?"

"She hanged herself."

Hanneke closed her eyes and put a hand over her mouth.

"From her favorite oak tree. I found her myself." Gideon's voice had taken on a tone that was pained, and bitter and unforgiving. "Tabitha killed herself after the man from the big house paid his gambling debts by selling away our four-year-old twins, Sarah and Amy."

Hanneke thought she might be sick.

"He came right into our cabin one night and took the girls from their sleep," Gideon continued. "He refused to tell Tabitha and me where they were going. Just somewhere deeper south. There was no way to find out, much less get them back."

Abruptly, he shoved to his feet and stalked away, disappearing into the woods.

Hanneke watched him go. A salty lump had formed in her throat. She was crying out right now. She had once impatiently wondered if Gideon cared whether he lived or died. His story explained a lot.

And…*Lieber Gott*. Did Hiram Aubuchon know that Gideon was himself a runaway? Did Levi Cox? That would cast a whole new light on their ongoing animosity.

Hanneke waited for a long time, sitting on the log, watching the skeletal branches sway in the wind. Gideon did not come back.

Chapter Twenty-Three

The next morning, Clara Steckelberg hosted a small dyeing bee for neighbor women. When Hanneke arrived, Clara gave her a long, loaded look. Although Hanneke wasn't sure exactly what it was loaded with, she tried to thank Clara with her gaze, and clasped her hands to reflect profound gratitude.

Then she pulled a clean and whole folded grain sack from her basket. "I'm going to put this in the corn crib," she murmured. Clara simply nodded.

It was the first work party of the year, and Hanneke appreciated the normalcy of it. Clara did love to gather her friends together. Just then, Hanneke couldn't think of anything finer.

Getting to their farm had been challenging, though. The horse-kick bruise on Hanneke's shoulder was starting to fade, but the rest of her body had become a mass of livid purple, yellow, and green bruises. When Charles Steckelberg had come by early to offer a ride, he'd made the expected exclamations of horror about her appearance. Hanneke felt too stiff and clumsy to climb up into the wagon, so in the end, he simply put down the wagon bed's back end. She traveled to the Steckelberg place perched on the rear with her feet dangling, just as she and Jacobine used to ride into town on Market Day.

Clara had a big cauldron of water boiling over a fire built in the back yard. Hanneke had brought a winter's worth of onion skins to contribute, and other women arrived with baskets and sacks carrying the same. Simmered onion skins produced yellow, brown, or reddish hues. The women who kept sheep had been cleaning their fleeces during the winter months, and each brought yarn or unspun wool to dye. The ladies—many with knitting needles or darning eggs in their hands—would visit while the papery skins boiled until late afternoon, when the dyebath was ready to be strained and put to use.

Hanneke was dumping her offerings into the cauldron when Gerda Muehlhauser crept from the woodland trail to her house and approached the group. The two women hadn't seen each other since Hanneke had learned that Oscar Muehlhauser was working for Hiram Aubuchon. Gerda looked haggard today, and anxious. She stopped while still out of the circle and waited to catch Hanneke's eye.

Hanneke joined her. "*Guten tag*, Gerda." She could see Charles harrowing a field beyond them, smoothing the soil prior to planting. She expected that Clara had decided that today was the day to do so.

"Gracious! Are you all right?"

Hanneke waved the concern away with a quick, "Just recovering from a fall."

Gerda shifted her weight. "May I speak with you?"

It pained Hanneke to realize that Gerda felt a need to ask. "Of course," she assured the older woman. "Let's go into the house."

As soon as they were seated in Clara's comfortable, quiet parlor, Gerda began. "I'm sorry. I just need to tell someone."

"Tell someone what?"

"Oscar got drunk last night." Gerda twisted an embroidered handkerchief in her fingers. "He let it slip that he has not been helping a farmer with chores. What he's been doing is working odd hours for some slave catcher." Her expression suggested that she'd just found a dead rodent.

Hanneke didn't have the heart to say that she already knew that, and that she believed Oscar guilty of spying on her and reporting her journey with Gideon to Aubuchon. Since Oscar didn't really farm, he often went hunting to put meat on the table. He must know the local terrain well. If Oscar told the slaver how the journey had begun—what roads Gideon took—Aubuchon might have sent teams to cover several byways they might possibly travel. That could have led to Levi Cox and his companion spotting and attacking

Gideon's wagon.

What she hadn't known for sure was whether Gerda had understood what her husband was doing. Learning that Gerda had *not* been part of Aubuchon's efforts was an overwhelming relief.

Gerda leaned closer. "Oscar has put up broadsides about runaways! He… he's even helped track them down."

Oscar hasn't always tracked them down, Hanneke thought with some satisfaction. Oscar had not found her and Daniel.

"I didn't know who else to talk to." Gerda looked at Hanneke fearfully. "Am I correct in thinking that…you share my—my sentiments on this matter?"

Hanneke understood what Gerda was trying to say. "That's a fair assumption," she allowed. "But I do think it's best we don't discuss this issue with the others."

"Agreed." Gerda pursed her lips for a moment. "There's no one else I'd be comfortable talking with about such a thing anyway. I knew nothing about what he was doing. When he let it slip, I was horrified."

"I believe you," Hanneke said gently.

"How will God judge us?" Gerda's eyes glassed over with tears. "I should have known. I certainly have been enjoying the fruits of his labors."

Hanneke remembered again how pleased she'd been to see Gerda looking better on her last visit. "You had no way of knowing, Gerda. I'm confident that God will not judge you harshly."

Gerda made a *We shall see* gesture and slowly rose to her feet, leaning on the armrest for balance. "Thank you for listening, my dear. I need to get back home."

"Oh, stay for some food and company," Hanneke urged. "Clara's going to fry *wurst*, and she's making *Kartoffelpfannkuchen*." All German-speaking immigrants loved potato pancakes. Everyone was hungry for everything at this time of year, and she thought the gathering would do her friend good.

Gerda, though, shook her head. "*Nein*. Clara kindly invited me, as she always does, but you know I rarely leave home. I only came because I guessed you would be here."

They left the farmhouse. "I'll see you soon," Hanneke promised, but it hurt her heart to watch the frail figure plod back into the forest. Gerda was never comfortable around others. She'd been ashamed of her husband's drunkenness for years, and their poverty as well. Now Gerda felt the moral burden of her husband's disgusting work for Hiram Aubuchon.

Hanneke fought the sudden urge to stamp her feet and scream. Oscar Muehlhauser had not broken any American law. Celia and Daniel, she and Gideon, and other shepherds and lambs—*they* were the lawbreakers.

I will never understand, she thought, and went to join the others.

* * *

Charles drove Hanneke to Safe Haven Farm late that afternoon, with long skeins of golden-brown yarn spread about in the wagon. Minutes after being dropped off, as she was draping them over the garden fence to dry, she heard the sound of hooves clopping closer on the lane. Deputy John Barlow appeared and raised a hand in greeting. When he got close, he dismounted and tossed the Morgan's reins over a post.

He spoke without preamble. "I thought you were taking a few days to rebuild your strength."

Hanneke shrugged. "I am. Do you want to come inside?" The sun was setting in the western sky, so the temperature was likely going to dip.

Barlow tugged his felt hat lower and shook his head. "I'm on my way home, and don't want to leave Ulricke waiting. However, I learned something this afternoon, and I wanted you to know."

Hanneke went very still, one hand gripping the top of one of the woven-bough pickets that comprised the fence. "What is it?"

"Levi Cox is dead."

"What?" She blinked. "Levi Cox is dead?"

John crossed his arms impatiently. "*Ja*, dead. He was killed in a tavern brawl, and his body dumped in the river before any of us got there." He regarded her shrewdly. "You obviously knew him? I was afraid of that."

"I didn't know him. We'd never been introduced. However...I've heard the name. He traveled here with Aubuchon, right? That's all I need to know."

"Well, he won't be tracking anyone else. I helped fish him out of the Rock. The man was definitely dead."

A new thought struck Hanneke like a blow. *Lieber Gott.* If Cox was dead, Gideon must have killed him.

If he had, she didn't want to know about it. She loathed Levi Cox, and believed he was the hatchet-thrower on the road. He'd come looking for Daniel in the brickyard, and she had seen him attacking near Milton. She believed that his evil intent extended beyond making money. Nevertheless, she could not advocate actually *killing* someone—

"And word is that Aubuchon has also left. Empty-handed."

Hanneke tried to accept this news. Aubuchon was gone, and as long as Gideon had not murdered Levi Cox, she decided, she would not waste thought on the man or his death. How many times in the past few days had she heard something rustle in the underbrush and wondered if Cox was there? How many times a day had she speculated that she wasn't truly safe at her farm? How many hours had she lain awake, worrying that Levi Cox might be, at this precise moment, handcuffing Gideon…or worse?

The deputy tipped his head. "Are you all right?"

"*Ja,*" Hanneke said. "I am."

* * *

When the time came, nature smiled for Jacobine's and William's wedding day. Although the Steckelbergs had offered a ride, Hanneke chose to walk from Safe Haven Farm to Watertown, savoring the simple fact that she was able to do so. She saw a few green leaves on roadside shrubs, poking from miniscule buds. The sun felt warm on her shoulders. The young couple is being blessed, Hanneke thought, and was grateful.

The ceremony itself was a tiny affair, conducted by a pastor Hanneke had never before met. Karoline had been first disappointed, and then defiant, when their pastor refused to conduct the wedding. He didn't approve of mixed-race marriages, and in any case, he would not officiate at a marriage where the individuals involved were not orthodox Lutherans of the same

233

synod. William was willing to complete catechesis, but the pastor wouldn't say how long that would take. What William was *not* willing to do was face at the end of his studies an oral examination, in German, before the assembled congregation.

Hanneke didn't blame him.

"If we're going to do this," Karoline had told Hanneke with resolve, "we are going to do this properly." In the end, William found a willing pastor at St. Luke's Lutheran Church, a *"freie Geminde"* or free thinker congregation, composed primarily of Forty-Eighters who'd fled Europe after the failed 1848 revolution. They were meeting in the Buena Vista hotel while raising funds for a building, but Karoline refused to bend that far and insisted that the pastor come to her own home for the ceremony.

It was a small group that packed inside the apartment that morning—Karoline and Hanneke, Jacobine's friend Dora Hardke and her parents, Clara and Charles Steckelberg, Annie Bluewing, and her two girls. Hanneke had helped Karoline and Jacobine decorate the room with cedar boughs. All eyes were on the young couple.

Jacobine was reserved and solemn, but her blue eyes glowed. She'd always worn her flaxen hair in braids or a coronet, but today Karoline had fixed it in a complicated twist at the back of her daughter's head—a transformation Hanneke observed with a bittersweet pang. The promised new practical dress was a no-nonsense dark green wool from which Jacobine would no doubt get years of service, just as she'd wanted. The delicate lace collar and cuffs that Hanneke had knit, and the oh-so-fine shawl she'd just *barely* managed to finish in time, elevated Jacobine's attire to something special.

William was dressed in his Pomeranian finest: handsome black trousers, a white shirt, and a brocaded gold-colored vest beneath his coat. When he smiled at his bride, the depth of his happiness and pride was almost too intimate to watch.

Hanneke wondered, though, if there wasn't a very faint shadow in his eyes. He knows too much about the past, she thought, to be entirely at ease contemplating the future. She certainly understood. She thought about Gideon's destroyed family, and couldn't help thinking of her own dream, broken when Fridolin had died.

As the bridal couple took their vows, a heartfelt prayer burst forth from Hanneke's mind: God, please bless these two. Certainly, she and Karoline and Annie would do everything in their power to keep Jacobine and William safe and content.

Then, they were joyfully married. The blonde Pomeranian-American woman and the black-haired Ho-Chunk man faced their guests as a wedded couple for the first time. Hanneke felt a half-joyous, half-poignant twist beneath her ribs. She was extremely relieved that Karoline had relented and given her blessing to the union. Jacobine and William deserved every moment of happiness they could snatch.

William, with help from his male relatives, had built a small log cabin on a back corner of Hanneke's property. After the wedding service, William and Jacobine invited everyone to continue the festivities at their new home. Soon the building overflowed with well-wishers and laughter and good things to eat.

Ho-Chunk people arrived with baskets of food to gift the young people. Each of the Pomeranian women had scrounged in her own kitchen, and soon, a small pile of bowls, plates, cutlery, earthenware crocks, and other essentials were piled on the table. Karoline had sewn and hung window curtains of blue-and-white gingham. In Hanneke's opinion, they turned the raw cabin into a cozy home.

She was standing in a corner, sipping a mug of cider, when Karoline came to stand beside her. For a moment, they watched William and Jacobine enjoy an impromptu jig. A few people, both Ho-Chunk and white, chose to stand aside and watch. Others joined in the dancing.

"Have you heard any negative comments?"

Hanneke answered truthfully. "Not one."

Karoline nodded but murmured, "I do hope I've done the right thing." She looked lovely today—not so worn and tired as she'd been on the farm, when Hanneke had first known her. Her expression, however, was somber.

Hanneke took her hand and squeezed. "Look at those two," she whispered to her friend. "Honestly, I don't think you had any choice."

"I have come to love William," Karoline admitted. "And I trust him."

Hanneke leaned close, touching shoulders. "That's all any mother could hope for."

After a lovely afternoon at the cabin, Hanneke kissed the bride and groom, slipped away, and began walking home. She took the long way around, circling to Safe Haven Farm by road. To her shame, she had to admit that a bit of regret colored her mood. Part of it came from the loneliness of attending a wedding as a still-young widow. It had reminded her that she'd never had the chance to celebrate her own wedding here, in her new home country.

That was an old ache, but there was more, too. The truth was, Gideon's story had been haunting her. She hadn't seen or heard from him since the day at the Bluewings' camp when she'd urged him to speak of his sorrow. *I hope I didn't do more harm than good,* Hanneke thought, stepping aside to leave space for a passing buggy. Every instinct had assured her that telling his story was the best thing Gideon could do. Still, she'd been tiptoeing in new territory. She had comforted many people in her life, but this level of evil and loss was incomprehensible.

Well. She couldn't undo what was already done. She might never see the man again, and she *had* promised him that she'd never speak of his personal life again. Hanneke honestly didn't know if he was willing to call upon her again when he needed help on the local Underground Railroad. Her friendship with Charlotte Stofeldt was also over, even though John Barlow had decided against bringing charges.

If I never hear from Gideon again, I will simply look for new ways to work for abolition, Hanneke vowed to herself. After stiffening her spine and pushing back her shoulders, she felt better.

It didn't take long to approach her farm. *Perhaps I'll spend extra time with my animals this evening,* Hanneke thought. She'd been absent too often of late. Although William had taken superb care of them in her absence, she owed them personal attention—

She stopped abruptly in the lane before she could even turn into her own drive. *What under heaven…?*

CHAPTER TWENTY-THREE

Smoke was rising from her chimney.

For a moment or so, she simply stared. As much as she'd longed for this very sight, it made no sense. Why was a fire burning inside her home? Apparently, someone had broken in. Aubuchon was gone. Cox was dead. How afraid should she be?

It took Hanneke a moment to settle herself and walk up the drive. She detoured to the side of the porch and grasped a sturdy hoe she'd recently brought outside. When she was composed, she walked slowly up the drive and around to the back of the house.

As she turned the corner, the kitchen door opened, and Gideon Sparrow stepped outside. "I hope you don't mind," he said without preamble. "I knew you were going to the wedding today—"

And how did you know that? Hanneke wondered silently. She didn't ask.

"—so when I arrived here before you did, I took the liberty of warming your house."

"How did you get inside?" Hanneke demanded. "Did you break the lock?"

Gideon shrugged. "Picked it."

Of course, lock-picking was one of Gideon's skills. She would look for a different style of lock the next time she went to Watertown.

"I really didn't think you'd mind." Gideon sounded more perplexed than defensive.

Hanneke didn't have an inkling of what was going on. "Warming the house is fine," she said carefully, walking closer to the small back porch and putting down the hoe. "But…what are you doing here?"

Gideon shoved his hands in his pockets and walked down the steps to meet her. "I came to talk to you."

"What about?"

"First…I wanted to tell you that after a lot of thought, I've come to believe that your involvement in this business should be your choice. Not mine."

Hanneke felt her eyebrows arch.

"However, I also figured that at this point, other than maintaining your barn as a refuge, you might be done with the Underground Railroad. If the need ever arises again, do you want me to call upon you?"

"I do think so," Hanneke murmured, nodding. She was still struggling to understand what was happening. Walking past him, she sat on the edge of the back porch.

After a pause, he sat nearby, contemplating the woods beyond the outbuildings. A flock of sandhill cranes made their gangly-elegant way across the sky over the farm, calling to each other for reassurance.

"I do want you to call upon me if the need arises," Hanneke confirmed. "I'm still cleaning up from the last trip, though. I need to replace all of the laundry items I stole, and add in some knitted goods as well. It's the least I can do."

Gideon looked taken aback. "Well…all right."

"The other thing leaving me hesitant is more opaque." Hanneke rubbed her knees. "These two excursions have changed me. Brought out things in me I didn't know I had, both good and bad. I'm still thinking that through."

Gideon picked up a pebble and tossed it into the yard. "I'd worry if you said the two trips *hadn't* changed you."

He gave her room to reflect for a few minutes, which she appreciated. I may not know exactly who I am anymore, she thought, but I can't go backwards. I have to keep moving into the future. I am a capable woman and shall face the future with confidence.

She turned to Gideon. "I definitely do want to stay involved in the Railroad. I want to learn how to do this better."

He tipped his head slightly, contemplating her. "It will break your heart."

"I know."

He nodded. Evidently, that was all that needed to be said.

A few chickens pecked at the barren soil, making *tuck-tuck-tuck* sounds. Some of her precious Cotswold ewes had left the stable and come outside to enjoy the sunshine. Puffy white clouds sailed overhead.

Gideon shifted restlessly. "I also came by with a question."

"Yes?"

He drew a deep breath. "I wanted to see if you would like to go for a wagon ride one day."

Hanneke's forehead puckered in confusion. "A ride? You mean…a runaway needs help?"

"No." Gideon looked oddly patient, like a schoolteacher talking to a particularly slow child. "I mean a wagon ride. Just for a few hours."

Hanneke took pains to keep her jaw from dangling. I must have misunderstood, she thought. Even if she knew what to say, which she did not, it seemed certain that she had misunderstood Gideon's meaning.

"I just thought…." He shrugged again. "With the weather finally warming… it might be pleasant. Perhaps you could even pack a picnic." He scuffed one boot in the dirt. "I don't really know how people do that. What they bring. I've never been on a picnic."

Nein, Hanneke mused silently, I don't suppose you have. She threw a glance at him. His face was closing. A muscle tightened in his jaw.

She felt panic rising inside. She wished that the stars were out so she could connect with her husband. *Fridolin,* she tried. *I don't know what to do.*

Fridolin did not answer in words. But for a moment—just a moment—she sensed him grinning. She remembered his smile—the way it shone from his face, the way it created tiny crinkles at the corner of his eyes. She had missed Fridolin's smile…but he was sharing it now, she was certain.

Hanneke cupped her elbows in her palms and took a steadying breath. "A ride does sound pleasant. And I will pack a picnic lunch."

Gideon closed his eyes for a few seconds. He didn't look pleased, exactly, but definitely more positive than he had a moment before.

Hanneke thought about going for a wagon ride with a man who had no idea what a picnic was like. Gideon had no idea what an everyday life was like. She could never really understand Gideon's life experiences, any more than he could understand hers.

Perhaps that should have frightened her. It did not.

A breeze *shushed* softly through the nearby trees. A robin hopped along the foundation. Arion, Gideon's horse, tossed his head several times. Gideon had left the bay roan's reins looped over the fence.

Hanneke felt as if she were tiptoeing across a narrow ledge. She heard herself say, "Would you like to come inside? Stay for supper?"

Gideon hesitated. Perhaps he was also tiptoeing. "I think so."

A small smile took shape on Hanneke's face. "All right, then." She walked past him, marched up the steps, and went on into the kitchen. She had no idea what someone from Arkansas might like to eat but she did have a few smoked sausages left, and some wrinkled potatoes, and the rhubarb Frau König had given her. She could put a decent meal together with those things.

Gideon's bootsteps sounded on the steps behind her, and she smiled.

A Note from the Author

This tale of freedom-seekers and slave catchers springs largely from my imagination. Slave catchers did travel to Wisconsin, but they tended to gather in the eastern ports such as Racine, Kenosha, Milwaukee, and others. There are no records of slavers haunting Watertown.

Nonetheless, such activity does not seem impossible. Scholars believe that over a hundred enslaved people fled through Wisconsin on their way to Canada, but the people who helped them generally did not keep records. Who knows how many Black people ran through the state? While the numbers never equaled those of eastern states, enslaved people from areas like Arkansas and Missouri might well have escaped through Wisconsin.

Choosing appropriate and respectful language to describe African Americans trying to reach Canada proved challenging. I avoided the derogatory terms that were in common use in the 1850s, but it wouldn't make sense for Hanneke to reference "freedom-seekers" either, or to refer to "enslaved people." Searching for middle ground, I did rely on "runaway" and "fugitive." I also respectfully acknowledge that some readers today may object to those terms, believing that they imply criminal behavior.

Although most locations are fictional, The Milton House Museum in Milton, WI, was and is a real place. This extraordinary building has been certified as an Underground Railroad site by the National Park Service and the Network to Freedom program. It has also been designated as a National Historic Landmark. At this time, The Milton House Museum is the only certified Underground Railroad site in the state that can be toured by the general public. See https://miltonhouse.org/ for more information. Nancy and Joseph Goodrich were also real people, although of course they were used fictionally here.

Descriptions of Charlotte Stofeldt's *fachwerk* housebarn are based on the 1850 Kliese housebarn (also known as the Langholff housebarn) near Watertown. I had the great good fortune to tour this private property while writing this book. Architectural historians have identified a number of these rare structures in Dodge and Manitowoc counties, which were home to many Pomeranian and other Prussian immigrants.

Acknowledgements

I'm grateful to the many people who helped make this book possible, including Chuck Werth, Alan Pape, Elaine Langholff, Marilyn Koepsell, and Terry Schoessow. Material made available by the Watertown Historical Society and the Trinity Freistadt Historical Society was invaluable. Special thanks to Keighton Klos, Executive Director at the Milton House Museum, and site staff and volunteers.

Laurie Rosengren Haselden and Barbara Ernst offered essential editorial assistance. My friends at Write On, Door County provided a beautiful and quiet writing space.

Warm thanks to editors Verena Rose and Shawn Reilly Simmons at Level Best Books.

I'm indebted to all the readers who have opened their hearts to Hanneke. And as always, deep gratitude to my husband Scott for decades of support.

About the Author

Kathleen Ernst is a social historian, educator, and bestselling author. Kathleen's forty-three published books encompass mysteries, historical fiction, poetry, and non-fiction. The Hanneke Bauer historical mystery series feature a newly-arrived German immigrant in the 1850s. The Chloe Ellefson Mysteries feature a historic sites curator whose knowledge of the past helps solve contemporary crimes. Kathleen's children's books include twenty titles for American Girl.

Honors for Kathleen's work include multiple Agatha nominations, an Edgar nomination, a Lovey Award for Best Traditional Mystery, the American Heritage Women in the Arts Recognition Award for Literature from the National Society of the Daughters of the American Revolution, a Major Achievement Award from the Council for Wisconsin Writers, the Sterling North Legacy Award for Children's Literature, and an Emmy Award for Children's Instructional Programming. Her books have sold 1.9 million audio, eBook, and printed copies to date.

Kathleen lives in Middleton, Wisconsin, with her husband Scott and feline muse Eliza.

AUTHOR WEBSITE:
  kathleenernst.com

SOCIAL MEDIA HANDLES:
www.sitesandstories.wordpress.com
www.facebook.com/kathleenernst.author
www.youtube.com/user/KathleenErnst

Also by Kathleen Ernst

Lies of Omission: A Hanneke Bauer Mystery

The Solace of Stars: A Hanneke Bauer Mystery

Kathleen also writes the Chloe Ellefson mysteries, featuring a historic sites curator, as well as children's novels, poetry, and nonfiction.